"Why'd you  Whisper Cr

The sleepy ques_____e turned and saw that Joni's eyes were open. She still looked sleepy, and amazingly huggable.

He shrugged. "I don't know. It's home."

She shook her head. "I'm serious, Hardy. The way Witt has treated you... Why didn't you take a job with some architectural firm in Denver or Chicago? You could have made more money."

"Is that what you think I should be doing? Making more money?"

"No. It's just that I wondered why. You had a way out." She pushed her hair back from her face. "It's all about Karen, you know. It's all about this feeling of unfinished business. At least for me."

Before he could say a word, she'd disappeared into her room. He turned back to the window and stared out into the teeth of the blizzard. Yes, it was unfinished business that had brought him back. But not Karen. Not Witt.

Joni.

"Lee crafts a heartrending saga...."
—*Publishers Weekly* on *Snow in September*

RACHEL LEE

A JANUARY CHILL

MIRA®

ISBN 1-55166-802-5

A JANUARY CHILL

Visit us at www.mirabooks.com

Printed in U.S.A..

A JANUARY CHILL

1

The November evening was frigid and blowing dry snow so hard it stung. Joni Matlock came through the back door of the house, taking care to stomp the snow off her boots, then removed them and set them by the wall on the rag rug. Her feet instantly felt cold, because the mudroom wasn't heated. Shivering a little, she shook out of her jacket, tugged off her knit cap and hung both on a peg next to her mother's.

Then she darted into the kitchen and gave thanks for the heat that made her face sting. Her mother was sitting at the table in the dining room, visible through the open doorway, apparently busy with her needlework.

"Mom," Joni said, "you put too much wood in the stove again."

Hannah Matlock looked up with a smile. "I get cold, honey. You know that."

"It must be eighty in here." But Joni wasn't complaining too seriously. It felt good after the bitter chill of the dark evening outside. On the trip home from the hospital where she worked as a pharmacist, her car heater didn't even have time to start working. She felt like an ice cube.

"There's fresh coffee," Hannah said, bowing her head over her stitchery. "And I thought I'd just heat the leftover pot roast for dinner."

"That sounds good."

Joni poured herself a mug of coffee and whitened it with a few drops of cream. Real cream. She couldn't stand the nondairy creamers. Then she stood in the doorway between the kitchen and dining room, sipping the hot brew and watching her mother stitch.

At fifty, Hannah's hair was still as black as a starless night, a gift from her Ute ancestors. Her face, too, held a hint of the exotic in high cheekbones, and was still nearly as seamless as her daughter's. Her eyes were dark brown, almost as dark as her hair, and Joni had always envied them because they seemed to hold mystery.

Joni, for her part, had bright blue eyes. Hannah always said Joni's eyes had captured the sky. Joni felt differently about them. Blue eyes were a lot more sensitive to the light, and all winter long she had to hide them behind sunglasses.

The women were alike enough, however, to be sisters.

Joni joined her mother at the table, cradling her mug in her cold hands. "How was your day?"

"Delightful," Hannah said. She rarely said anything else. "Well, there was one bad spot. I had to help put down Angie Beluk's dog." Hannah worked as a veterinary assistant four mornings a week.

"I'm sorry," Joni said, feeling a pang. "What was wrong?"

"Cancer." Hannah sighed and snipped her thread. Then she put her hoop to one side. "Poor Angie. She had Brownie for sixteen years."

"That's so sad."

"Well, it happens, unfortunately. On the brighter side, we delivered a litter of pups. What about you? How was your day?"

Joni sipped her coffee, feeling the heat all the way down to her stomach. "Oh, the usual. I rolled pills, mixed elixirs, chatted with a dozen people...."

Hannah laughed. "You make it sound so boring!"

Joni smiled back at her. "It's not. But it sure isn't the height of adventure."

Something in Hannah's face softened. "Is that what you really want, Joni? Adventure?"

After a moment, Joni shook her head. "Not really. Remember the curse, 'May you live in interesting times'? I'll settle for ho-hum, thank you very much. Want me to put the pot roast on to heat before I go change?"

"No, honey, I'll do it. You just go on up."

"Okay." Taking her mug with her, Joni rose and disappeared into the living room, in the direction of the stairs.

Hannah stared after her, a faint crease between her

eyebrows. Maybe, she thought for the hundredth time, she had made a mistake in moving them fifteen years ago to Whisper Creek after Lewis died.

She had told herself at the time that it was for Joni that she had brought them here, but now, in retrospect, she wondered if she hadn't really done it because she was afraid herself. After all, staying in Denver had meant finding reminders of Lewis around every corner and in every familiar face. She had tried to go back to work but had found being in the hospital again was just impossible for her. Every sound, every smell, reminded her of Lewis and the fifteen years they had shared.

So maybe she hadn't really done it for Joni. Maybe she had been lying to herself when she justified the move by assuring herself she was taking the child away from all the bad influences to a quiet community where kids didn't hang around in gangs and kill innocent doctors who were crossing a parking lot on the way to save lives.

Maybe she had been lying to herself when she argued that Joni would be better off near the only family either of them had, Lewis's brother, Witt.

Maybe those had all been excuses because she was unwilling to face her own fears and her own pain— and her shame.

But she hadn't really wondered about it until lately. Not until three years ago, when Joni had finished her schooling and moved back into her old bedroom while taking a job at the little mountain hospital just outside town. For the first time it had seriously occurred to Hannah that she might have crippled Joni in some way.

Because what could a twenty-six-year-old woman possibly want in this town? There was no adventure, few single men of her age, nowhere to go on Friday night other than a movie theater and a couple of bars. Why hadn't Joni taken a job somewhere else? Her pharmacy degree and her grades surely would have given her her pick.

But Joni had chosen to come here and live with her mother. Not that Hannah minded. It just made her feel terribly guilty.

As did her secret, the one she had never whispered to a soul. Over the years she had almost convinced herself it wasn't true, but lately...lately every time she wondered if she had gone wrong somehow with Joni, the thought came back to haunt her.

Maybe she had made it worse by keeping it so long. Maybe she had deprived Joni of something essential. Every time the thoughts rose in her mind, she shied away from them, telling herself that the truth would have made no essential difference, that all she had done was protect herself and her child from shame.

But she hadn't really protected herself, because the shame still burned in her, making her squirm inwardly. Reminding her that her motives had never been as pure as she had told herself. Keeping her

from the one thing she wanted more than anything
apart from Joni's happiness.

But it was too late now, she told herself. She had
made her mistakes, and there was no way to mend
them. She had to believe that, at the very least, she
had taken good care of her daughter.

Sighing, she rose from the table and went to put
the leftovers in the microwave to warm. And she
tried not to think of the terrible secret she guarded.

Upstairs, Joni's room was like an oven. The heat
from the woodstove downstairs funneled up the stair-
well and filled the bedrooms. It was one of the reasons she was always trying to persuade her mother
not to put so much wood in the fire.

Smothering a sigh, she battled to open the argu-
mentative bedroom window and let some of the overpowering heat escape into the frigid night. The icy
chill that only a few minutes ago had been making
her so uncomfortable now actually felt welcome as
it sucked some of the heat out.

Her room was blessed with a walk-in closet large
enough to be a dressing room—which was a good
thing, since the room itself barely had enough room
for the four-poster double bed and a rocking chair.
The closet was chilly, since it had been closed all
day, and she shivered a little as she changed swiftly
into what she called her "compromise clothes," a
pair of chinos and a long-sleeved cotton shirt. She
wouldn't suffocate at the temperature her mother pre-

ferred, yet they would prevent her from shivering in the drafts that always stirred in this old house.

Downstairs, she found Hannah humming quietly as she set the table. Hannah frequently hummed, though she never sang out loud, and Joni always found the sound comforting. Taking the plates from her mother's hands, she finished the job.

"So not one exciting thing happened today?" Hannah asked.

"Not really." Joni put the porcelain candleholders in the middle of the table and lit the red tapers that were left from last Christmas. Every year, Hannah went overboard scattering red candles around the house for the holiday. Then they spent all the next year burning them. "Pneumonia is going around again. You be sure to stay away from anyone who's coughing, Mom."

Hannah gave her a wry smile. "I *used* to be a nurse."

Joni laughed. "You're right. I'm terrible about that."

"I don't mind. But I *will* remind you. And the same goes for you, Miss Smarty-Pants. Don't forget to wash your hands."

They exchanged understanding looks.

Hannah returned from the kitchen, carrying the casserole dish that held the remains of the pot roast. Using a big steel spoon, she began to dish out the food. "How bad is it? Are many people getting sick?"

"Bob Warner said the wards are almost full. The docs think this is going to be the worst winter in years."

Hannah clucked her tongue. "Well, tell Bob that if they need extra hands, I'll be glad to come in and help. I'm not *that* rusty."

"He knows that." Joni gave her a wicked grin. "You've been practicing on dogs and cats for a long time."

"Child, you are terrible. The skills aren't all that different."

Joni pursed her lips. "I'm sure. And you know how to pin a patient down."

Hannah looked over the top of her reading glasses at her daughter. "That can be useful on *any* ward."

Then they both laughed and sat at the table, facing each other across the candles.

The best thing about living with her mother now, Joni often thought, was how they'd become such good friends. Her going away to college seemed to have given them just the distance they needed to cross the mother-child barriers, and what had grown between them since was something Joni wouldn't have traded for anything.

"So," Hannah said, "apart from pneumonia, what else happened in your day?"

Joni hesitated, knowing the family position on Hardy Wingate too well to suppose the news would be greeted warmly, but then decided to go ahead and tell her mother anyway. "I saw Hardy Wingate today. Apparently his mother is in the hospital with pneumonia.''

Hannah looked up from her plate and pursed her lips. ''Joni…''

''I know, I know. Witt hates him. Well, you don't have to worry about it, Mom. Hardy will barely talk to me.'' Which was a shame, she thought. She'd had a crush on Hardy years ago, and while she'd outgrown it, she still thought he was attractive. And nice, despite her uncle Witt's opinion.

''Well,'' said her mother after a few moments, ''I'm sorry Barbara is sick.''

Apparently it was okay to feel bad about Hardy's mother.

After supper Hannah went back to her needlework and Joni did the dishes. There was a small window over the chipped porcelain sink, and she found herself pausing frequently as she washed to look out into the night. The hill there was so steep she could almost look over the neighbor's roof toward downtown. She did, however, have an unimpeded view of the night sky, and since the moon was full tonight, she could even see the pale glow of snowcapped mountains in the distance.

Whisper Creek had sprung up around silver mines in the 1880s, nestled on the eastern edge of the valley between two mountain ranges. The town itself was built into the hills, and many of the houses clung to steep terrain. It had never grown large enough to spread into the valley to the west, where the land was flat and open. Her uncle Witt owned a lot of that land out there. Not that it did him any good. Runoff from the tailings left in the hills by miners a century ago had tainted the water and consequently the land. Brush was about all that grew out there, and even it was thin.

The land hadn't always been poor. Back when the first Matlock had purchased it with the money he'd made from his own silver mine, it had been verdant with promise. But after about forty years or so, the cattle had started sickening and dying.

Uncle Witt hadn't even tried to do anything with the land. What could he do? It would take more money than he had to reclaim it, and even though the EPA had declared the town and the area around it a Superfund site, there didn't seem to be much improvement.

Joni sometimes looked at the land, though, trying to think of things that could be done with it. The view, after all, was spectacular. But who could come up with the money to turn it into a resort? Everyone in town talked about ways to draw tourists to the area, to give the economy another base apart from the unreliable molybdenum and silver mines, but so far no one had been able to ante up the investment money.

Realizing she was daydreaming again, Joni quickly returned her attention to the dishes. After a busy day at work, where inattention could cost someone's life, she generally felt mentally drained and had a tendency to zone out when she came home. Today had been an exceptionally busy day, as the altitude, the dryness of the air and the low temperatures seemed to weaken people's resistance.

Then there had been Hardy Wingate. She felt almost guilty for even thinking about him, but his face popped up before her mind's eye. He'd looked exhausted, she thought. His square, bronzed face had been paler than usual, and his gray eyes had been bloodshot. He'd been in the hospital cafeteria, swallowing coffee in the hopes that caffeine would keep him going.

Seeing him, she had walked over to him and joined him. He'd looked at her almost hesitantly, as if expecting her to say something nasty. Or as if she were on some list of prohibitions he didn't want to break.

"Hi," she'd said, sitting across from him anyway.

"Hi." His voice had sounded strained, weary.

"Are you sick?" It was a pointless question. He looked exhausted, but he didn't look ill.

"My mother. I was up all night with her in intensive care."

"I'm sorry." And she truly had been. Still was. Barbara Wingate was a lovely woman. "Pneumonia?"

"Yeah."

"How's she doing now?"

"Better. They said I could go get some sleep."

She pointed to the coffee. ''That's a great sleeping potion.''

For an instant, just an instant, he looked as if he might crack a smile. But then his face sagged again. ''I'll be here all night.''

''I don't think so. You'll collapse, yourself, if you don't get any sleep.''

''I'll be fine.'' Then, without another word, he tossed off the last of his coffee, rose and walked away.

And now, standing at the sink, Joni heard herself sigh. He hadn't even said goodbye, as if simple social courtesies were forbidden, too. And all because of Witt.

The phone rang, and she heard her mother pick it up in the living room. A little while later, Hannah's laugh wafted to her. Good news of some kind. That was a plus. God knew they could use some.

Not that life was all that bad, but there were times when Joni thought they were all dying in this little town. Silver prices were lousy, and the silver mine was on minimal operation, which meant a lot of miners were on layoffs that were supposedly only temporary. The molybdenum mine was doing better, but there was some talk of cutbacks there, too.

This had always been a boom-and-bust town, and it looked as if they were once again on the edge of a bust.

And she didn't usually feel this down. She wondered if maybe she was getting sick, too, then decided she just didn't have time for it.

She drained the dishwater, rinsed the sink and was just drying her hands when her mother came into the kitchen.

"Witt's coming over," Hannah said. "He said he has some good news."

Not for the first time, Joni noticed the way Hannah's face brightened and her eyes sparkled when Witt was coming over. It was the only time Hannah ever looked that way.

"Great," she said, although after talking to Hardy Wingate today, she was feeling surprisingly unreceptive toward the idea of seeing her uncle. Silly, she told herself. The feud was more than a decade old, so old they should all be comfortable with it. Why was she feeling so uncomfortable? Because she was afraid Witt would look into her eyes and read betrayal there, all because she had talked to a man she'd known since her school days?

How ridiculous could she get?

Witt arrived fifteen minutes later, apparently having walked from his house across town. When he stepped in through the front door, he brought the frigid night in with him, and Joni felt the draft snake around her bare ankles.

Witt was a bear of a man, over six feet, and broad with muscle from hard labor. He filled the doorway and then the small living room as he stripped off his coat and muffler. A grin cracked his weathered face, and his eyes, as blue as Joni's, seemed to be dancing.

He wrapped Joni in a big hug, the way he always had, his arms seeming to make promises of safety and eternal welcome. Even when she was irritated with him, which she was every now and then, Joni couldn't help responding to that hug with one of her own.

"You're cold," she told him, laughing in spite of herself.

"You're warm," he countered. "You're singeing my fingers."

"That's because Mom keeps it so hot in here."

Witt released her and turned to Hannah. "Still a hothouse flower, huh?"

Hannah laughed but shook her head. "Sorry." The truth was, as Joni knew, her mother had spent too many cold nights as a child, and keeping warm made her feel as if she lived in the lap of luxury, even if the lap was a small, aging Victorian house on the side of a hill in a tiny mountain mining town.

"Well," said Witt, greeting her with a much more restrained hug than he had given Joni, "if I suddenly dash out into a snowbank, you'll know it's because my clothes started smoking."

Hannah laughed; she always laughed at Witt's humor, Joni thought, not for the first time.

Hannah offered her usual gesture of hospitality. "I was just about to make coffee. Join me?" Hannah never made coffee in the evening, but she always said this same thing to a guest. Long ago, when she'd been eight or nine, Joni had asked her why.

"Because," Hannah had explained, "it's polite to offer refreshments to a guest, but I don't want them to feel like they might be putting me out, so I always say I was about to do it."

Joni had thought that was kind of silly. Why not let your guests know you were doing something especially for them? But she'd been watching Hannah's hospitality charm people for years.

"Sure," Witt said, following her toward the kitchen. "Coffee's great, but yours in the best."

He always said *that*. For some strange reason, tonight that irritated Joni. What was wrong with her? she asked herself. Why was she getting so irritated by things that were practically family rituals?

They gathered at the dining-room table, another family tradition. The only times they ever gathered in the living room were at Christmas or when they had company from outside the family.

Hannah brought out a coffee cake she had baked that day and cut a large slice for Witt. Joni declined.

"All right," Hannah said when they all had their coffee. "What's the good news, Witt?"

He was grinning from ear to ear, wide enough to split his face. "You'll never guess."

Hannah looked at Joni and rolled her eyes. Joni had to laugh. "I know," she said to her mother. "He bought a new truck. Cherry red with oversize tires."

Hannah laughed, and Witt scowled. "You'll never stop teasing me about that truck I drive, will you?"

"Of course not," Joni told him. "It's a classic. Older than me, and so rusted out I can see the road through the floorboards."

"Well, just so you know, I *am* gonna buy a new truck."

No longer joking, Joni put her coffee mug down and looked at her uncle in wonder. "Are you okay? You're not getting sick?"

"Jeez," Witt muttered. "She'll never lay off. Hannah, you should have got the upper hand when she was little."

"Apparently so," Hannah agreed. But her eyes danced.

"No," Witt told his niece, "I'm not sick. I'm not even a little crazy. And if trucks didn't cost damn near as much as a house, I'd've bought a new one years ago."

"So what happened to make you buy one now?" Joni asked.

"I won the lottery."

Silence descended over the table. It was one of the longest silences Joni could remember since the news that Witt's daughter, her cousin Karen, had been killed in a car accident. Silences like this were frought with shock and disbelief.

It was Hannah who spoke first, almost uncertainly. "You're kidding."

Witt shook his head. "I'm not kidding. I won the lottery."

"Well, wahoo!" Joni said as excitement and happiness burst through the layer of shock. "Double wahoo! That's wonderful, Uncle Witt! Enough to buy a new truck, huh?"

But Witt didn't answer her. Instead, he simply looked at her and then at Hannah. Another silence fell, and Joni felt her heart begin to beat with loud thuds. Finally she whispered, "*More* than enough to buy a truck?"

Hannah's dark eyes flew to her daughter, then leaped back to Witt. She reached out a hand and touched his forearm. "Witt? How much did you win?"

Witt cleared his throat. "It's…well…kinda hard to believe."

"Ohmigod," Joni said in a rush, feeling hot and cold by turns. "Uncle Witt…" She turned to look at her mother, as if she could find some link back to reality there. But Hannah's face was registering the same blank disbelief. Things like this didn't happen to people they knew.

"It's…" Witt sighed and ran his fingers through his hair. "I won the jackpot."

"Oh my God." This time it was Hannah who spoke, her tone prayerful. "Oh, Witt, that's a lot of money. How much?"

"Eleven million." His voice sounded almost choked. "Of course, it won't be that much. The payout is over twenty-five years, and there's taxes and stuff but, um…"

Joni, always great at math, calculated quickly. "You'll still be bringing home almost two hundred thousand a year," she said. "My God. That's incredible." Then, as a sudden, wonderful exuberance hit her, she let out a whoop. "Oh, man, Uncle Witt, you're on easy street now. So you get the new truck and a lot else besides." She grinned at him, feeling a wonderful sense of happiness for the man who had been like a father to her since the death of her dad. "It couldn't happen to a nicer guy. So, are you going to Tahiti?"

He laughed, sounding embarrassed. "Nah. Not unless Hannah wants to go."

Hannah's eyes widened; then her cheeks pinkened. "Tahiti? Me?" She waved away the idea. "What on earth would I do there? Besides, the winnings are yours, Witt."

His face took on a strange tension, one Joni couldn't identify. "So what then?" she pressed him.

"I haven't had a whole lot of time to think about it, Joni. Jeez, I just found out last week."

"Last week? You've been sitting on this for a week?" She couldn't believe it. She would have been shrieking from the rooftops.

"Well, I didn't exactly believe it. I wanted to verify it first. Then…well…" He hesitated. "I don't want the whole world to know about it, not just yet."

"That's understandable," Hannah said promptly.

"But you must have been thinking about what you want to do with the money."

But Joni's thoughts had turned suddenly to a darker vein, one that left her feeling chilled. She'd heard about lottery winners and how their lives could be turned into absolute hell by other folks.

"Just put it all in a bank, Uncle Witt," she said. "Put it away and use it any way you see fit. And just remember, you don't owe anything to anyone."

His blue eyes settled on her, blue eyes that she sometimes thought were the wisest eyes she'd ever looked into.

"I *do* owe something, Joni," he said slowly. "Everyone owes something. I'm thinking about building a lodge on the property. You know how long this town has wanted something like that. It'd make jobs for folks around here, jobs that don't depend on a mine. And if we had the facility, I'm sure the tourists would follow. God knows we've got plenty of snow and hills."

But the chill around her heart deepened. Because the simple fact was, when there was a lot of money involved, nothing was ever that simple.

"Well," said Hannah briskly, "this calls for a celebration. Let me get you a glass of Drambuie, Witt. What about you, Joni?"

"No thanks, Mom." She hated to drink. Besides, something about this didn't feel right. Witt was looking strange, and Hannah was looking disturbed, and there was suddenly an undercurrent so strong in the room that Joni could feel her own nerves stretching.

But she'd had that feeling before with her mother and her uncle. It had been there ever since she could remember, the feeling that things were being left unspoken. It was so familiar she hardly wondered about it.

But all of a sudden it seemed significant. And just as suddenly, Witt's news didn't feel like anything to celebrate.

The chill settled over her again, this time a strong foreboding. In her heart of hearts, she knew nothing was ever going to be the same again.

2

Hardy Wingate sat at his mother's bedside and tried not to give in to the anxiety that was creeping along his nerve endings. Barbara was better, they told him. She'd passed the crisis. But he couldn't see it. She was still on oxygen, she still had tubes running into her everywhere, and the only improvement he could see was that she wasn't on a respirator anymore. Her breathing was still labored, though, and he knew things could change in an instant, no matter what they told him.

He touched her hand gently, hoping she could tell he was there. Since last night, when he'd brought her in, she hadn't seemed to be aware of much. Which was probably a good thing. He hoped she wasn't suffering.

But he was going crazy, sitting there with nothing to occupy him but worry and guilt. And memories. God-awful memories of sitting beside Karen Matlock's bedside twelve years ago, just before she died. Just before Witt Matlock threw him out.

He didn't blame Witt for that, but it had hurt anyway. And sometimes it still hurt. Like right now, when he was reliving the whole damn nightmare because he had nothing to occupy his thoughts.

He'd picked up a paperback novel at the gift shop earlier, some highly touted thriller, but it hadn't been able to hold his attention. Either J. W. Killeen was losing his touch or Hardy Wingate just didn't have the brainpower left to focus on it.

So he sat there holding his mother's hand, trying not to think about how frail it felt, trying not to think about Karen Wingate and that hellish night twelve years ago. But trying not to think about things only seemed to make him think about them more.

Or maybe it was talking to Joni Matlock earlier in the cafeteria that was making him think so much about Karen. Back in high school, when he'd been dating Karen, he'd gotten to know Joni because the girls were close. But since Karen's death…well, he hadn't had a whole lot to do with the Matlocks since then.

And even in a small town like this, it was possible to avoid people if you really wanted to. Right after the accident, he'd gone away to college. By the time he got back, Joni had gone away to school, and since her return three years ago, the most he'd seen of her was across the width of the supermarket or Main Street. Which suited him fine.

But then today, out of the clear blue, she'd come up to him while he was having coffee in the cafeteria and had joined him. What had possessed the woman? She knew what her uncle thought of him. And she must have noticed that he'd been working on avoiding her. Hell, the reason the width of the street was always between them was that he was perfectly willing to cross the damn thing to get away when he saw her coming.

Then, like nothing in the world had ever happened, she plopped down with him at the cafeteria table. Weird. And he'd been within two seconds of jumping up and walking away when she'd asked about his mother.

Now, he couldn't ignore that. He couldn't be rude in the face of that kind of politeness. His mother had raised him better than that. So he'd been stuck, and he'd had to talk to her.

And all the time he'd been itching to get away. He supposed it was stupid, after all this time, but he didn't want any more trouble with Witt Matlock. That man hated him.

Well, why the hell not? He hated himself.

He froze suddenly, his heart stopping in his chest as he realized that his mother was no longer breathing. Caught in a vise of fear, he lifted his gaze to her face. Then, just as he was reaching for the call button, she drew a long, ragged breath. Then another. The tortured tempos of life resumed.

He waited breathlessly for a long time, but Barbara

seemed to have taken a firm grasp on life once more. The tightness in his chest eased a little, but as it did, he felt the burn of unshed tears in his eyes.

"Hang in there," he heard himself tell her in a rough whisper. "Hang in there, Mom."

Even as he spoke the encouragement, he wondered why. Maybe she was as tired of it all as he sometimes felt. As he felt right now. Sometimes it just didn't seem worth the effort.

But he wasn't ready to lose her yet. He probably never would be, but she was only fifty, and he figured he shouldn't have to be losing her for a good long while yet.

As soon as he had the thought, bitterness rose in him, burning his throat like bile. Karen had been too young, too. Only seventeen. Life and death didn't care about things like youth.

But Barbara kept breathing, difficult though it was, and the heart monitor kept recording her steady, too-rapid beats. He watched the lambda waves form on the display, one after another in perfect rhythm, checked the digital readouts and saw that her blood pressure was steady, her pulse a constant eighty-five. Too fast, but strong. Strong enough. Not like it had been with Karen.

For a few seconds he was suddenly back in the ICU twelve years ago, watching the monitor, all too aware despite his lack of knowledge that the ragged pattern of Karen's heartbeats wasn't a good sign. Aware that the rattling unsteadiness of her breathing was terrible. Aware that those low numbers on the blood pressure monitors were dangerous.

Aware that no one was doing anything for her just then. Wondering why, ready to go grab someone and demand they help her. Sensing that they had done all they could.

Then Witt had come into the cubicle behind him.

"Get out!"

He jerked, as if the words had been spoken behind him right now instead of twelve years ago. He came back to the present with the feeling of someone who had just taken a long, rough journey. His heart was pounding, and his face was damp with sweat. God!

There was a rustle, and the curtain was pulled back. Delia Patterson entered, giving him a slight smile and a nod as she approached the bed. She checked the IV and made a note on a clipboard.

"How is she?"

Delia, a slightly plump woman with the champagne-blond hair that a lot of older women adopted to cover the gray, looked at him. She'd known Hardy all his life. "You can see for yourself."

"Delia..."

She shook her head. "I can't make any promises. And I'm not the doctor. But..." She hesitated. "We might see some difference by morning. Maybe. The doctor put her on some pretty powerful antibiotics, Hardy. But no one can say for sure, understand?"

He nodded, hating the uncertainty. He'd always

hated uncertainty, but life seemed to deal out very little else.

"You staying all night?" she asked.

"I plan to."

"That waiting-room couch is mighty hard." She glanced at her watch. "And you've been in here longer than the allowed ten minutes."

"For God's sake, I'm just sitting here holding her hand."

She nodded. "Okay, I'll give you another ten."

"Thanks."

On the way out the door she paused and laid her hand on his shoulder. "If she's more alert in the morning, she's going to need you then, Hardy. You might consider getting some serious sleep tonight."

"I want to be here. In case."

She nodded. "But I can call you if…anything changes. You could be here in ten minutes."

"That might be too many minutes. Thanks, Delia, but I'm staying."

"And probably catching pneumonia, too." She shook her head. "We're overflowing into the hallways. Have you been immunized?"

"Who, me?"

She shook her head, muttered something and walked out. Hardy felt a faint smile curling the corners of his mouth, but it faded as he turned back to his mother. She was fighting for her life, and if she could summon the energy to do that, then he could damn well stick it out with her.

After ten more minutes Delia kept her word and banished him to the ICU waiting room. Much to his relief, there were only two other people there. Given Delia's description of patients overflowing into the halls, he'd figured the waiting rooms would be getting full, too.

There was one couch. It didn't look too healthy, as if it hadn't been cleaned in a long time, and it didn't offer any extra padding for comfort. In fact, he thought minutes after he'd stretched out on it, the floor was probably more comfortable.

So what? He could handle it for forty minutes until Delia would be obliged to let him back into the ICU.

But as soon as he closed his eyes, Joni Matlock filled his mind's eye. Everything was determined to torture him, it seemed. There couldn't be a worse possible time to start thinking about the Matlocks. Thinking about Joni inevitably led him to thinking about Karen, and tonight he didn't want to remember how the best medical treatment in the world hadn't been able to save Karen, not with his mother at death's door.

But good time, bad time, right time, wrong time, it didn't make a bit of difference. His thoughts wouldn't leave him alone, and they seemed bound and determined to focus on Joni.

Okay, he told himself. Think about Joni. Think about her until you're bored and your mind decides to go somewhere else.

So he thought over their conversation earlier. It

had been brief. He figured she'd picked up on the fact that he really didn't want to talk to her. She'd been polite, concerned the way any stranger would be. Nothing more. Nothing to get all bent about.

Except that he couldn't forget those blue eyes of hers. It wasn't just that they were pretty, though they certainly were. It wasn't just that they were as arrestingly blue as a clear mountain-morning sky. It was the way they seemed to speak to him. They'd only talked for three minutes, if that, but when he'd walked away, he'd had the feeling they'd shared an entire subtext, her eyes to his.

But those eyes had always made him feel that way. They'd always drawn him and spoken to him. If life had treated them all differently, he might have gotten to know her better. Instead, he avoided her the way he avoided Witt. Because some things were better left buried, and there was no way he could talk to Joni Matlock without remembering Karen Matlock.

As easy as that, his thoughts turned on him and began to twist into dark corridors. Swearing under his breath, he sat upright and forced himself to remember where he was. He had to stop beating himself up over the past. He knew that. It was done, and he couldn't change any of it.

But when it got dark, on nights when he couldn't sleep, he could still hear Karen's scream as the other car swerved straight at him, could still remember her screams as they lay in the mangled wreckage of his car. Could still remember Witt looking at him out of cold, dead eyes and saying, "You killed her, boy. You killed her."

The sounds and smells of the ICU had brought it all back to the surface, bubbling up like explosive gases in the swamp of his brain. His hold on the present, he realized, was getting mighty tenuous.

Shoving himself to his feet, he went out into the brightly lighted corridor to pace. But that, too, was familiar, and he realized with a sickening plunge of his stomach that yesterday and today were starting to fuse in his weary brain. He wasn't sure from one minute to the next which year it was and who was lying in the ICU near death.

God, he thought he'd gotten over the worst of this a few years ago, but now here it was again, rearing up to bite him on the butt. He deserved it; he knew that. But deserving this kind of torture didn't mean he had to like it.

He passed his hand over his face, trying to wipe away the images that seemed to be dancing at the edges of his vision, horrific images that were burned forever into his mind. Feeling desperate, he glanced at his watch and realized it was only two minutes until they would let him in to see Barbara one last time before they shut down visiting hours for the night.

Stupid, he thought. Family members ought to be able to visit patients in the ICU round the clock. What difference did it make if it was midnight, 2:00 a.m. or 8:00 a.m?

But they were strict about it, and he didn't want to squawk too loudly right now, especially since he'd been pushing the limits all day and the nurses had been letting him.

He was standing right outside the ICU door when Delia opened it.

"Last call," she said, pursing her lips. "Ten minutes and you're outta here, Hardy. Then you're going to go home and get some sleep. With this pneumonia going around, we ain't got *no* room for exhaustion cases."

He gave her a wan smile and made his way to the cubicle where his mother lay. No change. At once relief and disappointment filled him, but he reminded himself that he'd been told not to expect a miracle. Morning. He'd been told again and again that she might be better in the morning. It was so hard to believe right now, though, as he stood at her bedside, holding her hand gently and murmuring nonsense to her.

Ten minutes later, when he was evicted, nothing had changed. He had the panicky feeling that his mother was slipping slowly away from him, so slowly that it was almost undetectable. And he couldn't really blame her.

Life had been hard on her for a long time. First there had been his drunken bum of a father. Then, when Lester had left, there had been the two jobs she worked to keep Hardy and herself clothed and sheltered. She'd even continued working two jobs so he could go to college. Then she'd helped him start his construction firm, working the endless hours right beside him as they built the business. Now that things were finally going good, it seemed somehow so unreasonably unfair that she should be at death's door.

But maybe she'd had enough. He could hardly blame her. He knew he hadn't lived up to her dreams for him. There was the accident with Karen's death, which had certainly hurt her, too, and then his refusal to date anyone, though she kept encouraging him to. She wanted grandbabies, she said, but he couldn't bear the thought of caring like that again.

So maybe she was just fed up. Her life had been one major disappointment after another.

And the thoughts running through his brain were doing nothing at all to ease his panic.

When he stepped blindly out of the ICU, he bumped into someone. It took him a moment to recognize Joni. "What are you doing here?" he demanded roughly. It was a question he had no right to ask, and he realized it almost as soon as the words came out of his mouth.

But she didn't take it amiss. "I was worrying about you and your mother. How is she?"

"Pretty bad," he admitted reluctantly. "We probably won't know anything till morning."

"I'm sorry."

He gave her a short nod.

She reached out tentatively and touched his forearm briefly. "Let me buy you a cocoa?"

He looked down at her and shook his head. "Joni, you're courting disaster. You know what Witt thinks of me."

"Yeah. But I happen to disagree, and I'm over twenty-one. Cocoa?"

"The cafeteria's closed."

She gave him a wink that made him feel strangely light-headed. Lack of sleep, he told himself.

"Hey," she said, grabbing his hand, "I work here, remember? I know where the good stuff is hidden."

She took him away from the ICU toward the reception area, then steered him through a door that said Employees Only.

Inside was a staff lounge. A nurse was sitting on an easy chair with her shoes kicked off, eating a snack. A man in scrubs was stretched out on a couch with a cushion over his face.

Joni waved at the nurse, then put her finger over her lips as she looked at Hardy and pointed to the sleeping man. He nodded.

She made two mugs of instant cocoa, passed him one, then indicated he should follow her. They left the lounge and went to sit in the reception area.

"See?" she said. "Insider knowledge."

"Thanks." He hoped it didn't sound as grudging as it felt, because the cocoa was hot and delicious and contained the first calories he'd put in his system since a sandwich at noon.

"You look awful," she told him.

She hadn't changed a bit, he realized. She was still

the mouthy fourteen-year-old who'd pestered the living bejesus out of him and Karen sometimes. Even back then, he'd tried to be understanding. A kid who'd lost her daddy and moved to a town that didn't easily make room for new arrivals—yeah, she'd had a reason to be a pest. Everybody else in the world had kind of ignored her.

"Have you slept within recent memory?" she asked.

"I've dozed here and there. Don't give me hell, Joni. I'm not up for it."

"Okay." She sipped her cocoa and looked at him from those amazing blue eyes.

"Don't you need to get home and get some sleep yourself?"

She shrugged. "I'm not on duty tomorrow. Day off."

"Even with the epidemic?"

"I might be called in," she admitted.

"Then go get some sleep."

"Are you trying to get rid of me?"

They stared at each other, letting her words hang in the air between them. Neither of them wanted to mention Karen, he realized, but she lay between them as surely as if she were there.

"I'm trying to keep you out of trouble with your uncle," he said finally.

"My problem, not yours."

He cocked an eye at her. "What put you in such a feisty mood?"

"I don't know. Maybe it's realizing that age doesn't necessarily make a person wise."

He sipped his cocoa, wondering what she was getting at, and almost afraid to ask. He didn't know Joni at all anymore, he reminded himself. Since Karen's death, until today, they hadn't passed more than a dozen words.

"Can you keep a secret?" she asked finally.

"Sure. But you shouldn't be telling them to me."

"I've got a reason."

She always had a reason. He remembered that from way back when. According to Joni, she never did a thing without good reason. He had his own thoughts about that.

"Witt won the lottery," she told him. "But don't tell anyone else."

"Yeah?" He felt a mild interest. "That's neat. You all going to take a vacation in Hawaii?" His mother had always wanted to do that. It pained him that he hadn't yet been able to make that dream come true for her. This year, he promised himself. Somehow, if she made it through this pneumonia, he was going to get her to Hawaii, if he had to move heaven and earth.

"I suggested Tahiti." She gave him a smile that struck him as uneasy and sad. Despite all his overwhelming emotional exhaustion because of the last twenty-four desperate hours, he still managed to feel a pang for Joni.

"What's wrong?"

"Not a thing," she said. "It's a lot of money."

"Well, that's a good thing," he said generously. "Witt's worked hard in the mine all his life. You can't begrudge him an early retirement."

"I'd never do that. No, I'm really pleased for him."

"So, is he going to Tahiti?"

She shook her head. "No."

"Seems a shame. But maybe it wasn't enough for the trip."

She looked at him sideways. "How about eleven million dollars?"

That set him back on his heels. Numbers like that were usually attached to major construction jobs, none of which he'd so far managed to garner for his company. "Wow," he said after a moment. "Wow. But it doesn't pay out in a lump sum."

"No, but even with the payout schedule it's a lot of money."

"I guess he *will* retire."

"Actually..." She hesitated. "He's thinking about a career change."

"That's cool." Like he cared.

"He's...um...thinking about building a resort on that property he owns west of town."

And suddenly Hardy understood why she was mentioning this to him. He looked straight at her and felt the entire world hold its breath for a few seconds. Then he said slowly, "Joni...are you sure you know what you're doing?"

Her mouth tightened, and she looked away. When she faced him again, her eyes were moist. "When Karen died, I didn't just lose my best friend. I lost my other best friend, too."

In spite of himself, he felt his throat tighten a little, and he cleared it. "Joni…"

She shook her head, silencing him. "It's been twelve years, Hardy. Twelve years! And ever since we talked this afternoon, I've been thinking about how much Witt's anger has cost *me*. And you, too. Karen would never have had to sneak out with you that night if Witt hadn't thought you weren't good enough for her. And you and I could still have been friends except for Witt. Damn it, Hardy, it's not right. And Karen had the guts not to let it keep her away from you. Maybe I've got the same guts, finally."

"Joni…Joni, it's not a matter of guts. It's a matter of not raking up a whole lot of…unpleasantness. Not at this late date. After all this time, Witt's not going to change his mind about me. It'll just open old wounds for everyone."

"Maybe they need to be opened." A tear spilled down her cheek. "This money's a bad thing, Hardy. I've been feeling it ever since Witt told me about it. The only way to avoid the bad things is to turn it to some good. You could build that lodge better than anybody."

"You don't know that. There's no way you can know that."

"I *believe* it."

He knew what she was offering him. Witt would never, ever, have asked him to bid on the project, would never even have let him know it was up for bid. But if he could just give Witt the best bid... maybe he'd get the job anyway. And it was exactly the kind of job he knew how to do, the kind of job he was constantly looking for. It could benefit them both.

He shook his head. "Witt will never agree, no matter how good the bid is."

"I have some influence, Hardy."

"That may be. But you don't want to get crosswise with your uncle, Joni. He and your mom are the only family you have."

"Well, you do what you think best. But I'll tell you right now, the next time you cross a street when you see me coming, I'm going to cross it, too." She drew a tremulous breath. "It's like...it's like I can feel Karen telling me to do this. I know that's crazy, but it's what I *feel*. I'm not going to let Witt tell me who I can be friends with anymore. And neither should you."

He looked at her, wondering if she were getting sick or slipping a cog. All this time... Yeah, all this time. He suddenly remembered that it hadn't been Joni who'd been avoiding him. No, he'd been the one avoiding her. Because of Witt. Because he was scared to look into that abyss yet again. Because he'd managed to put his guilt on the back burner finally, and getting involved with the Matlocks was only going to make him face it all over again.

He closed his eyes, the memories surging in him, filling him with blackness. "It won't work, Joni."

"You don't know until you try."

He did know, though. He knew in his deepest heart that Witt would never give him the job. But he also knew in his deepest heart that he wouldn't be able to live with himself if he didn't try.

Why, he wondered, did nearly every damn thing in his life have to be just beyond his grasp? It seemed to him that life had always been teasing and tantalizing him with promises it snatched away before they were barely fulfilled. And, God, he hoped his mother wasn't another one of them.

When he looked at Joni again, his eyes felt swollen and hot, and his heart hurt almost too much to bear. "What's the point? It won't happen."

"Maybe, maybe not," she said. "But you'll never know if you don't try."

A great philosophy, but words were cheap. Hardy had absolutely no doubt that he was going to find himself disappointed once again.

But what the hell, he thought. After a while you got used to being kicked.

But all that faded away at four-thirty in the morning when Barbara Wingate awoke, her fever gone and her gaze once again aware.

So maybe, Hardy thought gratefully, you didn't always have to get kicked.

It was a thought that kept him smiling the rest of the day.

3

Wind whipped the snow into a whiteness that erased the world as Joni drove home from work on a chilly January afternoon. A blizzard was moving through the mountains, and she was beginning to wonder if she'd stayed a little too late at the hospital. She didn't have all that far to drive, though, and she reminded herself that she would be driving through this kind of weather at least a dozen more times before winter blew its last white breath over the Colorado Rockies. Heck, some years she drove through this until June.

It was two days after New Year's, and she was feeling as good as it was possible to feel in the wake of the holidays. She wondered if she would have her usual letdown or if she was finally old enough not to get so high on anticipation that she would inevitably crash after New Year's.

Probably not, she decided. Nor was she sure she

really wanted to outgrow the magical, excited feeling that always preceded Christmas for her.

When she got home and had left her outerwear in the mudroom, she went to find her mother. Hannah was sitting in the living room, reading.

"Miserable out there," she remarked to her daughter. "Did you have trouble getting up the hill?"

"No. But I wouldn't want to try it in an hour." The stack of mail was on the table by the door, and she flipped through it, pulling out her credit card bill and the utility bill that she paid as part of her share of the household costs. Then she came to a thick manila envelope that wasn't addressed to anyone.

"What's this?" she asked.

"Witt left it. He said it's the request for bids he had a lawyer draw up." Hannah smiled. "He was as excited as a kid. Apparently he's sent a bunch of them out to firms in Denver, and now he can't wait for the replies."

"So why did we get a copy?"

Hannah laughed. "I think he wanted to show off a little."

Witt liked to show off for her mother, Joni thought. She often wondered why the two of them had never gotten together. They were both widowed, after all. But...sometimes she sensed there was an invisible wall between them. Some kind of barrier the two refused to cross.

Silly, she told herself. She was imagining things. "I guess he won't mind if I look at it."

"I guess he was hoping you might," Hannah replied. "Witt's like any other man. He wants to hear how brilliant he is."

The statement carried the warmth of affection, and Joni laughed. She tucked the envelope under her arm and headed upstairs.

"Trust me," Hannah called after her, "it'll put you to sleep."

But Joni had other thoughts in mind, and she eagerly pried the envelope open when she reached her room. A stapled stack of papers came out, and a quick scan told her most of it was boilerplate, establishing rules such as how the bid should be presented. But there was a specification, too, one that she was able to determine required an architectural proposal for a thirty-room lodge. The other details didn't matter to her. What did matter was the due date on the request: January tenth.

She was jolted by the nearness of the date. Witt must have sent these out early last month or even in November to the firms in Denver. They would need at least a month to respond.

The due date was only a week away. And Hardy probably hadn't even seen this yet.

She checked the date again to be sure she wasn't mistaken. This was fast, awfully fast, but maybe it had to be, so construction could start as early as possible in the spring.

But why had it taken Witt so long to drop this copy off for her mother? Had he deliberately done this so it wouldn't fall into Hardy's hands? But why would he even suspect it would? No, it must be that he'd only now gotten a spare copy from his attorney.

Eight days. If Hardy was to have any chance of responding to this, she had to get the papers to him right away.

But even as she jumped up from the bed, ready to dash out into the blizzard once more, a thought yanked her back. If she did this, Witt might never forgive her.

Her pulse racing, she flopped onto the bed and stared at the cracked ceiling, thinking about that. It was all well and good to believe that Witt ought to forgive Hardy. The police had blamed the drunk driver for the accident, and Joni couldn't understand why Witt persisted in believing Hardy was responsible—except that Hardy wasn't supposed to be seeing Karen, and if Karen hadn't climbed out the window that July night, she would probably still be alive.

But Karen was dead, and Witt honestly believed that Hardy was responsible. There was, she supposed, a possibility that Witt was right. Maybe he knew something about what had happened that she didn't. But it was more likely, she believed, that he simply needed a scapegoat, and since the drunk driver hadn't survived the accident, Hardy was the only person left to blame.

Taking this proposal over to Hardy would be seen

as a betrayal. Witt might never forgive her. But then she decided that was ridiculous. Witt always forgave her. He would be mad, sure, but he would forgive her once she explained.

Explained. It occurred to her that maybe she'd better be able to explain this to herself before she tried to explain it to Witt. Common sense dictated that she just stay out of this. It wasn't her problem, nor was it her feud—as Hardy had made patently clear since their talk that night at the hospital. He was still avoiding her like the plague.

But it *was* her problem, she decided. She loved Witt, and she liked Hardy. It pained her that Witt had carried such anger all this time. It meant that he wasn't healing.

Karen would want her to do this. She believed that in her soul. They'd been like sisters, especially after Joni moved to town, sharing everything—their hopes, dreams and feelings. Sharing Witt as a father, and Hannah as a mother. Sharing Hardy's friendship, although only Karen had dated him.

Karen wouldn't like to see her father so bitter and angry, and she wouldn't like Hardy to miss this opportunity. There was not a doubt of that in Joni's mind. Karen, had she been here, never would have allowed this state of affairs to continue for so long.

But Karen wasn't here, and Witt was. She hated to have Witt angry with her and always had. She loved him so much that she wanted to be perfect for him, although it was an impossible goal.

And sometimes, dimly, she realized that she'd spent the last twelve years trying to replace his daughter for him. Maybe it was time to grow up and accept that she couldn't replace Karen, and that she had to live her own life as she saw fit.

Sitting up, she went to the closet and pulled out a small photo album she kept on a shelf beneath a stack of sweatshirts. Almost all the pages were empty, but that was because she only had a half-dozen photos of Karen.

Oh, Witt had shoe boxes full of pictures of his daughter, but these photos were special. These photos had been hers and hers alone, taken with a cheap camera that hadn't lasted beyond a couple rolls of film. In retrospect, she wished she'd photographed Karen more often, instead of wasting film on scenery. But she hadn't guessed what was going to happen.

So here they were, her six private memories of Karen. The first snapshot, her favorite, showed her and Karen sitting on the bleachers at the high school football field. They had both laughed and acted silly that afternoon at football practice, full of the high spirits and joy of youth. Hardy had snapped that photo of them just before practice had started. She could still remember how he had looked all suited up for the game, holding her silly little camera in his big hands.

The next photo, one she would never, ever let Witt see, was of Hardy and Karen. Snow was falling, and the flash had bounced off it, giving the couple in the photo a dim, background look. But they were holding each other, hugging, their faces pressed close as they grinned into the camera.

Where the first picture always made her smile in memory, this one always made her ache.

They had been so young. So sure that the world was their oyster. All of them. And maybe it had been, only instead of finding pearls they'd all found lumps of coal.

Her throat suddenly tight, Joni closed the album without looking any farther. She knew the photos by heart, anyway. She'd wept over them on enough cold, dark nights, lying up here, unable to believe that Karen was truly gone.

There was such a feeling of unfinished business, but not just for Karen, who had died. Lately she had been thinking that they'd all somehow gone into stasis since Karen's death. As if they were in some kind of emotional suspended animation. All of them: Witt, who had never recovered from his grief; Hannah, who...who just seemed to be getting through the days. Herself, who always felt as if she was just marking time. And Hardy, who, as far as she could tell, hadn't even dated.

They were all unfinished lives, and for so long none of them seemed to have taken any real steps to move forward emotionally.

Karen wouldn't have liked that. And it was time, Joni decided with a stiffening of her shoulders, that someone pushed them past their frozen emotional states.

Scooping up the request for bids, she tucked it under her baggy green Shaker sweater and set out on her personal mission to thaw the glacier that had swallowed them all.

"Where are you going?" Hannah asked as Joni passed her in the living room. "Supper's almost ready."

"I won't be long," Joni replied, not even breaking step. "I just need to run over to…Sally's. Back in a sec."

"Be careful out there. It's getting really bad."

No kidding, Joni thought after she'd tugged on her parka, hat, mittens and boots, and stepped outside. It had been bad enough when she'd come home from work, but now the wind was blowing so hard that ice crystals stung her face, and the street lamp two houses down was nothing but a glow in the snow-hidden night.

If she'd had to go either up- or downhill to get to Hardy's house, she would have stopped right there. But he lived three blocks over on a cross street, a level run. She could make it.

The night was mysterious and threatening, the whipping snow hiding the landmarks, making the world look unfamiliar. Leaning into the wind, squinting against the stinging snow, she slipped and slid down the drifting street. The sidewalks, caught as they were between two deep snowbanks, were already filled with the snow they caught, and the going was easier on the street. There was no traffic at all to give her any problems.

It was so lonely out here. There was something about being out in the middle of a snowstorm alone that left her feeling cut off and solitary to her very soul. The little bits of warm light that reached her from the street lamps and the glow from nearby windows only made her feel lonelier somehow.

She'd always felt this way on cold wintry nights, walking down darkened streets with no other soul in evidence, but tonight was even worse than usual, as if all the empty places in her heart were filled with a cold, whistling wind she couldn't ignore. Nor could she shrug off the feeling.

Hardy's house was just another one of the small Victorians lining the streets in this part of town, but unlike the rest, his was a showplace renovated through his own hard work and skill.

Even back in high school, Hardy had loved to work with his hands and with wood. He'd replaced the gingerbread on the house during those years, spending painstaking hours in the school shop, because he didn't have the tools at home, whenever he didn't have to work. Karen had spent a lot of those hours with him, watching him, admiring his growing skill. Occasionally Joni had joined them.

But since Hardy had come back from college, he'd transformed the exterior, getting rid of the ugly aluminum siding and replacing it with wood, hanging new shutters, rebuilding the huge porch. She imagined he'd done a lot of work on the inside, too, but she didn't know, because she'd never been invited in, not since Karen's death.

At the foot of the porch steps, she hesitated, forgetting the snow that sliced at her cheeks. This was nuts, and she didn't delude herself about it. Hardy might tell her she was crazy, to get lost. Sometimes she wondered if he agreed with Witt's opinion of him.

Then there was Witt. He would forgive her. Maybe. He certainly hadn't been able to forgive Hardy all these years. But she was different, she told herself. She was his niece. His brother's daughter. He couldn't possibly treat her the same way he had treated Hardy.

That was what she told herself, anyway. She was well aware that she didn't believe it one hundred percent as she climbed the steps and finally rang Hardy's bell.

A minute passed before the door opened. Hardy stood there in stocking feet, looking rumpled in jeans and a gray sweatshirt with the sleeves pushed up.

"Joni?" he said as if he couldn't believe his eyes. "What the hell are you doing here?"

It wasn't exactly a warm welcome, but Joni hadn't expected one, not the way things were. But she wasn't doing this for herself, or even for Hardy, really. She was doing it for Karen.

Before she could formulate a response, the wind ripped around the corner of his house, splattering her face with ice needles.

"Damn," he said under his breath and reached out, taking her arm and pulling her inside. He closed the door behind her, shutting out the bitter night.

"Thanks," she murmured, her thoughts scattering as she got a look at the inside of Hardy Wingate's house.

Polished wood greeted her everywhere, from the original plank floors to the polished stair railing rising to the second floor. Colorful old rugs were scattered around the foyer, and the walls were painted a creamy white. Through the door to the right she could see a living room filled with beautiful period pieces, and to the left was the dining room, with a long Queen Anne table and chairs.

"I didn't know you liked antiques," she blurted.

"These aren't antiques," he said almost impatiently. "I made them myself."

She looked up at him. "When do you have time?"

He shrugged. "I've been doing this for years. Keeps me busy in the evenings. What do you want?"

He wasn't even going to ask her to take her coat off, she realized. Not even a civilized, neighborly offer of something hot to drink before she left. She was, however, stubborn enough not to allow him to rush her. What she was about to do deserved at least that much consideration.

"How's your mother?"

"Getting better. Still exhausted. She sleeps a lot. She's sleeping right now. Did you want to see her?"

She could tell he doubted it, and she couldn't blame him; she certainly hadn't tried to come see Barbara in the last two months. "No," she said slowly. "I came to see you."

"Big mistake. Witt'll have your hide."

"Witt's not entitled to my hide. I'm a grown woman." She smothered her exasperation. "And it's all irrelevant, anyway." Shoving her hand up under her jacket, she tugged the envelope out from under her sweater and offered it to him. It was warm from her body. "Here. The request for bids on Witt's lodge."

Hardy hesitated, looking at the envelope as she held it out to him. "Joni…" He trailed off as if he didn't know what to say.

"You've only got until the tenth to submit," she said, thrusting it toward him. "I'm sorry I couldn't give you more time, but I just got this today. You'll have to hurry."

He still didn't take the envelope. He stared at it as if it might explode at any moment. Then, slowly, he dragged his gaze from it and looked straight at her. "Witt is going to kill one of us if I take that."

She shrugged, all too aware that he was right. "I can handle it."

"Joni, why are you doing this? Why?"

She looked down, studying the braid rug beneath her feet, watching the melting snow drip from her boot and disappear into the rug. "Karen would want me to."

For the longest time Hardy didn't say anything. He didn't even move or seem to draw a breath. Just as she was about to look up at him, to make sure she hadn't shocked him into a stroke or something, he spoke.

"Take your jacket and boots off," he said roughly. "You need something hot to drink, and I'm boiling water for tea."

"I need to get right home," she said, mindful that Hannah would ask questions if she was gone too long. She wasn't comfortable with the lie she had already told, and she didn't want to have to tell too many more of them.

"You've got time enough for some tea. If you're worried about your mother, call her."

Hannah wasn't the biggest part of her problem, Joni thought gloomily as she tugged off her boots and hung her jacket on the coat tree. Not by a long shot.

She followed Hardy into the kitchen, which was behind the dining room toward the back of the house. Here, too, loving care was displayed in a brick floor and gleaming modern appliances complemented by beautiful oak cabinets and tiled countertops. Hardy waved her to a round oak table.

"Earl Grey okay?" he asked.

"Great." She wasn't much of a tea connoisseur,

and she would have been content with ordinary old orange and black pekoe.

Hardy brought two steaming mugs to the table, both dangling tags over the side. "Sugar? Cream? Lemon?"

"Black's fine."

Apparently he felt the same, because he sat across from her, dipping his tea bag absently while he studied her. "Karen's been gone a long time," he remarked. "I doubt any of us could know what she'd want."

"She'd want for her dad not to be so angry and bitter," Joni said firmly.

"And me submitting a bid is going to change his mind?" The question was full of disbelief.

"If you submit a good one, it might force him to face how unfair he's been to you."

"Are you so sure that he's been unfair?"

The question jolted Joni. What was he talking about? The cops had said the accident wasn't his fault. The other driver had steered right into them and Hardy hadn't been able to evade him. "It wasn't your fault," she said urgently.

"Maybe not." He dragged his eyes away from her and looked toward a corner of the kitchen. "And maybe it was. The point is, Joni, nobody except me *really* knows what happened that night. I can't blame Witt for thinking I should have done more. I think about that a lot myself."

Horror gripped her like vines of ice around her heart. "No, Hardy."

"Yes, Hardy," he said almost mockingly. He looked at her. "I've replayed those thirty seconds in my mind so many times, and I keep reaching the same conclusion. I didn't have enough experience at the wheel. Maybe I should have sped up instead of slowing down. Maybe I could have spun the wheel more. Maybe if I'd known that drunk drivers steer right into lights I would've had the presence of mind to turn mine off. Maybe I should have gone left instead of right. I can think of a dozen things I could have done differently. Maybe the outcome would have been different."

He leaned forward, his gaze burning into her. "And if I can think that, why shouldn't Witt? I don't blame him for how he feels."

She hated to think of Hardy feeling this way. "Hindsight's always twenty-twenty."

"No it's not," he said harshly. "It just asks a lot of pointless questions. But this isn't getting us anywhere. I can't bid on this project. I'd just be wasting my time."

"You don't know that." Anger began to burn in her.

"And you don't know that Witt might have a change of heart."

"You don't know that he won't. My uncle isn't a stupid man, Hardy. He wants to build the best lodge he can afford. He doesn't want it to be second-rate, or fail because it isn't attractive enough.''

"And he can get any one of a dozen decent architects and general contractors anywhere between Denver and Glenwood Springs.''

"He said he's doing this to make jobs for local people.''

Hardy shook his head in exasperation. "Noble intent, but I'm sure he's not thinking of me as local people. Christ, Joni, you still go off half-cocked, don't you?''

Another time she might have bristled, but right now she didn't want to argue with him. It would only make it easier for him to refuse to bid. "I'm not going off half-cocked. I've been thinking about this for months now.''

He just looked at her.

"Hardy, it's time for this to end.''

His eyebrows lowered, and something in his jaw set. "Have you considered that you're proposing to pick at one very large scab? That if you keep this up, someone may well wind up bleeding?''

"It's been twelve years,'' she said. It sounded like a mantra, even to her. "Enough is enough. Don't chicken out, Hardy.''

She tossed the envelope on the table and rose, ignoring her tea. But before she could reach the kitchen door, his voice stopped her.

"How are you going to explain to Witt that you don't have your copy of the bid package?''

She shrugged, refusing to look at him.

"Jesus H. Christ," he said under his breath. "Drink your damn tea. I'll make a copy of it."

She faced him then. "You're going to bid?"

"No, I'm going to save your altruistic butt." Snatching up the envelope, he disappeared into the back of the house, where his office was. Moments later, she heard the sound of a photocopier warming up.

He was going to bid, she told herself. There would be no reason for him to make a copy otherwise.

But even as she lied to herself, she knew she was doing it. He was just making sure she didn't have any excuse to leave without her copy of the request for bids.

He was taking care of her again, the way he'd always tried to in the old days. Part of her wanted to resent it, and part of her was touched that he still cared enough to do it, even after all these long years.

A few minutes later he returned with two sheafs of papers. One was her copy, carefully restapled at the corner. The other, unstapled, was clearly his copy.

"There," he said, returning hers. "Look, this isn't some kind of morality attack, is it?"

Confused, she looked at him. "Morality?"

"Yeah. You're not on some moral high horse, thinking that you're going to teach us all to be better people, are you?"

"No. God no! I'm not that conceited."

"No?" He put his palms on the table and leaned toward her, looking straight at her. "Then what is this, Joni? Are you saying our feelings aren't valid? That Witt doesn't have a right to be angry with me? That I don't have a right to feel it's better to avoid the man?"

She felt hurt, because she didn't at all like the way he seemed to be seeing her. Her eyes started stinging, and her throat tightened up. Pressing her lips together, she snatched up the envelope, stuffed the papers into it and headed for the door, picking up her jacket as she went.

"Joni..."

She didn't want to look at him, but something made her turn around anyway. "I think...I think I'm ashamed of my behavior," she said thickly. "I think I've let Karen down. You and I were friends, Hardy. We were *friends*."

Hardy stood at his open door, watching her dash down the street. Not until she stopped and pulled on her jacket did he close the door.

Damn her, he thought almost savagely. Damn her eyes. What was she doing, shaking all this old stuff out of the woodwork at this late date? What was she hoping to accomplish? Did she think some miracle was going to occur if he entered his bid? Did she think Witt was going to forget all his anger and bitterness just because Hardy Wingate could build a better hotel?

Not bloody likely.

"Shit!" He swore under his breath so his mother wouldn't be disturbed. He could almost hate Joni right now. She'd dangled a plum under his nose, something he would have given his eyeteeth to do, something that would have put him in a position to take his mother to Hawaii.

And considering that Barbara wasn't doing well at all, he desperately wanted to give her that trip. Since her pneumonia she'd been so frail, even needed a wheelchair some of the time. Her lungs had been damaged, leaving her breathless after even mild exertion. He needed to get her to a lower altitude, but she refused to go.

Swearing softly once more, he grabbed the bid packet from the table and went back to his office. A spacious two rooms he'd added to the house, it was like another world: gleaming real-wood paneling, wide picture windows looking out onto a snowy, night-darkened backyard, a freestanding fireplace. Worktables, model tables, drafting boards, two computers...

It was his eyrie. His escape. His dream-place. When he was here, he forgot everything except creating.

On the model table right now was the project he'd been working on for the last couple of months despite himself: a lodge for Witt Matlock. He had decided to fly in the face of the conventional for this one. Instead of following the Vail and Aspen trend toward Alpine looks in redwood and cedar, he'd cho-

sen to carry the Victorian charm of Whisper Creek
into the hotel. High spires, lots of gingerbread, a
porch that wrapped around. Beautiful.

Lines that sang. A creation that deserved to be
realized.

He stretched out his arm and prepared to knock
the whole thing to the floor, to wipe out the insane
dream that Joni had planted in his brain.

But he couldn't bring himself to do it. Instead, he
dropped onto a stool and simply sat staring at the
model. Seeing it not as it was, but as it could be
when finished. Somebody else could build it, he told
himself. It didn't have to be Witt. Some other inves-
tor would come along, especially if Witt built a
lodge.

That was what Witt probably wanted. A long, low
building, the rustic log-cabin type. A male sort of
retreat. That would be like Witt, to want something
of that kind, not this Victorian froufrou.

But he knew he was lying to himself. He was lying
to himself about a lot of things, and had been for
many years. It was a poor excuse, realizing that de-
luding himself was the only way he could remain
sane.

Squeezing his eyes shut, he clenched his fists and
wondered why he couldn't just keep on pretending.
Wondered why Joni had suddenly decided she had
to take action when this whole mess had been carefully buried years ago.

Did she suspect? he wondered. Had she always

suspected at some unconscious level? And if Joni had, had Karen? And maybe Witt?

It was something he'd never really admitted to himself, and sometimes, over the past twelve years, he'd managed to convince himself he was imagining the whole thing.

But the heavy weight of guilt in his heart didn't let him fool himself that easily. It wouldn't let him forget for long.

The night he'd taken Karen out, the night she'd been killed…he'd begun thinking about breaking up with her.

Because he'd just started to realize that he was falling for someone else.

And that someone else had been Joni.

4

The drive to Denver took nearly four hours, even with the high speed limit on the interstate highway. Witt was impatient all the way, and glad of Hannah's company to keep him distracted.

"I still don't understand why you want me to come with you," Hannah said as they were at last traveling through the suburbs, passing the Westminster exits.

"It's simple," he said, as he had yesterday when he'd insisted she ride shotgun. "I want a second opinion on the proposals."

"But I don't know anything about hotels, Witt."

"But you know the kind of place you'd like to stay in if you were taking a vacation in the mountains."

"I doubt that." She looked at him with a vaguely amused smile. "It's one woman's opinion, Witt."

"It's one more than just mine."

"Aren't these things decided on the basis of cost?"

"Partly. That has to be taken into account, of course. But whatever it costs, I want to be sure it's appealing." He didn't want some boxy-looking place that could be any one of a hundred other motels and hotels in the state. "I want something special."

She nodded and settled back in her seat. Out of deference to her, Witt had troubled to lay a metal sheet across the floorboards so the wind of their travel wouldn't be blowing up through the holes.

Hannah had never criticized his truck, unlike Joni, who was apt to tease him mercilessly about it. But Hannah didn't seem to have very high expectations, which he found a little strange in a woman who'd been married to a doctor. Instead, she seemed content with whatever she had, meager though it might be. And she never criticized his truck.

"I'm still gonna get that new truck," he told her, for some reason needing to know how she would react.

"I imagine you'll enjoy that," she said.

"Wouldn't you be more comfortable?"

Her dark gaze settled on him. He could feel it, even though he wasn't looking at her. He'd always been able to feel Hannah's gaze. "If I was worried about that, we could have taken my Jeep."

He kept his eyes on the road. "Seems like you could worry a little more about such things, Hannah. Look after your comfort a bit better."

"I'm content."

That was what she always said, that she was content. And he always wondered whether to believe her. Maybe she was just trying to convince herself. Or maybe she meant it. God knew he had no way of knowing the truth.

The lawyer's office was on a quiet street, in a professional building full of doctors and other lawyers, and surrounded by older residences. Jim Loeb's office was on the second floor, a spacious suite that suggested he did quite well in business and real estate law. A very ordinary man with brown hair and eyes, his wide smile saved him from being plain.

He shook Witt's hand warmly and didn't even blink when Witt introduced Hannah as his business partner. Hannah did, though. She opened her mouth as if she wanted to argue the point, then closed it tightly.

"How do the bids look?" Witt asked when they were all seated with cups of coffee.

"Well…" Jim sighed. "I was hoping for a larger response. Apparently a lot of firms don't want to get tangled up in jobs in such a small, out-of-the-way town. But we did get three, and they all look pretty good to me."

He opened a large portfolio on his desk and passed some eleven-by-seventeen color drawings to Witt. "These are from the first bidder."

"Not too bad," Witt muttered as he looked at the

half-timbered Tudor-style structure. "But not exactly exciting."

Jim nodded. "I know. But given the price constraints…well, I think this bid was off-the-shelf, if you know what I mean."

"Yeah. Something these folks have done before. What's next?"

The next was a log cabin-style structure, two stories high, looking like a piece of Fort Laramie. Witt actually liked that better. At least it had rustic charm. Hannah wasn't exactly thrilled, though. She didn't say anything, but she didn't seem especially interested. "Okay. And the last one?"

"This one's interesting," Jim said. "It came from someone we didn't approach. I guess one of the other prospectives must have turned it over to him. Anyway, I checked on him. He's solid, even if he is relatively new to the business. And he seems downright eager. Come on, I'll show you."

He took them down a short hall into another room where a polished conference table held a scale model of a two-story Victorian structure that looked like a grand hotel out of the past.

"Ohh…" said Hannah.

Witt couldn't mistake her enthusiasm, even though she said nothing more. Of course, he had nearly thirty years of learning to read that often-inscrutable face of hers. There was a smile in her dark eyes, just a subtle hint around the corners.

He looked at the model again and admitted to himself that he kind of liked the fact that the architect had gone all out, building a model rather than relying on drawings. He liked the idea that the guy apparently really wanted the job.

But he was no pushover. "Can I afford this?"

"Actually," said Jim, "you can. The bid's reasonable, well within what the bank's willing to go with."

"I don't know." He wasn't quite sure why he was resisting. "I wasn't thinking Victorian."

Hannah broke her silence. "It would fit with the rest of the town."

It would. It would fit perfectly. Especially with the Main Street improvement project that had resulted in Victorian streetlights and brick sidewalks.

He walked slowly around the table, looking at the model, which was painted in the candy colors so popular on Victorians. "It's cheerful," he said finally.

"It's beautiful," said Hannah, then clapped a hand to her mouth as if she were talking out of turn.

"That's why I brought you along," Witt said. "Talk to me, Hannah."

"The others are ordinary, Witt. This would be a landmark."

Surprisingly, Jim nodded. "Might even get you some coverage in the major papers and some magazines. And look at this." Bending over the table, he swung back part of the model, opening one of the wings for inspection. Inside were the rooms, a few of them even decorated with fancy doll furniture, rugs and fixtures.

"Wow," said Hannah, a smile curving her mouth. "Can I take this home and play with it?"

Jim laughed, and Witt had to grin. "Some doll-house, huh? Well, if I decide to go with this guy, you get to keep the model."

Hannah colored faintly. "I don't have anyplace to put it, Witt. I was just being enthusiastic."

"You'll have a place to put it," he said with a firmness that had her looking strangely at him.

"Okay," Witt said, looking at the model again, trying to wrap his preconceived ideas around this un-expected model of his future. Hannah liked it, and that was a big plus as far as he was concerned. "It's got the owner's apartments and everything?"

"It does," Jim confirmed.

"And you're sure this guy is okay?"

"I checked him out. He's only been in the busi-ness solo for five years, but he hasn't had any prob-lems. His clients seem to be happy. He has a repu-tation for keeping on schedule and on budget."

"Sounds good. And the overall price?"

"Smack between the log cabin and the Tudor style."

"Hmm." He couldn't reject it on those grounds, then.

"Witt?" Hannah spoke. "What's wrong? Don't you like it?"

"It's just not what I had in mind. I'm going to have to think about it."

"What don't you like?"

"Nothing. Really. It's just I wasn't planning on Victorian." A silly thing to be resistant about, especially when Hannah seemed to like the design.

"Well," she said, "it has to be *your* decision."

Jim spoke. "If you don't like any of them, Witt, we can put out requests for more bids. Acceptance is contingent on you liking the designs, as well as on the financial side of it."

"It's not that I don't like it," Witt said again, feeling a little beleaguered. "Maybe it's the colors. Wouldn't all white with black shutters look better?"

"More traditional, certainly," Jim agreed.

"Let's take a look at the bids, okay?"

Jim nodded and led them back to his office. He'd pulled out the salient parts of all the bid packages and had them ready for Witt to look at without the boilerplate in the way.

Witt read through the first two slowly, making mental notes about the time lines, about the lists of materials, thinking about all the little details these guys had considered, things he might never have thought about if he'd spent a year working on something like this.

The he turned to the final bid, the one for the Victorian. And he saw the name at the top of it.

"Hardy Wingate?" he said, his voice muffled. Beside him, he could feel Hannah stiffen.

Jim looked at him, his brow furrowing. "Is something wrong?"

"Yeah," said Witt, tossing the papers down on Jim's desk. "I wouldn't do business with that jerk if he was the last architect on the planet. I'll think about the other two, Jim. I'll call you in a day or two."

He and Hannah were in the car climbing back into the mountains before he spoke again. "I'm sorry, I forgot I was going to buy you lunch."

"Don't worry about it."

He nodded once, briefly, then pounded the steering wheel with the palm of his hand. "Goddamn it! How the hell did Hardy get hold of that bid package?"

Hannah spoke uncertainly. "You heard what Jim said. One of the other firms must have passed it along to him."

"Yeah. Yeah." But his gut was burning, and he didn't want to think it was all as simple as that. "Imagine him having the gall to bid!"

Hannah folded her hands in her lap. "He put an awful lot of work into it."

"And why the hell did he do that? He must've known I was going to turn him down."

"Maybe."

"There's no maybe about it." He glared at her, as if she were somehow at fault, then slapped his hand against the steering wheel once more.

"Witt…"

He hated it when she did that, starting to speak, then checking herself, leaving him wondering what the hell she had decided to say. But he knew from long experience that pressing her wasn't going to get her to spit it out.

"Damn it," he said again, and turned off the highway. "I'm getting lunch. Son of a bitch thinks I'm going to hire him to build my lodge after he killed my daughter?"

"Maybe not," Hannah said quietly.

"What's that supposed to mean?"

"Maybe he doesn't expect anything at all from you. Maybe he just has dreams, too, Witt."

"Well, fuck him."

Neither of them said another word until they stopped at a fast-food place and ordered chicken. Hannah had her usual thigh with coleslaw. Witt, who burned calories faster in the mine than he could sometimes eat them, ordered two breasts, mashed potatoes and gravy, biscuits and baked beans.

They took a table in a quiet corner. The place wasn't busy, probably because it was the middle of the afternoon. Halfway through his first chicken breast, Witt looked up. "He did it just to tweak my nose."

Hannah, who was nibbling at her coleslaw, merely looked at him.

"Well, what the hell else could he be up to?"

"Maybe," she said carefully, "he just wants the job. Or maybe it's an olive branch."

"Olive branch! Hah! He should never have taken Karen out behind my back."

"Maybe not. But you need to remember that she was your daughter, and she chose to go with him even when you forbade it."

"She wouldn't have done it if he hadn't been urging her."

"Mmm." Hannah said no more. Instead, she filled her mouth with a spoonful of slaw.

God, Witt thought, he *hated* it when she went inscrutable on him. That "Mmm" said volumes. She didn't agree with him but wasn't going to say so. Ordinarily he could ignore that kind of stuff from her, but today he was itching for a fight so badly he could hardly stand it. And Hardy Wingate was nowhere around to fight with. Which left Hannah. And what did that say about him?

"Sorry," he grumbled, and attacked his second piece of chicken. The food, which he ordinarily enjoyed, tasted like sawdust today. For a bit, he stared out the window beside him, noticing that dark clouds were gathering over the mountains to the west. Apparently the clear sunny day was about to give way to some more snow. Well, that was fine by him. The way he was feeling, getting snowed in would suit him just fine.

He tried to tell himself he shouldn't feel so bent, but he felt bent anyway. It wasn't as if Hardy Wingate had done anything new to him. All the guy had done was set himself up for a major disappointment. Asking to get kicked, really.

So what maggot was gnawing Hardy's brain, any-

way? For all the nasty things Witt had thought about
Hardy over the years, he'd never thought the guy was
stupid. And this was stupid. Had he thought he was
going to slip one by, that maybe Witt wouldn't notice
who the bidder was?

He would have liked to think Hardy was that un-
derhanded, but in his mind's eye he could still see
the pages of the bid, every one clearly marked Hardy
Wingate, Architect.

No, he hadn't been trying to pull a fast one.

"Olive branch?" he said, returning his gaze to
Hannah.

She was holding her foam coffee cup in both
hands, her lunch barely touched. "Yes," she said.

He sometimes hated her calm and her monosyl-
labic answers. Sometimes he wished she would get
all ruffled. Angry, even. He'd only seen her that way
once, but afterward it had been as if all the doors
had shut. Probably better that way, for both of them,
but a guy could wish.

"Well," he said, "it's a hell of a way to do it.
And I don't give a damn, anyhow. My daughter's
dead, and I'm not likely to forget that fact."

"Of course you're not."

He barely heard her agreement, because he could
almost, but not quite, hear the three or four sentences
she *hadn't* spoken. "What are you thinking?"

Hannah shook her head and sipped her coffee.
"It's a pretty hotel."

"Too fuckin' bad."

"Witt, please."

"Sorry." He knew Hannah didn't like that word, but he was that mad. Mad because he had a feeling someone was trying an end run around him, and he didn't like that feeling. Mad because he had a gut-deep suspicion that Hardy hadn't come up with this harebrained idea on his own. Hardy was definitely *not* that stupid.

But then, his opinion of Hardy Wingate had never been that low. Even back when he'd objected to Karen dating him, he hadn't thought Hardy was all that bad. A little wild, like most boys his age, but not as wild as some. It was just that at the time, given Hardy's background, Witt had feared the boy wasn't going anywhere, and he hadn't wanted Karen to tie herself down to some miner. He'd wanted better things for her.

And he'd feared that Hardy's character hadn't been fully set yet, and that he might turn out to be a twig off his father's tree. A useless alcoholic. Hadn't turned out that way, obviously, but Witt didn't have a crystal ball. He'd just wanted what was best for Karen.

But Karen was dead, and he held Wingate directly responsible, and he wasn't going to make any excuses for that. None at all.

And he sure as hell wasn't going to give the guy a million-dollar job. Jesus, no. Every time he saw Hardy, all he could think of was Karen.

Hannah stirred, and Witt looked at her, asking, "Aren't you going to eat?"

"Somehow I don't have much appetite when you get mad."

"I'm not mad."

She shook her head.

"Okay, so I'm mad. Except that…that's not exactly the word I would use, Hannah."

She sipped her coffee and nodded encouragingly, but he didn't have any more to say. Finally she said, "Maybe you're not as angry as you are hurt."

He shied away from that. It sounded weak, somehow. "The hurt was a long time ago."

"That isn't what I meant." But, as usual, she wouldn't tell him what she *had* meant. That was Hannah. Like talking to a goddamn riddle.

He sighed in irritation and shoved his lunch aside, his appetite long since gone. Reaching for the coffee he still hadn't touched, he popped a hole in the plastic lid, then swore when it burned his tongue. Some days he felt cursed, and this was turning into one of them.

It didn't help when he realized Hannah was looking amused. "What's so funny?" he demanded.

"Not a thing."

"Quit lying to me."

Her amusement faded, but she didn't answer directly. "Sometimes," she said, "folks start acting like flies caught in a spiderweb. Twisting this way and that and just getting more stuck."

Witt didn't like that image one bit, especially since he had the niggling suspicion she might be right about him. "What are you saying?" The question was truculent, and he expected that in her usual way she would avoid answering. She surprised him.

"Look into your heart, Witt. Do what you know is *right*."

And the way she said "right" let him know that she didn't mean he should do what he felt like doing. Funny how doing the *right* think was often the wrong thing in terms of how you felt about it.

"I *am* doing the right thing. I ain't letting any murderer build my hotel."

For once her face wasn't inscrutable. It was downright disapproving. Right now he didn't give a damn. Right now he wasn't prepared to nitpick the fine line between murder and killing, or the one between deliberate and accidental. Because the result was always the same, regardless: Karen was still dead.

Joni beat her mother home by about twenty minutes, so she started making lasagne. As a rule, she hated cooking, but there were times, like now, when the routine and rhythm of it could soothe her. She desperately needed soothing.

All day she'd been acutely aware that Witt and Hannah had gone to Denver to review the bids. She had no idea if Hardy had bid and couldn't even guess what Witt's response would be if he had. Would Witt suspect her involvement? Part of her hoped not, while another part of her scolded herself for being spineless. She ought to just fess up and have it out with Witt.

But now that she'd taken the drastic action of trying to mend fences with Hardy, all she could think about was how much she loved Witt.

She browned some hamburger, then dumped store-bought spaghetti sauce into the pot with it to simmer. She put the water on to boil for the pasta and stirred the ricotta mixture in a blue bowl.

Then, for a bit, she had nothing to do but wait, and waiting gave her time to think. For a week now she'd been trying to avoid that, but life wasn't cooperating.

She loved Witt. She loved him at least as much as she'd loved her father. He'd been a good uncle before her father's death, and she'd adored him, but from the day she and Hannah had moved up here, after Lewis was killed, Witt had stood in for her dad.

He'd been there every time she had needed him. He'd treated her with every bit as much affection and warmth as he'd treated Karen, and she and Karen had often pretended they were sisters, not just cousins.

Since Karen's death...well, since Karen's death, Joni had often felt she needed to fill that hole in Witt's life, and Witt had seemed to take her even more into his heart. It wasn't that she had replaced Karen for him, but that, lacking Karen, he had lavished even more love on Joni.

She would have done just about anything for him. So why had she done this? What had compelled her, after all this time, to rock what was a very dangerous emotional boat?

Remembering her reasons now was surprisingly difficult. All she knew was that she had felt compelled, as if some shame deep within her had demanded she act. Shame at having abandoned Hardy after the accident because Witt had blamed him?

Maybe. Or maybe it was something more. But she honestly didn't know what.

And that scared her a bit, the feeling that something was going on deep inside her that was out of her control.

Hannah came in just as Joni was layering the lasagne. "Oh, good," she said. "I'm starved, and that's just what I'm in the mood for." She paused to kiss her daughter's cheek.

"Didn't Uncle Witt buy you lunch?" Joni's heart had started to race with anxiety.

"Yes, of course he did. But he was so upset I couldn't really eat."

"What was he upset about?" She tried to ask casually, and wondered if she sounded natural. She didn't know. All she knew was that her cheeks felt hot and her heart was pounding.

"Hardy Wingate bid on the hotel."

"Really?" That sounded too weak. Her hands were trembling as she sprinkled Parmesan and mozzarella over the top of the lasagne. The aluminum foil rattled as she pulled it off the roll and covered the baking dish.

"Here," said Hannah, nudging her out of the way. "Let me put that in the oven. You're shaking."

Joni was beginning to wish she could fall off a mountain.

"What's the matter?" Hannah asked. "Didn't you eat lunch?"

"I did. Sure. I'm just…shaky." Lies. Oh, God, she hadn't thought about all the lies she would have to tell because of what she'd done.

Hannah put the baking dish on a cookie sheet to catch any spills, then slipped it into the oven and set the timer. "You'd better go sit down," she said to her daughter. "You don't look well."

Joni felt terrible, all right, but only emotionally. Shame at her duplicity was filling her. Her legs feeling weak, she went into the dining room and sat in a chair where she could watch her mother bustle around the kitchen preparing to make the garlic bread.

Hannah put the loaf of French bread on the cutting board and sliced it in two, putting half the loaf back in its plastic bag. Then she paused, her knife hovering over the bread and, without looking at Joni, said, "Why did you give Hardy that bid package?"

"Mom…" But Joni couldn't speak, neither to tell the truth nor to prevaricate. Her heart slammed hard, and she sat mute.

Hannah turned her head and looked at her. "That's

what you did the night you said you were going to see your friend. When we had the snowstorm? Why did you do it, Joni?''

All the explanations she'd given herself when she made up her mind to draw Hardy into this were gone from her brain as if they'd never existed. Empty, anxious, shamed, she simply looked at her mother.

"I don't suppose," Hannah said after a moment, "that we need to tell Witt that. He's mad enough as it is. I can't see what good it will do to have him angry with you. What's done is done."

That didn't make Joni feel any better. She watched as her mother began slicing the bread diagonally.

"I suppose," Hannah said presently, "that you'll give me an explanation eventually."

When Joni finally spoke, her voice was a thick, tight croak. "I had reasons."

Hannah nodded, putting her knife aside and going to the refrigerator for butter. "I'm sure you did, Joni. You always do."

Joni couldn't tell if that was a mere statement of fact or a sarcastic comment. And, honestly, she didn't really want to know. She just wished she could remember why it had seemed so important to her to give that bid package to Hardy a week ago. And wondered why all that determination seemed to have deserted her.

Nothing more had been said by the time they began to dine. Hannah offered no information about the bids she had seen, her silence telling Joni as clearly as any words that her mother wasn't happy with her.

Well, she hadn't expected anyone to be happy with her. Even Hardy hadn't been. But she didn't like feeling cut off from her mother. Hannah's disapproval had always cut her like a knife.

Finally, unable to bear the silence any longer, Joni put down her fork. "It's wrong, Mom, Witt hating Hardy all these years. He didn't kill Karen."

"Mmm." Hannah said no more.

Feeling almost desperate, Joni said, "Witt's never going to heal if he keeps on hating Hardy."

"Really." It wasn't a question and carried the weight of disapproval. "Have you considered that Witt is grieving in his own way?"

"It's been twelve years!"

Hannah's dark eyes fixed her. "Joni, do you think I miss your father any less because it's been nearly fifteen years? Do you?"

"I..." Joni's voice trailed off, and her eyes began to burn.

"I think," Hannah continued, "that you've been arrogant. You have no right to decide when someone else's grief should end."

"But..." Again words escaped her.

"Grief isn't measured by calendars. And I thought you understood people better than that, anyway. Witt's anger at Hardy is the way he keeps himself from being torn up inside."

Joni looked down, her throat tight and her chest aching. "Karen wouldn't like it, Mom."

"No, she probably wouldn't. But Karen isn't here, and that's the whole problem."

Joni couldn't even bring herself to raise her head. She was suddenly hurting so deep inside that she didn't know if she could bear it. "We all miss her, Mom," she said thickly. "Including Hardy."

Hannah sighed. "Yes," she said presently. "We do. But opening up the wounds this way isn't good for anyone, Joni. Not for anyone."

She felt like a stupid child who should have known better, and somehow she couldn't reach into herself and find the force that had compelled her to rush headlong into this situation. Couldn't feel again the fire that had pushed her. And that left her feeling defenseless.

But still, despite that, she felt that the situation was wrong, that Witt's anger was a poison not a cure. And that Hardy was being treated unfairly.

"Hardy was my friend, Mom," she said finally. "He was my best friend, next to Karen. And when she died, I shouldn't have had to lose him, too." Then, having said all she could, she went up to her room and sat in the quiet, staring out the window at freshly falling snow.

It hurt, she thought. It still hurt like hell. And maybe that was what had compelled her to reach out to Hardy.

Because, dear God, even after twelve years, something inside her was still bleeding.

5

A couple of days later, Witt ran into Hardy at the hardware store. It wasn't unusual for that to happen; in a town the size of Whisper Creek, where there was only one hardware store, one pharmacy, one bank and one auto-parts store, such encounters on a Saturday were inevitable. Usually they both just turned away and pretended the other didn't exist.

But today Witt was in a different mood. When he saw Hardy buying some screws, he didn't walk away. Instead, he approached.

"What the hell," he said bluntly, "did you think you were doing bidding on my hotel?"

Hardy dropped a dozen screws into a small paper bag. He didn't reply immediately, as if trying to decide how much he should say. Finally he shrugged. "I'd like to build your hotel."

"In your dreams."

Hardy raised his gaze slowly and met Witt's angry

stare. "Exactly. In my dreams." Then he went back to counting another dozen screws.

Witt didn't like being ignored. And he didn't like being made to feel as if he was behaving badly. Hardy's calm just annoyed him more. "You have some nerve, boy."

"I'm not a boy anymore, Witt. Maybe you'd better keep that in mind."

"Oh, I do keep that in mind, just like I keep it in mind that my daughter would be a woman now—but for you."

Hardy dumped more screws into the bag, then folded the top of it carefully. Only then did he look at Witt.

"Yes, she would," he said quietly. Brushing past Witt, he headed for the checkout.

Leaving Witt feeling like an angry ass. What had he expected? That they were going to duke it out in the aisle?

Still disgruntled, he went to get the epoxy he'd come for. Fact was, he'd been gnawing on his anger like an old bone since he'd learned that Hardy had bid on the hotel. It was an anger he never entirely got over, but it had been a long time since it had been this fresh and hot. Mostly, he kept it buried as long as Hardy Wingate stayed out of his way.

But Hardy had just gotten very much in his way, and his anger was like the volcano was erupting again, consuming him with its red-hot heat. After all these years, it was unresolved.

Nobody had paid for Karen's death except him. The drunk driver hadn't even lived long enough to be arrested. And Hardy...Hardy, who hadn't taken good care of Karen, who'd been indirectly responsible for her death, was still walking around whole and healthy.

That stuck in Witt's craw like a boulder.

Out on the street, with his bag of screws in his hand, Hardy hurried away from the hardware store. He should *never* have let Joni tempt him with the prospect of building that hotel. All he'd managed to do was push Witt to the brink again.

He didn't want to do that. And it struck him that he must have been harboring some kind of hope that Witt would get over his bitterness or he never would have placed that bid. Stupid fool. After twelve years, Witt wasn't likely to change his mind about anything.

Trying to sidestep a dark feeling that was threatening to overwhelm him, he forced himself to consider why it was he cared about Witt's opinion. The man had never liked him. Never. So why should it matter so much that he was angry with Hardy?

Because, Hardy realized with a sense of shock that seemed to rock him to his very soul, he was never going to be able to forgive himself unless Witt forgave him. Christ.

"Hardy?"

He looked up and saw Joni hurrying toward him

down the snow-packed sidewalk. Instinctively, he glanced over his shoulder to make sure Witt wasn't standing in front of the hardware store watching. He wasn't.

"Are you crazy?" he asked Joni. Reaching for her arm, he urged her a little way down a side street in case Witt emerged from the store. "Your uncle's in the hardware store."

"Oh." She looked up at him, blinking those huge blue eyes of hers, making him wonder if something about her was going to remain eternally a child. Because right now... He shook his head. Joni was no child, and he wasn't going to patronize her by thinking of her as one.

"He's hopping mad about that bid of mine," Hardy told her. "He was trying awful hard to pick a fight with me."

"I'm sorry."

It was on the tip of his tongue to tell her that she invariably apologized too late. She always had. Joni had always been inclined to follow her impulses and to regret many of them later. But he bit back the criticism and said only, "That's okay. I should have known better than to bid." Then he summoned a wry smile. "Sometimes this town just isn't big enough for both Witt and me."

He'd hoped to get a flicker of a smile in return, but all he got was a sigh. She kicked the toe of her boot against the snowbank beside the walk and finally looked up at him again. "It was stupid," she said. "My mother figured it out."

"Figured out that you gave me the request package?"

"Yes. She asked me why I'd done it."

"And?"

Another sigh. "And all those good reasons I had just kind of evaporated. I couldn't even remember them. I just know this situation isn't right."

"To tell you the truth, I don't remember the reasons you gave me, either." He was actually beginning to feel some sympathy for her. "I *do* remember that your intentions were good."

"The road to hell and all that." She looked so downcast. "Well, I just wanted you to know that my mom figured it out, so it probably won't be long before Witt does, as well. I guess that won't make any difference in how they feel about you. But it's going to make my life miserable for a while. Which I guess I deserve."

There was a small coffee shop down the street, a place frequented mostly by some old hippies who had migrated here to live a more rural life and spent small fortunes on organic foods. The café was part of the Earth Mother Co-op, but anyone could shop there. He took her hand.

"Let's go get something hot to drink. That wind is cutting right through my jacket." Mainly because he'd been in a hurry and had grabbed the nearest jacket at hand, one that was better suited to the fall than the winter around here. He hadn't planned on standing outside having a conversation.

"Okay," she said. The circles that moved through the Earth Mother Co-op and the circles in which Witt moved almost never intersected. Small town or not, there were a few social boundaries over which gossip seldom passed. Witt would never hear about the two of them having coffee.

The co-op was warm, heated by a Franklin stove that was always well fueled. The floorboards creaked beneath their feet, and the aromas of grains stocked in open barrels filled the air, along with the delicious scent of fresh coffee and baked goods.

"Man," Hardy remarked, "I'm going to have to buy a loaf of bread."

Joni was apparently of like mind. She ordered a cinnamon roll with her coffee.

"Have you ever noticed," Hardy asked, "that many of life's most important conversations take place over food?"

Some of the sadness lifted from her eyes. "It's true. Mom and I always have our conversations over coffee or dinner."

"Yeah. Seems more sociable, somehow." But his mind wasn't really on the coffee the waiter put in front of him, or on the aroma of Joni's cinnamon roll.

"Okay," he said after a few moments. "If Witt asks me if you gave me the bid package, I'll tell him no."

"You don't have to lie for me."

"No, I don't. But I will. There's no point in having that ugliness fall on your head. I'm a grown man. I didn't have to bid."

"No," Joni said firmly. "I'll take my licks. I deserve them."

"You don't want this kind of trouble with your uncle."

"Why not? Maybe it'll clear the air."

Hardy shook his head. "Nothing's going to clear the air, not after all this time."

Sitting back, he sipped his coffee and wondered what the hell he was doing sitting here with Joni Matlock. Then he wondered, as he always did, if he would have been sitting here with Joni under better circumstances if he'd broken up with Karen when he'd first noticed his attraction to Joni.

Probably not, he told himself. None of them had been old enough to sustain a long-term relationship. If Karen hadn't died, he would have broken up with her. Joni might have agreed to date him, but probably wouldn't—out of loyalty to her cousin. And except for the possibility that Karen would still be alive, nothing would have changed. Not really.

But what good did it do to ask himself these questions? All he could do was wish Karen hadn't been in the car with him that night. And wishes were worthless.

Joni's mood seemed to be rising as the sugar in her roll began to hit her system. She looked less worried and tired, and more like her old self. Finally she even smiled at him and said, "Okay, it was a stupid idea."

While he would be the first to admit that Joni too often acted on impulse, and that sometimes her reasons weren't the most sensible, he didn't like to hear her put herself down that way. Casting his mind back over the years, he could remember dozens, maybe hundreds, of times when she'd put herself down. It was kind of strange coming from a woman who, as far as he could tell, ought to be spoiled rotten. Witt and Hannah both doted on her to an extreme degree. Maybe that was why she was so impulsive.

But it didn't explain why she was so quick to call herself stupid. A woman who had a graduate degree in pharmacy shouldn't be thinking of herself that way.

He shifted in his chair and leaned over the table a little, on an impulse of his own asking her, "Why do you always call yourself stupid? You're not stupid at all."

Her eyes were strangely haunted as they met his. "Maybe not," she said finally. "But I'm not the world's brightest bulb or I wouldn't keep getting into fixes like this. Well, I'll take what's coming to me. Maybe it was a stupid idea, but I was trying to make things better. I guess I ought to be smart enough to realize that if twelve years isn't making it better, nothing else is likely to."

She pushed her roll aside and stared into her coffee

cup. When she spoke again, her voice was muffled. "I hate to see people I care about hurting."

"We all do, Joni. But sometimes we've just got to let them hurt because there's nothing we can do. There's no way to make Witt stop hurting."

"But what about *you?*" she asked.

His heart turned over, and that was exactly what he didn't want to happen. Feeling a pull toward Joni was bad enough given the situation, but feeling any more was suicidal. Rising suddenly, he tossed a few bills on the table to cover their check. He picked up his coffee and looked down at her. "Been nice talking to you, Joni. But let's not make a practice of this. It's not good for anyone. Thanks for trying with Witt."

Then he turned and walked out, feeling her eyes on him every step of the way.

Born to hurt, that was what he was, he thought. Born to hurt everyone he knew.

He didn't make it but half a block before he ran into Sam Canfield. They'd gotten friendly after Sam had moved to Whisper Creek a few years back to take a job as a deputy. Sam's wife had died a couple of years ago in a skiing accident, leaving Sam looking haggard and haunted.

Sam was a tall man, far leaner than he used to be, and since his wife's death, he seemed to have hunched in on himself. His face had taken on deep lines, and his gray eyes had lost their sparkle. Although he was only thirty-five, his dark hair had begun to show streaks of gray.

"Hey, buddy," Sam said, his voice dragging Hardy's head up from his gloomy study of the slippery sidewalk. "You look like the world's coming to an end."

"Nah." It was Hardy's usual response. He wasn't comfortable admitting that sometimes he would like to cut his own throat, or find a hole in reality that would allow him to just slip out, like the fire door in a theater. The idea sounded stupid even to him.

"Right," said Sam, who'd been around the block of life often enough to recognize that for what it was. "Got some time? I'm thinking about stopping at the café for lunch, and I don't mind telling you, I'm tired to death of eating alone."

Hardy was agreeable. He didn't have anything that pressing today, and his mother, who was feeling a little better, had begun to insist she could make her own lunches, thank you very much.

They sat facing each other in a corner booth. Sam ordered a turkey sandwich and salad. Hardy went for a burger and fries.

"I try to eat healthy," Sam remarked. "The problem is, it's a lot harder to do when you're living alone."

Hardy nodded, leaning back to let the waitress put mugs of coffee in front of the two of them. Sam, he thought, was looking better than he had a while back. Some of the gauntness that had appeared after his wife's death had filled out. But there was still a haunted look in his eyes from time to time. Hardy decided not to mention it. He was never quite sure how to deal with grief. Mention it? Ignore it so as not to reawaken it?

"I hear you bid on Witt's hotel."

Hardy's head snapped up. "You know, the grapevine in this town is unbelievable. Where'd you hear that?"

"From one of Witt's cronies. My guess would be he's been sounding off a little."

"Probably." Hardy shook his head and decided to drink some coffee before he answered. But with the cup halfway to his mouth, he paused. "You know, this town is the damnedest place."

"That's one of the things I like about it," Sam remarked. He cradled his cup as if his hands were cold. "Something happens around here, damn near everyone knows who did it. Makes my job easy. On the other hand, everyone's going to know you were hanging out with Joni."

"I bet." Hardy flashed a smile, then sighed and sipped his coffee. "I thought going into the co-op would be safe."

Sam shrugged. "I dunno. How many people saw you and Joni head in there?"

"Well, *you* did, apparently."

"I'm not saying a word about that anywhere. Soon as I measured the gossip rate around here, I figured a closed mouth was my best protection."

"Other folks don't feel the same."

"Little enough to occupy them. Work and talking about the neighbors is it. Most of it's not mean-spirited, though. Just interested."

"Witt would have a cow."

Sam grinned. "Now, that's something you don't see every day."

Hardy laughed; he couldn't help it. Sam was putting things in perspective. "I'm worried about Joni, though. She loves that man like a father."

"Then don't be having coffee with her in broad daylight." Sam paused, sipped his coffee. The waitress came with their meals, asked if they needed anything else, then went back to the other customers. Sam cast his gaze around, apparently assessing the others.

Then he leaned across the table and said in a low voice that barely carried over the cacophony of the people talking and eating, "Maybe I recognize it because of my...loss. But I've seen how you look at that woman, Hardy. From clear across the street. Like a man who wants something so bad he can hardly stand it."

Hardy's first reaction was shock. He couldn't believe he'd been so transparent. Worse, he didn't want to believe that the aching inside him was that strong. He'd spent twelve years avoiding Joni like the plague, and for damn good reason. The whole idea that he was carrying some stupid kind of torch made him rebel.

He opened his mouth to tell Sam he was imagining things, but the lie wouldn't come. He couldn't even tell it to himself anymore. Part of the reason he'd been avoiding Joni was because he was afraid of what would happen if they got too close. Sort of like matter and antimatter. One humongous uncontrolled explosion, and then...nothing.

Because all he could be feeling was a yearning for a hope lost. He didn't even know Joni anymore.

"I don't need to do anything about it, Sam."

"Maybe not." Sam let the subject go and tucked into his lunch. Hardy followed suit, figuring that if they both had their mouths full they couldn't talk about anything uncomfortable.

But that didn't keep him from thinking uncomfortable thoughts. Later as he walked home, he wondered just how self-deluded he was.

The first words Witt said to Hannah as he stormed into her house were, "Joni gave that bid package to Hardy, didn't she?"

Hannah didn't know how to reply to the certainty in his tone. She didn't want to outright lie, but she also wanted to protect her daughter. In the end she said nothing at all.

"Don't bother to deny it," Witt said as if she had tried. "I talked to all the architectural firms. None of them passed the package on. You and Joni were the only other people with access."

Hannah sat in the armchair and watched Witt pace

a tight circle through the living and dining rooms. This house wasn't big enough for him, she thought irrelevantly. He dwarfed it, seemed confined by it. And right now he looked like a tiger pacing in a cage.

"Why did she do this to me, Hannah? She knows what I think of Wingate."

"She didn't do anything to you. Hardy made a bid. You can ignore it."

He rounded on her. "She *betrayed* me."

Hannah, who rarely argued with anyone, and who usually had little to say about the folly of her fellow human beings, couldn't ignore that. "That's going too far. You weren't betrayed."

"No?" He glared at her. "How would you feel if she went behind your back to someone who killed your daughter."

"Witt, don't be ridiculous."

"I'm not being ridiculous. That boy is the reason my daughter is dead."

"You daughter is dead because of a drunken driver."

"She's dead because Hardy Wingate encouraged her to slip out at night with him!" Witt roared the words, and Hannah heard the windows rattle. Another irrelevant thought slipped through her brain: time to caulk the windowpanes again.

This side of Witt appalled her a little, and worried her. She'd known him since she'd married his brother, and Witt wasn't prone to anger. He was ordinarily a reasonably quiet, self-contained man, calm in situations that had others shouting. And the degree of his anger, after all this time, troubled her.

"Witt…" Hannah spoke quietly.

He paused in his pacing and looked at her. The redness of his eyes made her heart ache. "What?"

"I think Joni was trying to help."

"Help what?"

Hannah hesitated, still reluctant to offer opinions of this kind. But, she decided, Witt really needed to take a good long look at himself. "To help you heal."

Witt practically gaped at her. "Help me heal? How the hell is this supposed to help me heal, for the love of God? She just ripped the wound wide open again."

"Think about that, Witt. She couldn't have ripped it open if it had been healed. And if you want to know what I think…"

"That would be refreshing," he said with a biting sarcasm that made her cheeks redden.

"What I think is that your wound not only never healed, but it's been festering for twelve years. And it's making you sick in your soul, Witt."

She was braced for an explosion, but it never came. For the longest time he didn't say a word. Then, finally, he sat in the other armchair and studied his hands.

"I've lost everyone, Hannah," he said quietly. "I lost my wife to cancer, I lost my brother to a mugger and I lost my daughter. I lived with the first two. I can't live with the last."

"I can see that."

"And it doesn't help me at all when my niece goes running around behind my back to the man who was responsible for Karen's death."

Hannah smothered a sigh, finally asking, "Tell me, Witt. Please explain this to me. Why do you hold Hardy responsible? Because all that happened was that he and Karen were in a car in the wrong place at the wrong time when a drunk came along. It's just like with Lewis, Witt. Lewis was in the wrong place at the wrong time when that mugger came across him. It's no different."

"It *is* different."

"That's what I don't understand."

He suddenly ran his fingers through his graying hair, then leaned back in the chair and closed his eyes. When he spoke, he sounded drained. "It's different. They were running around behind my back. Hardy was encouraging her to disobey me and run around behind my back."

The use of that phrase twice, after what he had said about Joni, chilled Hannah. The idea that he might be lumping her daughter in with Hardy frightened her more than anything ever had. And she wondered how she could prevent that.

"Karen," she said yet again, "chose to disobey you, Witt."

He shook his head and sat up straighter, looking

at her. "Hardy Wingate was the only damn thing she ever disobeyed me about."

"You don't know that."

"I *do* know that."

Hannah shook her head, "Witt, no parent ever knows all the things their kids do when they're not looking. Every child does things that their parents would be upset about if they knew. Joni's told me things about high school that, if I had known them at the time, I probably would have chained her in her bedroom."

The faintest flicker of humor appeared on Witt's face, giving Hannah an instant of hope. But then it vanished and was replaced by something cold. "Hardy's influence," he said flatly. "He was a bad influence."

"Hardy wasn't involved in most of Joni's hi-jinks."

"Then maybe *she* was the bad influence on Karen. Maybe *she* encouraged Karen to defy me."

"Witt!" Hannah was appalled. She couldn't believe what she was hearing. Her heart began to beat painfully, and she felt as if something inside her were crumbling. "Witt, no."

He jumped up from the chair and began pacing tight circles again. "What am I supposed to think? Here I have proof that Joni's been running behind my back to Hardy. Why wouldn't I think she was a bad influence on Karen?"

"You cut that out right now, Witt Matlock. Your

Karen was a lovely girl, but she was no angel. No child that age is, unless there's something wrong with her. Hardy didn't manhandle Karen into going with him. Karen went because she wanted to."

"I knew her better than that."

"I seriously doubt it." The desperation in Hannah's voice was tempered by a surprising dryness. He looked at her, something in his face suggesting he was about to speak, but then his mouth clamped into a tight line.

When he did finally speak, his voice was as rough and dry as gravel. "She wouldn't have disobeyed me, except for him."

"No," Hannah agreed. "She probably wouldn't have."

"So it's his fault she's dead!"

"No, it's not."

"Cut it out, Hannah. I don't want riddles."

"I'm not riddling. If Karen hadn't been wildly attracted to Hardy, she wouldn't have disobeyed you, no matter what Hardy encouraged her to do. And if you're honest with yourself, you'll admit it. She wanted to be with Hardy more than she feared your disappointment in her. That says something. Heavens, the two of them were probably imagining themselves as Romeo and Juliet!"

Witt heard something unexpected in that. "Are you blaming *me* for Karen's death?"

Hannah's heart nearly stopped in her breast. "No," she managed to say after a moment. "No. It wasn't your fault. Whether or not you approved, Karen was going to go out with Hardy. And whether or not you approved, they were going to be in the wrong place at the wrong time that night. That's *all* I'm saying, Witt. It's not your fault. It's not Hardy's fault. It was the fault of one drunk driver.''

But he didn't look as if he was buying it. Which didn't exactly surprise Hannah. He hadn't bought it during the last twelve years, why would he change his mind now? But she didn't want him chewing Joni up and spitting her out. And right now, she feared Witt was capable of that. She'd seen him angry before, furious the night his daughter died, but never before had she seen him angry with this cold edge.

''You know,'' she said slowly, trying to placate him, ''it *was* wrong of Joni to give the bid request to Hardy.''

''Well, hallelujah,'' Witt said sarcastically. ''The woman sees sense.''

''Don't you talk to me that way, Witt Matlock!''

He had the grace to look a little embarrassed. ''Sorry.''

''And well you ought to be. As I was saying, Joni was wrong. But it was a minor wrong, Witt. Minor. All you have to do is decline the bid.''

''Sure. And have you disappointed. And have that niece of mine upset with me. You think I don't see what she's up to? She figured she could manipulate me into accepting Wingate's bid for her sake. What's she doing? Sleeping with him?''

"Witt Matlock!"

"Wouldn't surprise me. Wingate's always been hell on wheels. Why wouldn't he enjoy getting back at me that way?"

"Getting back at you?" Hannah was beginning to wonder if Witt was losing his mind. This really didn't sound like him at all. Yes, he'd carried an anger at Hardy all these years, but nothing this paranoid. And he'd never talked about Joni this way. Never.

"Yes, getting back at me," Witt growled. "Maybe he thinks he's going to get even for me being angry with him all these years. Thinks he can do it by taking my niece away."

"Don't be ridiculous. Nobody's taking Joni away from you. And she's not seeing Hardy." Although at the back of Hannah's mind there was a niggling doubt, given the situation. But she couldn't believe Joni would hide something like that from her, regardless of what Witt might think. The two of them were too close now for that.

But her heart was beginning to break, because as she watched Witt and listened to him, she began to think he might create a rupture between himself and Joni. That he might make the same kind of breach he'd made with Hardy, one that might never heal. After all this time, she certainly knew how long he was capable of bearing a grudge.

And for the first time in all the years she had known him, Hannah began to wonder if Witt was the good man she had always believed him to be, or if he was a stranger to her. This side of him...this side of him seemed to belong to someone else. It didn't fit with all she knew of him.

That he held Hardy responsible for Karen's death was sad, but it wasn't a major thing, because Hardy wasn't a member of the family, hadn't ever been a close friend. From Witt's perspective, Hardy was a wild young man he had never really known. It was easy to carry a grudge against someone like that.

But Joni...Joni and Witt had been close for a long time. Surely Witt couldn't treat her the same way he had treated Hardy?

She opened her mouth, wanting to prevent that eventuality at all costs, ready to spill her shame and her secret and take the consequences.

But Joni chose that moment to come into the house. She froze when she saw Witt's angry face and glanced at her mother questioningly. Hannah nodded and kept silent with difficulty, waiting to see what tack Witt was going to take.

"Hi, Uncle Witt," Joni said brightly, her outward cheer belied by the tension around her blue eyes.

He glared at her.

Joni instinctively pulled back. Of course, Hannah thought; she had never been glared at by Witt that way. It was a look that would make anyone step back.

"Uncle Witt?" Joni said tentatively.

Hannah waited on tenterhooks, her fingers digging

into her palms as she saw the way Joni's chin first trembled, then thrust out. Her daughter might be too impulsive, Hannah thought, but Joni had never refused to take the consequences of her actions. Nor had she ever denied responsibility. But Hannah had the awful, awful feeling that that was not going to be enough this time.

Witt looked as if accusations wanted to burst out of him. Then he looked as if it all hurt too much and he couldn't voice anything at all. They were both wrong, Hannah thought. Both of them. And in that instant, she didn't know which of them she wanted to comfort more.

"You…" Witt's voice was hoarse. He cleared his throat and spoke again. "You gave the bid package to Hardy."

"Yes," Joni said steadily. "I did."

"Why?"

For a second Hannah's heart lifted. Witt was going to listen to Joni's explanation. It wasn't going to be so bad.

"Because," Joni said, "I love you, Uncle Witt."

His head jerked up and he thundered, "Don't give me that crap!"

Joni's temper rose just as fast as his. "It's not crap. I love you. And what you're doing is wrong. It's wrong and it's hurtful, not just to Hardy, but to me, too."

"You? *You?*" He whirled on Hannah. "See?

What did I say? She's sneaking around with Hardy behind my back. Sleeping with him like some slut!''

"Witt!" Hannah's voice cracked with horror. "Don't you dare! Don't you ever!"

"I'm not sleeping with anyone," Joni shouted, trying to divert her uncle's attention back to herself. Hannah knew what she was doing, didn't know how to stop her. But it had always upset Joni when Witt was annoyed with Hannah. Or vice versa.

Witt rounded on Joni again. "And I'm supposed to believe that? Hell will freeze over first! You didn't do this for me. I know better than that. *You* know better than that. You know how I feel about Hardy."

"And it's wrong, Uncle Witt! It's wrong! As long as you stay mad at Hardy, you're never going to heal."

"What a bunch of psychological hogwash! Well, let me tell you something, young lady. I don't care what your reasons are! I don't give a damn. You can sleep with that good-for-nothing piece of shit, you can marry him for all I care. What I care about is that you went behind my back. You betrayed me!"

"No!"

"Yes. And from this day forward I don't have a niece anymore. Do you hear me? From this day on I don't know who you are!" He turned on Hannah. "Or you either. I wash my hands of both of you."

Then he turned and stomped out the front door into the snowy night.

Hannah looked at Joni and saw she was trembling.

Looking down at her own hands, Hannah saw that she was, too. And right now, her heart felt as if someone had driven an ice pick into it.

"Mom?" Joni said. Her voice was plaintive, small, seeking reassurance.

"What did you think was going to happen?" Hannah asked wearily. Her throat felt tight, her eyes burned, she ached for both Joni and Witt, and she didn't feel she knew Witt at all anymore. Nor could she say what hurt worst.

"I knew he'd be mad." Joni's voice was broken, shocked-sounding. "But Witt...Mom, that didn't sound like Witt."

"He was wound up tighter than a spring," Hannah agreed. God, she wanted to crawl away to bed and end this night now.

"He doesn't usually say such hateful things."

"He doesn't usually get hurt this way." Hannah refused to ease Joni's conscience on this one.

"I've got to talk to him."

"Let him cool down first."

"No," said Joni, heading for the front door. "I can't let him think I... No, I've got to talk to him now."

The door slammed behind her, and Hannah thought numbly that Joni hadn't even been wearing a jacket. She was going to get awfully chilled out there.

But just a few moments later, Joni burst back through the door. "Mom! Mom, Witt's down in the snow. Something's wrong with him!"

6

Joni watched as the ambulance bearing Witt and Hannah pulled away. Hannah had told her to follow in the car, but for long minutes Joni couldn't even move. Heedless of the cold wind that was cutting through her flannel shirt and making her skin burn and ache, heedless that her stocking feet were cramping and icy from standing in a snowbank, she stared after the disappearing ambulance.

A heart attack, Hannah had said. A heart attack. Joni felt a crushing weight on her own chest as the thought struck her that she might have killed her uncle. He might die, and it would be all her fault for upsetting him so.

Something inside her seemed to cut loose and tumble into free fall. Her stomach plummeted as if she were riding a super-fast elevator...except that it didn't stop. It just kept on falling.

She might have killed Witt. He had been so angry, and it had all been *her* fault. Her selfish, stupid, impulsive fault. She been all hung up on what was right, what was best for all of them, and she hadn't stopped for one minute to consider that maybe she didn't know what was best.

She had the worst urge to just collapse into the snowbank and cry until she could cry no more. To give in to tears and let them wash away the terrible feelings of guilt and shame.

But they wouldn't do that, she knew. Nothing was going to wash away this mistake. This time her impulsive action had cost more than she had considered in her wildest imaginings.

Turning at last, she went back into the house. The heat indoors felt searing on her cold skin. Her soaked socks left wet footprints on the rugs and plank floor.

Her mother would need her. No matter her iniquity, she had to be there for Hannah.

She changed swiftly into dry jeans and socks, checked to make sure all the lights were out, then headed out, grabbing her parka, keys and purse. Fear filled her, making her shake, making it difficult to get the keys into the ignition of her car. Please, God, let Witt be all right.

She was never going to forgive herself, she thought as she drove. Never.

Another pang struck her, a blast of fear that felt like a cyclone ripping through her. For an instant, just an instant, she had to close her eyes at the force of it.

The next thing she knew, her car was sliding off the road into a snow-filled ditch.

"Damn it!" All the violent, tangled emotions she was feeling erupted as she shouted the curse and pounded her hand on the steering wheel. "Damn it!"

She had to get to the hospital. Hannah needed her. But pressure on the accelerator only spun the wheels. She wasn't going to get out that way.

Grabbing her purse, she turned off the car, got out and locked it. She would walk to the damn hospital. She'd failed everyone in her life, but she wasn't going to fail Hannah in this. She was going to be there for her.

The wind was cold, whipping down from the mountains to sting her cheeks and find every cranny in her parka. The denim of her jeans began to feel stiff against her legs, began to chafe as the moisture escaping her body froze in the fabric. Just what she deserved, she told herself angrily. Maybe less than she deserved.

As she hiked toward the hospital, she grew colder, and more fatigued. Hypothermia, she noted. Well, she could deal with a little of that. Was it so awful, anyway? Maybe they would find her frozen body beside the roadside in the morning.

But that thought, twisting into her brain, had an unexpected effect on her. It made her realize how childish she was being. How childish she had been. It was as if some part of her just kept refusing to grow up.

As if some part of her had died with Karen.

A tear stole out of the corner of her eye, burning her cheek. That was what was wrong with her, she realized. She had only the pretense of adulthood. An adult wouldn't have given the bid request to Hardy. An adult would have realized that the problem lay between Hardy and Witt, and that she had no business interfering. An adult would have known that reawakening the anger was hardly likely to heal the breach.

She heard the crunching of tires on the ice and snow behind her, and she moved over closer to the snowbank lining the road to give the driver more room to pass. But the truck didn't pass. It pulled up right alongside her and began pacing her.

She kept her eyes firmly fixed on the ground, refusing to look and give encouragement to some creep. Man, wouldn't it be perfect if she were murdered on the way to the hospital to be with Witt and Hannah? Talk about irony.

But that was a childish thought, too. A thought, she decided with savage self-perception, that resulted from a juvenile desire to avoid the consequences of her own actions. A desire to make everyone sorry they were mad at her.

"Joni?"

Recognizing the voice, she jerked her head up and looked at Hardy Wingate. He was driving his pickup right beside her.

"Are you okay?" he asked. "What are you doing

walking out here? I saw your car in the snowbank when I was on my way home, and I went to your house to see if you were okay. I got worried when no one was there."

"I'm fine."

"Then why are you heading to the hospital?"

"Witt had a heart attack."

His truck kept rolling slowly next to her. "Jesus," he said finally. "Joni, get in the truck. I'll drive you."

"I can walk."

"I don't know about that. You're shivering so hard I can see it. Come on, get in the truck."

It struck her that she was still behaving childishly, refusing a ride for no better reason than that she felt she needed to be punished. Giving in, she climbed in. Hardy turned the heat up, giving her a blast of it.

"I'm glad I saw your car," he remarked.

"Why?"

"You'd probably have frozen to death out here. It's down to twelve below, Joni."

"Really?" The idea was mildly interesting. It didn't often get that cold here, even at night. That explained why she was getting hypothermic.

"What happened to Witt? You said heart attack, but…"

Joni hunched her shoulders and realized she was still shivering, that even the inside of her parka felt cold now. "We had a fight. He…um…he…" A shudder ripped through her, and she had to bite her lower lip to hold the tears back.

"He found out about the bid? That you gave it to me?"

"Yes."

"Christ. I wonder who told him."

"I don't know but he, um, he…well, he disowned me. Then he stormed out. I went after him, and he was lying in the snow groaning. Mom said it was a heart attack."

"So you were following them to the hospital?"

"Yeah." She turned her face away from him, afraid he would read her shame and ugliness there. Her childishness. "It's…my fault."

Hardy didn't say anything right away. He focused on getting his truck over the hill just before the hospital, but when he pulled into the parking lot and up in front of the emergency-room exit, he turned toward her. "People get really really angry all the time, Joni. And they don't have heart attacks."

"But it was my fault."

"Sure, and you make the sun rise in the morning, too."

The sarcasm of his tone was like a slap in her face. "Hardy…"

He shook his head. "Maybe someday you'll realize you're not the center of the universe." Then he flashed the most disarming grin. "*I* am."

She wanted to fall into that grin. She wanted desperately to let it wrap her in warmth and hold at bay the reality she was facing. But she couldn't allow it. Responsibility, shame and guilt stopped her. "Thanks for the ride, Hardy."

"I'll go back and pull your car out of the snow. Do you have your keys?"

She shoved her hand into her pocket and passed the keys to him.

"Okay. I'll check in with you later."

She stood on the pavement for a half minute, watching him drive away, and wondered why she felt that she had just somehow been blessed.

The feeling didn't last long. It couldn't. Not when she had to turn and go into the waiting room. Hannah was there, looking more worn and worried than Joni could remember since her father died.

"How is he?" she asked.

"They're having trouble stabilizing him."

Joni looked into her mother's eyes, trying to read more information there and seeing only fear. "That's not good is it?"

Joni wanted to apologize to her mother, to beg forgiveness with everything that was in her soul, but from the look in Hannah's eyes, she knew this was the wrong time. Hannah didn't want to have to deal with her confession and guilt right now. At this moment Hannah didn't want to think about anything at all except Witt.

Reaching out, Joni took her mother's hand. "I'm sorry, Mom." She had to say at least that much, although she vowed to say no more.

Hannah squeezed her fingers but didn't reply.

Joni closed her eyes and leaned back in her chair, wondering if anything would ever be the same again. If Witt would ever smile at her again, or if he would continue to blame her. It was all her fault he'd had the heart attack anyway. Maybe the best thing she could do was go away. Leave him alone. Leave Hannah alone. Stop messing up their lives with the stupid stunts she pulled sometimes.

God, at her age she should have learned something. She should have learned that whenever she got a fixed idea like this in her head, she was probably bound for trouble. It wasn't the day-to-day stuff that was her downfall, it was her big ideas. Like when she had tried to fix up her college roommate with the basketball player. Ilsa had had a crush on him for months, and Joni happened to have two classes with Bill. They chatted a lot before and after class, and Joni had foolishly thought they were friends.

Even more foolishly, she'd developed the idea that Ilsa and Bill would be good for each other. So, after sounding Bill out a little...or so she thought...she had broken Ilsa's confidence and told Bill that Ilsa had a crush on him, and that they ought to go out together.

Bill had agreed to ask Ilsa out. Unfortunately, he had done so only because he liked Joni, and when Ilsa found that out, she had been so humiliated that she never spoke to Joni again. To this day, Joni suspected Ilsa still hated her.

That was the kind of mess she was always getting herself into. In her case, the road to hell was indeed paved with good intentions.

Well, she'd learned this time, she promised herself. She had learned. And if Witt survived...

The thought that he might not live struck her with full force again, and she opened her eyes to look at her mother. Hannah was pale, and the way her lips were moving, Joni guessed she was silently praying.

And suddenly, as the reality of the situation fully came home to her, Joni began praying, too.

The next two hours were the longest of Joni's life except for the night she had sat in this same emergency room and waited for word of Karen's and Hardy's condition. And she remembered all too clearly how that night had ended. Disbelief was no longer part of her makeup. People she loved and cared about *did* die, like her dad, like Karen. But this time was even worse, because this time she felt responsible.

Memories came back to haunt her: the look on Hardy's face when he'd come out of the emergency room and walked past her and her mother without saying a word. She had noticed the cuts and scrapes on his face, and known instinctively that Karen had to be so much worse.

She remembered Witt's face two hours later, when he had emerged from the ICU and said flatly, emptily, "She's gone." She remembered how that felt, as if the universe had carved a huge, empty hole in her, as if everything inside her were sinking into a black well of ice. Her heart had known what her mind did not yet grasp: the magnitude of her loss.

Her dad's death had been different. She'd been eleven at the time and remembered him coming in to kiss her good-night before he left for work. He always did that, even if she was sound asleep, but that night she had roused enough to say, "I love you, Daddy."

He'd scooped her up into a bear hug, murmuring, "I love you, Honeybee." The last words he would ever speak to her.

Morning had brought the news, too awful to comprehend. For days she had refused to believe it, sure that her mother was lying to her. She might have been only eleven, but she'd been aware that her father spent time with other women. She'd been able to smell it on him and read the sadness in her mother's face. So when she was told that he was dead, she at first clung to the desperate hope that her parents had separated and that her mother was lying to her.

But four days later, faced with the horrifying reality of her father's lifeless body in a coffin, with the nightmare of watching that coffin being lowered into the cold, dark earth, she had known the agonizing truth. Daddy was gone.

Forever. That word, bandied around so carelessly before, had suddenly taken on a dimension that stunned her mind. Forever. No more hugs from Daddy—forever. No more knock-knock jokes from Daddy. No more kisses or smiles or Saturday hikes in the woods. No more games of catch and softball. No more smell of his shaving soap. But worst of all, no more comforting Daddy arms to hug her.

She had learned the meaning of forever then. And the knowledge had stayed with her to the night of Karen's death.

Now here she was staring it in the eye again, and some part of her knew she wouldn't be able to handle it if Witt died. She could handle anything but that. Even if she never saw him again, she would be okay as long as she knew he was still on this earth. That awareness would comfort her even if he were gone from her life.

What she couldn't do was risk killing him. He had disowned her. She had made him so angry that he had disowned her, then had a heart attack. She decided that she would stick around just long enough to be sure he was going to be all right.

Then she would leave Whisper Creek.

It wasn't as if she could avoid him in this town. And she didn't want to come between Witt and Hannah. They meant too much to each other after all these years. They were two old friends who relied on each other so much that it would be utterly unconscionable to separate them.

So she would leave. It was the cleanest, easiest solution for them all. Hadn't her mother been hinting that she ought to try out the great big world before she buried herself in this small mountain backwater? Of course. And Hannah was right.

The arrival of Sam Canfield distracted her from her thoughts. He strode into the room, a look of concern on his face, and pulled up a chair facing her and Hannah. "I just heard about Witt. Is he okay?"

"We don't know," Hannah said.

Sometimes Joni hated her mother's restraint and calm. Anyone else would be pacing the floors, crying, worrying. Hannah sat there calmly, the fear in her eyes the only proof that she was feeling anything at all.

It would have been easier, Joni thought, if Hannah had gotten hysterical. At least she and Sam would have had something to offer. Some way to be useful.

"Earl Sanders called me," Sam said, referring to the sheriff. "I guess he heard the call on the dispatch. He'd have come himself except his wife and daughter are pretty sick.

Hannah nodded. "There's a nasty stomach virus going around."

How, wondered Joni, could she talk of such a thing at a time like this?

"Well," said Sam, "I'm aiming to stay away from the sick. Would you ladies like some coffee? I happen to know my way to the staff lounge."

"Thanks," Hannah said. "That would be real helpful."

Joni wanted to shake her head but realized it was

going to be a long night. "Thanks, Sam. I could use some."

He went off to get the coffee, leaving the two women to look at each other. Hannah reached out suddenly and patted her daughter's leg. "No news is good news," she said.

"I guess." The weight in Joni's chest was growing. "Mom, I'm going to leave."

"All right. I know you have to work in the morning."

"No, I mean I'm going to leave town. Just as soon as we know about Witt."

Hannah's dark eyes fixed on her, a long, steady stare. "What brought this on?"

"I did a stupid thing. Witt doesn't want to see me anymore. And…and I don't want to give him another heart attack."

"You didn't give him this one." Hannah took her hand and squeezed it. "Honey, people don't have heart attacks just because they get mad."

"I know that." Joni drew an unsteady breath. "I still feel responsible. And now that he's had one…well, it won't do him any good to upset him."

"Joni…" Suddenly Hannah shook her head. "Look, I'm not really up to discussing this at the moment. I'm too distracted. Just promise me you won't leap before you look. We'll talk about this tomorrow, all right? *Tomorrow.*"

Joni realized she was being selfish again, selfish and impulsive. Of course this discussion could wait until her mother's mind was at rest about Witt. "Tomorrow. There's no rush," she reassured Hannah. "I won't do anything sudden."

"Good." Hannah gave her a wan smile. "We ought to hear something soon."

She would know, Joni thought, clinging to Hannah's greater experience with medical things. Half wishing she had followed in her mother's footsteps and become a nurse. Or maybe in her father's and become a doctor. A pharmacist was pretty useless at a time like this.

Sam returned with the coffee. Joni sipped hers slowly, telling herself she needed the caffeine but hating the way the coffee was making her stomach burn. Finally she put the drink aside and jumped up, pacing the waiting room. All she could think was how sick Witt must be if it was taking this long to stabilize him. How touch and go it must be. How every minute of waiting seemed to bring the horrible possibilities even closer.

Then Dr. Weiss came into the waiting room. "Hannah? We've got him stabilized."

Hannah sagged with relief. It was that sag that told Joni just how tense Hannah had been. And that was when Joni realized her own knees were turning to water with relief. She collapsed on a plastic chair.

"Thank you," Hannah said.

Weiss nodded and went to sit beside her. "As far as we can tell at this point, he had a cardiac arrhythmia."

"How bad?"

"Bad enough that it almost killed him."

"And the prognosis?"

"Pretty good if he doesn't have any more trouble tonight. He'll be on medication for the rest of his life, but it's fairly effective stuff. I'd like to see him improve his diet, and before long I want to send him to Denver for an arteriogram, to be sure we haven't missed a blockage. But he should recover completely."

They were allowed to go in and see Witt, but Joni hung back, afraid of distressing him. "I'll see him another time," she told her mother. Lying. She was lying. She was never going to see Witt again.

Then she hurried out of the emergency room into the frigid, dark mountain night.

Hardy towed Joni's car out of the snowbank. He considered taking it to the hospital and returning her keys, then decided against it. He didn't know how Hannah Matlock felt about him, but on the off chance she shared Witt's opinion, he didn't want to add to her upset in the midst of her other worries.

So he towed the car back to Joni's house and parked it in her driveway. Then, having no other choice, he went back to the hospital to wait the night out.

It was cold, and he didn't want to keep his engine running for fear fumes might overcome him, so he sat in the main lobby, keeping an eye on the emergency-room entrance.

It was just after midnight when he saw Joni come hurrying out, heading for the road. Jumping up, he hurried outside and called her name. At the same instant, Sam Canfield came out of the emergency room and called her.

"I'll take her home, Sam," Hardy said, waving to the deputy. "You look after Hannah."

Sam nodded and went back inside.

Joni never missed a stride. Hardy had to run to catch up with her. When he did, he had to stop her by seizing her hand.

"Joni, wait up. I'll drive you home."

It was a dark night, starshine gleaming off snow and without a moon, and by rights when she looked up at him, her face should have been a pale blur with dark holes for eyes. Instead, he felt the full force of her anguish like a gut punch. It was like Karen had died all over again. "Witt?" he said instinctively.

"He's going to be okay."

"Thank God."

She tried to tug her hand from his, but he wouldn't let her. "I'll take you home, Joni."

"I'm not going home. Not ever." The words were forceful, but full of pain.

"No?" He felt momentarily flummoxed. He couldn't exactly force her to go home, but he was damned if he was going to leave her wandering around out here all night in the cold. God, she would be dead in an hour. "Where are you going to go?"

"Anywhere."

"Right. That's a great plan. Are you going off half-cocked again?"

The look she gave him should have withered him. She tugged her hand again but he still wouldn't let go.

"Think about this, Joni. Just stop feeling sorry for yourself and think about this."

"Feeling sorry for myself? What makes you think I'm feeling sorry for *myself*? I nearly killed Witt! The best thing I can do for him is stay away."

"Maybe. Maybe." He sighed, feeling his earlobes turning numb. "Look, let's have this conversation in my truck. At least we'll be out of the wind before one of us gets frostbite. We'll talk it over, and you can make some kind of plan."

Apparently, either because of the cold or because her upset had cleared enough that her brain was kicking into gear again, she didn't feel like arguing anymore. She went with him to his pickup and climbed in. The leather seats were like sitting on ice cubes. He turned on the ignition, the Chevy coughed to life, and he hoped like hell the heater would start blasting soon.

"Let's be practical about this, Joni," he said. "You can't hike down the mountain tonight, and I don't think you're in any shape to drive." That gave him another pang. Suddenly he didn't want to take her home, where she would have access to her car. He didn't know if she was feeling suicidal, but she sure wasn't being rational.

She still didn't say anything. Hardy found himself thinking a stupid thought: that he was once again in the unenviable position of having the life of someone Witt loved in his hands. He hadn't been able to save Karen, but maybe he could save Joni. Witt could disown her all he wanted, but he wouldn't stop loving her. Witt didn't stop loving easily. There had been enough proof of that in the last twelve years.

"Okay," said Hardy, not knowing what else to do. "You can come stay with my mother and me until you get this all sorted out."

The heater had finally begun to blow air that was perceptibly warmer, and almost as if it were thawing Joni, she gave a huge shudder and nodded. "Barbara won't mind?"

"Hell no. She'll be glad of someone to talk to besides me. You want to stop and get some clothes?"

"I guess I better. Where's my car?"

He had been afraid she was going to get around to that. He was suddenly wishing he'd left it in the snowbank. "In your driveway."

"I'll drive myself to your place, then."

He shook his head, his heart inexplicably thudding. "Not tonight. You're too upset, okay? You can get the car in the morning."

He feared she would argue, but she didn't. She merely nodded. And that was so unlike Joni that a deeper fear began to gnaw at him. Maddening as she'd always been at times, he didn't want to see her act like a whipped puppy.

But he didn't say anything about it. Instead, he put the truck in gear and headed for her house. And he found himself a little amazed that he was once again all tangled up with the Matlocks.

Life could be such a bitch sometimes.

7

Barbara Wingate welcomed Joni warmly, even though she had been sleeping. Once a strong woman, illness and the years had taken a toll on her. She appeared frail, almost tiny, and her hair had turned snow-white. Only her lively dark eyes were the same. She came down the stairs, leaning heavily on the railing, and urged Joni into the kitchen for something warm to drink.

Hardy filled her in on the night's events, sparing Joni the effort.

Barbara shook her head. "That Witt Matlock. He always had a tendency to go overboard."

As did Joni. Hardy looked at her, thinking she was an awful lot like her uncle. Which wasn't surprising.

"Well," said Barbara as she brought out a box of instant cocoa and put the kettle on to boil, "he'll come round. He always does."

Hardy wasn't inclined to agree with her, having been the object of Witt's wrath for more than a de-

cade. And he didn't know that he was all that concerned about it, anyway. But Joni was, and it was
Joni he worried about.

"He disowned me," Joni said, her voice trembling. "He said he never wanted to see me again."

"I'm sure he did," Barbara answered. "What
were you thinking, child? You had to know he was
going to be furious."

Joni bowed her head. "I don't know, Mrs. Wingate. I don't know anymore. He's gotten mad at me
before, but not like this."

"Hmm." Barbara tore open three packets of cocoa
mix and poured one into each mug. "Sounds to me
like you were counting on his love for you. Not a
wise thing to do, Joni."

Hardy wanted to silence his mother, to tell her to
lay off Joni, who'd been through quite enough tonight. But Barbara was a mother, and for mothers
silence was rarely golden. And Hardy had never figured out a way to get her to keep quiet about anything.

"Maybe," Joni admitted. "Maybe I was."

Barbara nodded and paused to touch the younger
woman's shoulder before she poured boiling water
into the mugs and passed them around. The three of
them sat there for a few minutes, stirring cocoa, waiting for it to cool enough to drink.

"You know," said Barbara, "this is almost like
déjà vu."

Joni looked up, and Hardy asked, "What?"

"Well, Karen used to sit right there and drink cocoa with me," Barbara said. She smiled at Joni. "You two are very different in appearance, but I can still see a resemblance."

"Karen used to do this?" Joni prompted.

"Well, yes. When she was in high school, sometimes she'd slip out of the house and come over here. You remember Hardy had that job at the movie theater? He was out late some nights, and I guess she was pining for him a little. She'd come over here, and we'd sit and talk for hours."

Joni was amazed. "I never knew."

"Me neither," Hardy said.

"Well, we talked about private things. At least, things *she* wanted to keep private. She wasn't very happy with her dad. Too strict, she said. Now, I didn't put much stock in that. I think all children that age think their parents are too strict. But she especially didn't like the way he talked about Hardy. 'He doesn't know Hardy,' she'd tell me. I had to agree." Barbara smiled fondly at her son. "Witt never did see Hardy clearly. I think he was always seeing Hardy's dad, in his mind's eye."

Joni nodded. "I think so, too."

"Anyway, we'd sit here and talk, and she'd tell me all the things that upset her, and then she'd go home. She was a nice girl. I liked her." She nodded at Joni. "I think I'd like you, too, if we had a chance to talk."

"Thank you."

But none of the hurt in Joni's gaze eased, and
Hardy wished he could think of something to say that
would make her feel better. "Witt'll get over it," he
said finally. "Mom's right. You're blood kin, Joni.
He won't stay mad at you forever."

"Maybe not. But for right now…right now I'm
going to stay away from him. I don't want to give
him another heart attack."

Barbara clucked but finally said, "You might be
right for a little while. He needs some recovery time.
After that…after that I somehow don't think he's going to be quite so angry."

But it was obvious Joni didn't believe that, and
Hardy couldn't blame her. Witt had a track record of
staying angry for a long, long time.

Barbara leaned over and covered her son's hand
with hers. "Can you go up and check to be sure the
heat registers are open in the guest room? I can't
remember, but I may have closed some of them."

Hardy went willingly, sensing that his mother
wanted some private conversation with Joni. Maybe
she could think of something to help.

But when he got to the guest room, he paused
suddenly, unable to take another step. The anguish
he had seen on Joni's face hit him again, a one-two
punch. And he realized that not even twelve years
had made him care any less about that woman. Not
one bit less. He was still drawn to her as he had been
back then. Still found furtive thoughts of drawing her

close, of feeling her body pressed to his, lurking around the corners of his mind. He still wanted her.

And that was a damnable thing to be feeling at a time like this. An ugly thought gripped him, an almost atavistic pleasure that Witt had disowned her, because now Hardy didn't have to stay away from her. But the thought so appalled him that he trampled it into the mud at the back of his brain. God, maybe he was every bit as disgusting and terrible as Witt thought.

Feeling about as low as slime, he opened the registers to take the chill off the guest room. Then he took a moment to compose himself, well aware of how perceptive his mother's eyes could be. Well aware that Joni had more than enough on her plate right now and didn't need one more damn thing.

When he returned to the kitchen, he found Joni and Barbara still sitting at the table, still sipping cocoa. If they'd been talking about anything, he couldn't tell. He certainly didn't get the feeling they'd stopped talking on his account. So he took his seat again and waited to see what would unfold.

"Tell you what," said Barbara a few minutes later, as if completing some earlier thought, "you can stay here with us for a while, Joni."

"Oh, no," Joni said hastily. "Mrs. Wingate, I couldn't do that. It would be such an imposition."

"No imposition at all," she said firmly. "I could use somebody to talk to in the evenings besides Hardy."

Yeah, right, thought Hardy. Like the whole ladies' group from the church didn't keep her in a positive social whirlwind. This house was full of middle-aged women most evenings. But there was something more important than that. "Mom, maybe it wouldn't make things better for Joni if she stays with us. You know how Witt feels."

"Witt doesn't have to know. I'm not telling him, and neither are you. And I don't think Hannah will, either."

"But I was just going to leave town," Joni protested. "Find a job somewhere else."

Barbara shook her head. "Not right now you aren't. Your mother will probably need your help the next few weeks. Because you know who's going to take care of Witt, don't you?"

Hardy looked at Joni and saw a trapped expression in her eyes, as if she were some small animal caught in a snare.

"Besides," said Barbara all too wisely, "running never got rid of a problem. You won't feel one bit better if you put a continent between you and Witt. When that idiot decides to come around, you need to be here."

Joni shook her head, but she didn't argue any further. A short while later, Barbara returned to bed, leaving Joni and Hardy at the table.

"How do you feel?" he asked her.

"Terrible. I feel like I'm messing up everyone's life."

"You're not messing up mine," he said gently.

"Right. You really want me under your roof."

"I invited you, didn't I?" Then he said something calculated to annoy her, hoping it would drive away some of the self-pity she was drowning in. "I'd do the same for a stray cat."

Her head jerked up, and he saw her blue eyes flare, and for an instant she looked so much like Witt that he was amazed. But just for an instant, because the person she truly resembled was Hannah, and after the flare, her composure returned. "You're a jerk, Hardy." It was a phrase from their high school days, a way she had teased him over nonsense.

And he gave the same reply he always had. "I work at it."

A smile flickered over her tired, pinched face, then faded like autumn color. "There's no way to fix this," she said. "No way. I was so stupid."

"Well, I was, too. Nothing you did would have made a lick of difference if I hadn't submitted that bid."

"Why did you? You were so certain this would happen."

What could he say to her? That a part of him hadn't wanted to disappoint her? In the scheme of things, that was probably as important as not being able to pass up such a great opportunity, no matter how remote. He would never have forgiven himself for not trying. But it would have been even harder to forgive himself for disappointing Joni.

He couldn't tell her that, though. So he sighed and shrugged and said ruefully, "I guess I'm every bit as impulsive as you are."

She nodded slowly. "I feel guilty."

"For giving me the bid prospectus?" He already knew that and wondered why she needed to say it.

"Yes, but for other things, too. I feel guilty for still being alive when Karen's dead."

"Me too." He'd recognized that a long time ago and figured he deserved the self-inflicted emotional flogging. Like Witt, he would probably never forgive himself for going against Witt's wishes.

"I felt like this was something I needed to do for Karen," Joni continued, her voice low and thick. "I felt I owed it to her. It sounds so silly now, but..." She shook her head. "Twelve years is a long time. You'd think we'd all be past this crap by now. But I'm not, Hardy. I'm not at all. I feel like something inside me is frozen in time. And I guess I gave you the bid package to make time stop standing still...."

Her voice trailed away into tears, and she pushed her mug aside, putting her head down on the table. He hesitated a few moments, listening to her sobs, then, helplessly, he went to her, kneeling beside her chair and gathering her into his arms.

She turned to him, seeking comfort, clinging to his neck while her tears soaked the shoulder of his flannel shirt. He let her cling, enjoyed her clinging, and realized that her grief was reaching him in places that had been ice-cold for a long time. Making him ache. Making him want to cry, too.

"I'm sorry," she sobbed over and over. "I'm sorry."

He didn't know exactly what she was sorry for, so he guessed at it from the things she'd said. Sorry that Karen's death had had such an emotional impact on her that she somehow had been unable to grow past it? She wasn't the only one with that problem. Witt certainly hadn't. And Hardy himself...well, in some ways he'd been frozen in the ice of that night, too. It was like they were all going through the motions, a bunch of automatons who'd had something essential cut out of them.

Her tears were hot as they soaked his shirt, and he welcomed them. At least one of them could still feel something besides anger. Because Hardy was angry. He didn't like to look at that, and he pretended it wasn't so, because he didn't want to be like Witt. But he was angry through and through at the rotten blow life had dealt him and Karen. Angry through and through that she had died so young and he'd been left to face her father's wrath. Angry that he couldn't get past those fateful moments in time.

Angry that the only way he could ever have Joni was to hold her while she wept. Angry because he knew Witt was going to forgive her but would never forgive him, and he would have to give her back to her uncle. And angry at himself for having such muddled, selfish thoughts.

When all was said and done, Hardy Wingate hadn't liked himself at all since the moment he had realized that he wanted Joni more than Karen. And he had hated himself since Karen's death. God, what a tangle.

"Sorry," Joni said again. But her sobs were easing, and finally she pulled back from him, hunting up a napkin to dry her tears.

"Stop being sorry," Hardy said, and was relieved that the words didn't sound harsh. He hadn't wanted them to be, but in his current emotional turmoil, he couldn't be sure that anything he said was going to come out right. "You don't have to be sorry for crying. You don't have to be sorry for feeling guilty you're still alive—God knows, I'm feeling it, too—and you don't have to be sorry for anything else."

She didn't answer him, just sat there scrubbing her cheeks with a paper napkin until they looked red. "It's weird," she said minutes later.

Deciding she was through crying and being held, he straightened and pulled out a chair beside her, just in case. "What is?"

"What a mess we all are. People die, Hardy. Even young people. I've known others who've lost sisters and school friends. Witt lost his wife and brother. You and I both lost our fathers. But there was something about what happened with Karen...."

Maybe in his case, thought Hardy, it had something to do with the fact that he had a big ugly secret inside him. One that would probably plague him forever. He didn't know about Witt and Joni, though. What would they have to be feeling so guilty about?

But the suggestion made him think about Witt a little differently. Maybe Witt wasn't just being unreasonably angry at Hardy over something that Hardy, had he had a choice, would have given his own life to prevent. Witt hadn't gotten that angry at the mugger who killed his brother.

Then he realized that he was sitting there silently, lost in thought, not saying a word to Joni. "Sorry," he said, shaking himself. "I have a tendency to get lost inside my own head sometimes."

"It's okay. I do sometimes, too."

"I don't know what to say," he admitted. "Maybe it *is* weird how we've all reacted. That frozen-in-time feeling you mentioned…yeah, I feel it, too. When you said it, I all of a sudden recognized the feeling. I've been living with it for a long time and didn't even realize it. It's as if something stopped that night."

"Exactly. That's what I was hedging around when I came up with all those other reasons for what I did. I knew something was wrong. Something… Jeez, Hardy, none of us have been completely right for twelve years. Maybe it has something to do with the way Witt's reacted. I don't know. I just know…I've been marking time. Waiting, always waiting. Going through the motions."

"Yeah." He felt that way, too. So much of his life

was spent just going through the motions. As if more than Karen had died that night.

"Anyway…" Joni shook her head and wiped at an errant tear. "I made something happen. I made us all…I don't know. But it wasn't what I hoped would happen. I didn't think I'd nearly kill my uncle."

"I'm not sure you can blame yourself for that heart attack, Joni. I don't think anybody can build up enough crap in their arteries in ten minutes of being mad to cause a heart attack."

"Maybe not. But the stress…that played a part, Hardy. So I'm going to be leaving. Just as soon as I can find a job somewhere else."

He didn't know how to argue with her, though he very much wanted to. The little time they'd spent together since she'd hatched her scheme had made him realize that he was still very interested in her. That he still liked her a whole lot.

Not that that mattered. He didn't deserve her and never would. He was too hollowed out by his guilt, and by the recognition that if he just hadn't been such a chickenshit, Karen wouldn't have slipped out with him that night.

He couldn't inflict himself on anyone else. And Joni sure as hell deserved a whole heart, not the gutted remains of one. But a man could dream, and dreaming about Joni was easy. Even now, with her eyes all red from crying and her nose stuffy, he still wanted her close. Closer still. But he had no right to reach out, certainly not just to satisfy himself.

He also reminded himself, in a moment of blinding wisdom, that he didn't really know Joni anymore. He knew his memory of her, but those twelve years had still passed, no matter how familiar she seemed to him. He didn't really know the woman she had become.

All of those thoughts were hopping around in his head like a case of fleas, distracting him from the Joni who was sitting there beside him right that minute. It was a bad habit of his, to grow introspective even in the midst of conversation. He hadn't always been that way, but since Karen...

Everything in his life seemed to be ''since Karen.'' God. They were all basket cases.

But Joni, too, seemed to have turned inward. She sat with her forearms on the table, the forgotten cocoa between them, twisting her fingers as she frowned. An array of emotions swept over her face, moving too fast for him to identify. She was thinking about Witt, of course, about his heart attack. And castigating herself for her part in it.

He couldn't really blame her for feeling that way. The heart problem must have been brewing for a long time, but the explosion of rage had probably precipitated it. He wanted to reach out and take her hand, to give her silent comfort, but he didn't know if he would be overreaching.

Shit. Why was he making so much out of this? She was a friend, albeit one he hadn't been close to for a while, and she needed a temporary port in a storm. That was the only way to look at it. Anything else was wistful dreaming based on things long gone.

"Look," he said, "you don't have to sort it all out tonight. You go home in the morning and talk to your mom. She knows Witt better than anybody, and she can help you make up your mind about what to do."

She lifted her head and looked at him so sadly he felt his chest ache. "Which room is mine?"

"Top of the stairs, left."

"Thanks." She rose to leave, but in the kitchen doorway she paused and looked back. "I *know* what I have to do. I have to leave. I can't stand this situation anymore."

Then she turned and was gone. And he sat there, wondering if she might not be right about it after all.

8

Hannah was home and sound asleep when Joni returned at seven in the morning. She must have stayed at the hospital most of the night, Jodi thought.

Joni, who'd slipped out of Hardy's house before she had to face either him or his mother, started a pot of coffee, then sat at the dining-room table while it perked. At least she didn't have to go in to work. She wouldn't have trusted herself to count pills or do anything else accurately. She was exhausted, and far too upset.

Part of her wanted to go over to the hospital and see Witt. She wanted to stand beside his bed and, when he opened his eyes, tell him she was sorry. The rest of her knew that would be both foolish and risky. If he was still angry with her, he wouldn't be able to handle it. No, going over there would be a selfish thing to do. Purely selfish, and she'd already been too selfish about this situation.

It was time to put Witt first. And Hannah. To make

sure that they were okay. What did it matter that she had some wild, crazy feeling of having been encased in glass for twelve years? Frozen in time. Heck, she was surprised that Hardy hadn't told her she was crazy.

Anybody else would have. And they would probably have been right.

Regardless, she was getting the hell out of this town. Soon. Away from all this. Into a world where everything hadn't stopped because one person had died.

The coffee finished brewing, and she got up to pour herself some. After she filled the mug, she turned back toward the dining room and was startled to see her mother, wearing a white terry-cloth robe, standing there.

"Where were you last night?" Hannah asked, dark rings beneath her eyes.

"I stayed with a friend."

"Do you have any idea how worried I was?"

"I can't seem to do anything right anymore." The words came out bitterly. "I'm sorry. I figured you'd be too preoccupied with Witt."

"Not too preoccupied to notice you weren't here when I came home. I went to your room to fill you in."

"How is he?"

"Much better. Mind if I get to the coffeepot?"

Joni wasn't accustomed to that kind of sarcasm

from her mother, and it hurt. She stepped quickly aside to clear the way, then returned to the table.

Hannah joined her. The two of them sat there quietly for a while, then Hannah offered, "They said Witt probably didn't suffer too much permanent damage to his heart. There's some, of course. They think he might have been having the attack when he came over here so angry."

"I'm sorry." Joni couldn't bring herself to look at her mother.

"What I'm trying to say is, his extreme rage may have been part of the heart attack. Often, in the early stages, people get very angry."

Joni nodded but didn't feel any better. "Still, he wouldn't have had anything to get angry about except for me."

"He might have found something else. Regardless, I don't want you to take anything he said too much to heart. A lot of that may have been his illness, not you."

"Maybe." She lifted her head. "I'm still going away, Mom. I can't hang around and cause him another heart attack. I need to get out of this town. I need to get away from all this. I'm never going to escape Karen's death if I don't. Anyway, no matter what you say, Witt disowned me. He said he never wanted to see me again."

Hannah compressed her lips, as if holding in some overwhelming emotion. "You have to do what's best for you, Joni. I've always said that, haven't I? But before you decide to cut Witt out of your life permanently there's something…'' Her voice trailed off, and she drew a deep breath.

It was so unlike Hannah to be hesitant that Joni looked up, forgetting her preoccupation with her own feelings. ''Mom?'' Her concern grew to fear as she saw tears well in Hannah's dark eyes. Her mother never cried. Never.

''Mom?''

Hannah drew a quick breath, compressing her lips again as she sought control. When she spoke, her words were strained and her lips trembled. ''I had a lot of time to think last night, honey. A lot of time. I thought about you as much as Witt. I thought about what he'd said and how it made you feel. And I thought about some of the things I've done that…perhaps weren't so right.''

''Mom, you've never—''

Hannah interrupted her. ''You don't know everything about me, Joni. No one does. And as I was sitting there last night, waiting to hear about Witt, I realized that, well, I may have done a very bad thing to you. And to Witt. That maybe he wouldn't be so bitter if I'd told him the truth. Only now I can't, because it would upset him so much. It might kill him. And you…maybe I've cheated you out of something irreplaceable. Maybe the last twelve years would have been easier on everyone if you both had just known…''

Hannah's voice trailed off again as she fought to

hold back tears. Joni jumped up from the table and went to get the box of tissues from the end table in the living room.

When she came back with it, Hannah thanked her and snatched one to blow her nose.

"I'm sorry," she said, dabbing at her eyes. "I feel like such a sham. I'm so full of shame."

"About what?" Joni found it absolutely impossible to believe her mother had ever done a thing to be ashamed of. It just didn't fit Hannah's character at all.

Hannah expelled a long breath and took a sip of coffee, as if she needed something to reinforce her. "You can't tell Witt this right now. Promise me."

"I promise. I don't expect to be speaking to him any time in the near future, anyway."

"You may change your mind. The thing is…you need to know this before you make any decisions. Maybe you should have known it all along. Joni, Witt is…Witt is your father."

9

The room still looked the same. The humming of the refrigerator hadn't changed, nor had the scent of Hannah's rose potpourri, or the smell of hot cast iron from the woodstove. Everything was the same, familiar.

But it had all changed. It was never, ever going to look the same again, Joni realized. It was as if the surprise of Hannah's statement had driven her mind out of her body and placed it on some high, icy pinnacle. She was still using her own eyes, ears, nose and mouth, but she was removed. She was thousands of mental miles away.

Speaking felt almost as if she were trying to manipulate a ventriloquist's dummy. "You're lying." The words came out flat. Thick. Strange. The voice belonged to someone else.

"No," Hannah said, her voice catching. "It was...it was a mistake. Neither of us meant to..."

"You cheated on my father." Which gave her an

interesting perspective, Joni-on-the-icy-mountain thought with incredible clarity. She had always wondered why her mother had tolerated her father's cheating.

"Once," Hannah said. "Only once."

Once was enough. Once might have been a million times. What did any of it matter? All she had was her mother's word....the word of a woman who had lied to her for twenty-six years.

Her thoughts were starting to get confused, starting to hurt. The icy mountain was no longer far enough away, and she felt herself coming back to the dining room that would never look the same, the mother who would never look the same and a heart that felt as if it was going shatter.

"You lied to me," she said to Hannah. Her tone was glacial. "You cheated and you lied. And Uncle Witt cheated on his brother. My God, the two of you have a whole lot to be proud of, don't you?"

"Joni..."

But Joni had had enough. Shoving her chair back from the table she ran upstairs to her room and bolted the door.

She was Witt's daughter. The thought hit her like a bowling ball, and she fell facedown on her bed. Witt was her father.

Funny how only twenty-four hours ago that thought might have made her happy. Funny how bad it felt now.

Then she gave in to the tears and cried until she could cry no more.

Hannah wept her way through two cups of coffee. She didn't weep often. In fact, in her entire adult life, she had wept three times. The first was when she discovered Lewis was cheating on her. The second was when Joni was born. And the third was when Karen died. She hadn't wept for Lewis when he died. Whatever she had felt for him was long since dead by then, the marriage a convenient front for him and his career. A safe haven for Hannah, who somewhere deep inside didn't especially care for men and didn't want to be bothered by them.

Except for Witt. Witt had somehow always been different. Well, so had Lewis, until she had learned the truth about him. But Witt had never let her down the way other men had. Never. Until last night.

She had to mend that rift somehow. She had to find a way to keep Joni from running away until Witt was well enough that they could talk. And maybe there was a bit of selfishness in that, too. Hannah wasn't blind to her own faults. But with Witt so ill, she needed the comfort of Joni more than ever.

Except by choosing to tell the truth as a way to keep the family together, she might have successfully driven Joni away for good. She didn't know. And she was far too tired from the long night to know if her thoughts were making any sense.

She had just known that she couldn't let Witt die

and Joni run off...at least not until they knew the truth. Witt couldn't hear it right now, but Joni could.

Maybe, she thought, watching Witt so near death had made her acutely aware of the passage of time and of all the things she had put off for too long. Like telling the truth.

She had never told Lewis the truth. If he'd suspected, he'd never said a word. Too much had happened that particular New Year's Eve, and maybe Lewis had felt too guilty to look too closely at things. Or maybe he had never suspected. She'd certainly never been unfaithful to him again.

Not that she would have thought of it as being unfaithful, not when Lewis was busy having affairs. Hannah had been protecting herself by playing Caesar's wife, and she cherished no illusions of martyrdom.

But now... Oh, God, now. Maybe she had been wrong to spring this on top of the pain Joni was feeling from last night. But she had feared allowing any time to pass, time in which Joni might harden her heart to Witt.

And Witt...if he weren't so sick, she would shake him until his teeth rattled. How dare he treat Joni that way? What was the matter with him? Why was he nursing an anger so old it ought to have died by now? Why couldn't he see reason on the subject? Why was he willing to risk driving Joni away—and her, too—by clinging to his hatred?

She loved Witt. She'd always loved Witt. And

she'd always believed he was a better man than this. It hurt her to her core to think she might have been mistaken in him all these years.

Oh, she had known he didn't like Hardy Wingate, and why. But for a long time now she'd thought his dislike of Hardy was just a deeply ingrained habit. Until that day at the lawyer's office when he'd been so angry about Hardy's bid, she hadn't realized that the feeling was still very much alive in him. Alive and strong, strong enough to sweep Joni up in its wrath.

God, what was she going to do? If Witt wasn't ill, she would tell him the truth, tell him to come to his senses before he lost his other daughter. Maybe he would even listen. But she couldn't take the risk now. Maybe not for a long time.

Her stomach was burning from so much coffee, and she forced herself to get a glass of milk. She shouldn't have kept this secret for so long, she realized. She and Witt had been widowed only a few years apart, and as soon as they were both free of their marriages, she should have told him. She should have allowed him to be a *real* father to Joni, instead of just an uncle. And she should have allowed Joni to develop that relationship with him.

Now, in the midst of a crisis, she was using the truth as a lifeline. That wasn't fair to Joni. Not fair at all.

But she hadn't known what else to do.

* * *

A couple of hours later, Joni left the house without speaking to her mother. She considered getting into her car and driving until she felt she had put enough distance between them. Instead she decided to walk.

The day was gray and the chilly air was damp, hinting at more snow, but it wasn't terribly cold. Striding up and down the hilly streets, she kept waiting for her mind to stop feeling numb. She passed by people without saying a word, people she knew. Some of them stopped her and asked what was wrong. When they did, she gave them a wan smile and said she just wasn't feeling well. They expressed sympathy about Witt, then let her go on her way.

She lost track of time, lost track of where she was or how far she had walked...not that she could get lost in a town this size. The day was passing around her, and she didn't even notice.

Part of her realized that something was wrong with her, that she had withdrawn inside herself until she was barely a pinprick in her own mind. It was as if she needed to go away inside herself until she could adjust to the revelations and shocks of the last twenty-four hours.

As if she couldn't afford to feel a thing right now for fear the emotions would shatter her into a million pieces.

A long time later there was suddenly a broad, parka-covered chest blocking her path. Reluctantly she looked up from the snowy gravel road she was walking along and saw Hardy Wingate.

"Joni, what's wrong?"

"Nothing."

"Bullshit. Half the town is talking about the way you're walking up and down the streets like a zombie. Your mother called me—me—and asked me to catch up with you."

Joni blinked, still feeling as if she were a long way away and Hardy was talking to her from the other end of a tunnel. "Why?"

"Why? Because she's worried about you. Because she's had a dozen calls today about you. You think nobody's noticed? It's a small town, Joni. You can't walk these streets in a daze for hours without folks getting worried."

"I'm fine. I'm just thinking."

"Right. You're also freezing. Get in my truck."

She felt something then, the first thing she'd really felt since this morning's shock. "Who died and made you God?"

"Nobody. But apparently you don't have the sense to take care of yourself. Now get your butt in that truck before you freeze it off."

"I'm not going home."

"I don't care. Come to my place. Go to a hotel. But get yourself in before you freeze. Christ, don't you even realize that you're staggering like a drunk person? You're hypothermic."

She couldn't even summon the energy to stay angry, much as she wanted to. Nor could she get into the truck under her own steam. Nothing wanted to coordinate right, so he had to pick her up and put her in it. She hated him for that. She hated her mother for calling him. She hated the whole damn world.

The truck jolted over the rough, icy roads, then up the hill to Hardy's house. "You can stay with us," he said. "Until you figure things out or want to go home, you stay with us."

"Thanks." But she didn't care.

"Joni? What the hell is going on? This can't all just be because Witt pitched a fit. You *knew* he was going to have a fit. And surely you don't think that was the cause of his heart attack?"

"I don't care anymore."

"Yeah? Well, you're sure doing a great imitation of someone who cares a whole hell of a lot about something. People who really don't care don't try to commit slow suicide."

"I wasn't committing suicide."

"Then you're stupider than I could've thought."

He pulled into his driveway, then helped her out of the truck. Inside, he put her at the kitchen table. "I'm going to make some hot soup. Just stay there."

She watched him move around the kitchen with the ease of someone who was used to it. Once that might have interested her. Now she just felt numb. Numbness was good. Numbness protected her.

When he put a huge bowl of chowder in front of her, she didn't even have the will to pick up the

spoon. It was, she found herself thinking, a little difficult to accept that your entire life had been a lie.

"Joni? Eat."

Obediently, she picked up the spoon. The chowder
was tasteless, but it was hot, and as it settled in her
stomach she felt everything inside her beginning to
thaw. Her emotions began to thaw, too, splintering
like the ice on a spring river, shifting, cracking and
thundering as they collided.

Suddenly she was crying again. She dropped the
spoon into the soup and closed her eyes, letting the
huge, silent tears roll down her cheeks. They felt as
hot as flames, searing her.

"Do you want to talk now?"

Hardy's voice made her open her eyes. She saw
him through a blur, as if he were underwater.

"Joni?"

"It doesn't matter." The tears fell more heavily,
as if they were coming through a dam that had broken. No sobs wracked her; there was just the steady
flood from her eyes.

"Damn it," Hardy said. He jumped up from the
table and began to pace the kitchen. "Joni… God,
I'm going to kill Witt. I'm going to kill him."

She didn't answer that. What was the point? It
wasn't Witt, anyway. It was her mother. Apparently
Witt hadn't even guessed at the truth. But her mother
had known and had kept the secret way past reason.
She could understand Hannah not telling her while

Lewis was still alive, but what had been the excuse after that?

"It's not Witt," she said finally. Although it was. Snaking from somewhere deep inside her was a burning fury that a man who had grieved twelve years for his daughter was ready to throw her, his niece, away like so much trash he didn't need anymore.

Her tears stopped flowing, as if there was no more moisture inside her. She felt them drying on her face, making it feel stiff. Hardy stopped pacing and returned to the table.

"Talk to me, Joni. I can't help if you don't tell me what's going on."

"You can't help. No one can help."

"But it's not Witt?"

"No. Witt's just...I don't know. All I know is that if I don't get away from Karen I'm going to scream!"

Hardy looked at her, searching her face. On the surface, her remark was patently ridiculous. Get away from a girl who'd been dead for more than a decade? Yet he felt the truth in the words, however the sentence was phrased. Karen was probably more a part of their lives dead than she would have been if she'd lived.

"Will you get away from her if you leave town?"

She hesitated, then shook her head. "I guess not. I won't really get away from Witt, either. Damn Hannah!"

"What did Hannah do?"

What to say? Telling him the truth would only make it worse. It was better to let it lie. Yet she heard herself speaking, even as she fought to keep the words inside. "Witt is…my father!"

Hardy reeled. He wondered how a secret like that could have been kept in a town this size for all these years, then realized. Not even Witt had known. "Jesus."

He began to understand why Joni had been wandering the streets like a lost waif. If Barbara had told him something like that, he didn't know how he would have responded. It would be easy to laugh it off and say, "Well, at least I know I'm not the spawn of the town drunk," but he felt deep inside that he wouldn't feel that way at all. He would feel as if everything in his life was a lie. As if he couldn't trust his own mother. As if he didn't really know who he was.

"I'm sorry, Joni," he said, finding the words about as inadequate as anything could be.

"Yeah," she said, a bitter edge in her voice. "My mother's a cheat and a liar, my uncle's a cheat and an ass, and Karen's not just my cousin, but my sister. Which I guess means I'm never going to get away from her. Or Witt. Or anything…anything else." Her voice broke, then faded.

Hardy watched helplessly as Joni's entire face crumpled into a grimace of anguish. But she didn't weep again. Apparently she had no tears left. "I take it Hannah told you that this morning?"

She nodded.

"Jesus H. Christ. Why now? Wasn't there already enough going on?"

"She doesn't want me to leave."

"God." Frustrated, he shoved his chair back from the table and started pacing again. "I can't believe she used that as a weapon. Not now."

"I don't think she meant it to be a weapon."

He looked over his shoulder at her. "It doesn't matter, does it? It's still a crater in your life."

"Yeah." She drew a shaky breath. "Nothing feels the same. *I* don't feel the same. I feel... I don't know how I feel."

"I'm sorry Mom isn't here," he said. "She always has good ideas. I'm just... Hell, Joni, I'm just flummoxed. I don't know what to say."

"Neither do I." Her mouth trembled. "Everything just blew up in my face. All I can think is *ouch*."

He nodded. "Big ouch. Damn." Shaking his head, he paced some more, trying to absorb all this. Trying to absorb the fact that he'd invited another one of Witt's daughters into his house. Oh, man, wasn't that going to make a stink. "When's she telling Witt?"

"Not now. He's too sick."

"It might be wise to be two counties away when she does."

"If she does." It was odd, but having spat the horrible truth out to another person, she could almost feel the world stabilizing under her a bit. Not that she was going to get over this quickly, but she didn't feel quite so rocky as she had a few minutes ago. But nothing, absolutely nothing, was ever going to be the same again.

"It's amazing," she said slowly, "how fast your life can be permanently changed. All it takes is an eye blink."

"Like when the drunk driver hit Karen and me."

"Exactly." She didn't even mind him drawing Karen into the conversation again. "I just wish I had known sooner."

She picked up her spoon, sipped a little more chowder and thought she was doing well. She was going to be all right. Things no longer seemed as dire as they had that morning.

What had really changed, after all? They were all the same people they had been twenty-four hours ago. All that had changed were a few perceptions. Little things, really.

Just little things.

But as she watched her hand start to tremble again and felt her throat tighten until it hurt, she knew it wasn't going to be that easy.

Perceptions were everything. And hers had been irrevocably shattered.

10

Witt looked a lot better that afternoon. He was off the respirator, and his color had improved. Hannah, with a professional eye, watched the heart-monitor log steady lambda waves. There was a little glitch in them, which she didn't have the expertise to interpret, but she imagined it must come from the bit of heart muscle that had died last night.

He was sound asleep, so she sat by his bed, waiting for him to wake. In all the uproar last night, and then this morning with Joni, she had scarcely admitted to herself just how much she feared losing Witt. She loved her daughter more than life, but Witt was…Witt was the stability in her world. He was the shoulder she had always been able to lean on, the ear that was always willing to listen. He'd stood by her and Joni after Lewis's death, stalwart and ever ready to help them. She didn't know how she would have handled any of that, except for Witt. She would have been alone with her guilt, grief and shame, and what could she have done? Lean on Joni?

Joni had no idea how much Witt had spared her just by being there to support Hannah and to play father to Joni.

Joni, like all children, had taken her childhood for granted. She would never guess how much she had been sheltered and protected from, or how fast she might have had to grow up if Hannah had had no one else to lean on. But Hannah did. And she was honest enough to know that even if she had tried not to lean, in subtle ways she still would have.

So Witt had preserved Joni's childhood.

But Witt was like that. Frustrating as he was with his attitude toward Hardy Wingate, annoyed as *she* was for the way he had treated Joni, Hannah knew what a strong, generous and loving man Witt Matlock was.

Witt had raised his younger brother Lewis after their parents died. It was Witt who had gone to work in the mine to ensure that Lewis could go to medical school. And even after Hannah had married Lewis and could have supported him the rest of the way through school, Witt had continued to send the same monthly contribution, saying Hannah shouldn't be responsible for Lewis's education, despite the fact that Witt had started his own young family.

The end result was that when Hannah got pregnant with Joni and had to stop working for a while, Lewis had been able to finish school. Hannah and Lewis had been grateful, more grateful than they could say. Once they were making some decent money, they'd tried to pay Witt back, but he refused, saying it wasn't a loan.

And Witt had continued to work at the mine. Then Witt's wife had died, leaving him a single parent with a young daughter. Not too long after that, Lewis had been killed. It had been as natural as breathing for Hannah and Witt to get together and buck each other up. And neither one of them ever mentioned that night. The night Joni was conceived.

Maybe that had been a mistake. Maybe they should have been more honest with each other. Maybe if she'd told him years ago that Joni was his daughter he would have gotten over Karen better than he had. Or maybe, at the very least, he wouldn't have disowned her last night.

Hannah sighed, trying to banish the thoughts that were whirling in her head like a bunch of angry bees, all trying to get her attention. What was done was done. She couldn't change it. Now she could only hope to mend it.

Along about three, Witt stirred. He moved his arm, then his eyes sprang open, as if panic had seized him. Hannah heard the beep of the heart monitor speed up, and she reached out immediately to touch his hand.

"Witt, it's okay. You're okay." She rose and stood beside him, making it easier for him to see her.

"Hannah." He whispered her name, a raspy sound.

"I'm right here, Witt. Do you remember what happened?"

"No...."

"You had a heart attack. But you're fine now. You're going to be just fine."

But she saw the fear in his gaze, and she knew it wasn't going to be fine. How could it? It would be a long time before he stopped fearing that he could drop dead at any instant.

"What day is it?"

"Sunday. You had the heart attack last night. It's three o'clock in the afternoon."

He nodded and closed his eyes. "Work. Call Shep."

"I'll call him."

Then he turned his face to the wall and wouldn't speak another word.

And Hannah sat there for a long time, wondering just how much the stubbornness of one man was going to cost her.

Not knowing what else to do with a woman who was brokenhearted over problems he could do nothing to solve, Hardy coaxed Joni back into his office-*cum*-studio and showed her the model he was building for his next big bid. Much to his relief, she was actually interested in it.

In fact, it seemed to delight her.

"It's like a wonderful dollhouse," she said. She wasn't exactly jumping up and down, but it was the most emotion he'd heard out of her, other than grief, since he'd picked her up off the street a few hours ago. To his way of thinking, that was a major improvement.

"That's kind of the idea," he said. "Some people just build exteriors, but I like my models to open up so the customer can get a feel for the interior, too. It takes a lot more time, of course, but I think it pays for itself."

"Did you do this for Witt, too?"

He nodded and pointed to the far corner of the room. "That's a copy of the model I did for him. Go ahead and look at it."

"I never would have thought of making a hotel look like this," she said as she touched one corner of the model with her index finger. "Never."

"I wanted it to resemble one of those grand old hotels. Or even a large bed-and-breakfast. I was thinking homey."

"I like it."

He pulled out the stool at his worktable and started gluing some slivers of wood onto his new model, pretending to work when he was, in fact, watching Joni with an eagle eye.

He was seriously worried about her and didn't want her to be alone for a second. The problem was figuring out how to keep her from being alone without making her feel as if she were under guard.

And it terrified him, when he was honest about it, to once again have the life of one of Witt's daughters in his hands.

He tried to tell himself he was being too melodramatic, but he didn't believe it. Not after finding Joni wandering the streets in a near daze, half-frozen. He wanted to believe she would have found her way home eventually, but he wasn't sure of that at all. Right now he had the feeling she never wanted to lay eyes on Hannah or Witt again.

So maybe she would have gone to one of her girlfriends' houses. Maybe she would have discovered, even in her shocked state, that she still wanted to live.

Or maybe not. That possibility was keeping him on tenterhooks.

She seemed enthralled with the model, so he allowed himself to relax a bit and give a little more attention to what he was working on.

"It must take you a lot of time to build these," Joni remarked, moving on to another model.

"It keeps me busy. I generally do the modeling in the evening and on weekends."

"How come?"

"If I've got a job actually under way, I have to spend most days supervising and keeping things moving. So I try to treat the modeling like a hobby."

She came back to his worktable and sat across from him. "What exactly *do* you do?"

"I'm an architect, and I act as my own general

contractor. Which means I figure out designs for jobs, figure out the cost of building them, then bid on them. If I win the bid, I hire people to do the work and supervise them.''

"That must keep you busy."

"When I'm on a job. I'm between them now, so I've got a little time on my hands."

She nodded. "That won't last, will it?"

He shrugged. "It might. So far I've been jolting along, doing jobs, then sitting on my hands for a bit. It's okay. It's keeping me busy enough. And if things started to overlap a whole lot, I'd have to hire some permanent employees to help out. I'm not sure I want to do that yet."

"Why not?"

He shrugged. "Right now it's all my baby. I'm on top of everything. I don't have to rely on other people to do it right because I don't have the time to check up on them."

"I guess I can see that. Do you think you'll ever want to expand?"

"Maybe. I could see it if there was a lot of good work available. If…well, if I ever had a family, it'd probably be a good thing to do." He stole a quick glance at her, wondering how she would respond to that. And, as always when any such possibility passed his lips or entered his mind, he found himself thinking of Karen. As if Karen's death meant the end of all that for him, too. As if somehow he would be cheating on her if he married.

How the hell had his mind gotten into such a mess?

But apparently Joni's was in the same mess with him, because the first thing she said was, "You don't date much, do you? Not since…Karen."

He really wished he could laugh off the question or tell her she was crazy. Unfortunately, he knew he would be wasting his breath and wouldn't be fooling either of them. She'd hit the nail on the head when she had said it was as if they were frozen in time.

"I feel guilty," he finally admitted, thinking how stupid that sounded.

But she nodded as if she understood. "We're sick, Hardy. You know that? Most people would have gotten past this by now. Most people figure out how to get on with their lives."

He wanted to defend himself. Or maybe he wanted to defend her more. He knew the mire he was living in, but he couldn't see any blessed reason why Joni should be living in it, too. She hadn't been driving the car. She hadn't been planning to dump Karen. He had plenty to feel guilty about, but Joni didn't have one single thing to apologize for.

"I'm getting on with life," he finally said. "Most of it."

She surprised him with a faint smile. "Yeah. Most of it. It's the rest of it I've started worrying about. I got to thinking that maybe Witt was the reason I couldn't move on. The way he nursed his anger

against you, the way I was supposed to avoid you, it
kept it *alive*. Kept it fresh.''

He gave a sideways bob of his head, not quite a
nod, more of a ''maybe.'' ''And now that you've
broken the taboo?''

Her smile died completely. ''It didn't make anything good happen, did it? Which, I guess, just goes
to prove that Witt is always right. If Karen had listened to him, she wouldn't be dead. If I had just
listened to him, he wouldn't be lying in a hospital
bed.''

He didn't like the sound of that, but he didn't exactly know how to contradict her in a way that would
convince her. This was going to require some thinking. Heavy-duty thinking.

''I wish my mom hadn't told me that Witt is my
dad.''

He nodded, giving her room to speak.

''I mean, it's not just that I'm not who I always
thought I was. I'm not sure that even makes a difference. Part of me thinks it doesn't make any difference at all to *me*. It won't change my genetic
makeup, or my personality, or the color of my hair.''

''Right.'' He said it gently, waiting to hear the
rest.

''But it changes me emotionally, Hardy. And I
don't like the way it changes me. I don't like the
way it makes me feel about my mother. God! All I
can think is that she was a cheater, too.''

''Too?''

"My dad cheated on her. A lot. I figured that out by the time I was around eleven. I could smell it on him sometimes when he came home. Another woman's perfume. Another woman's body. I kept waiting for my mother to say something, but she never did. And by the time I was eleven, I'd figured out that she knew about it, too. But she never said a word."

Hardy felt his chest squeeze. "That's awful."

"It was…confusing. Instinctively I knew what he was doing was wrong. I didn't need anybody to tell me. And I'd get so mad sometimes, but I couldn't say anything. Somehow I knew I'd just get into trouble if I did. So I kept my mouth shut. And for a long time, I hated my dad."

Hardy wanted to reach out to her, but the model was between them. Maybe a good thing. Getting close to Joni was dangerous to what little peace of mind he'd managed to find over the years.

"Then I got indifferent. Developed the attitude that it wasn't my problem. But I never had a whole lot of respect for my dad. Now…now I don't have any respect for my mother, either. Maybe she didn't cheat all the time like he did. Maybe Witt was a one-time thing. But he was her husband's *brother*. And Witt…my God, he's so self-righteous sometimes, but he was still capable of cheating with his brother's wife."

"It does sound sordid," Hardy agreed, trying to keep his tone neutral. At the moment, he felt the best thing he could do for Joni was let her rant. And maybe, at some point, convince her to see a therapist. Because she had been seriously wounded, wounds so deep he wasn't sure she could get past them without professional help.

She jumped up from the table and started pacing the room, weaving among tables and desks, not even sparing a glance for the wide windows with their view of the snow-covered backyard.

That view was one that often brought him peace. But not today. Today it made an icy backdrop to a friend's crisis.

"Maybe," he said carefully, "it was one of those accidents."

"Accidents?" Her laugh was harsh, bitter. "You don't get in bed with someone by accident."

"Well, okay, it was a poor choice of words. One of those moments of passion. One of those moments when neither one of them was up to snuff. Up to saying no, for whatever reason. A little too much to drink, whatever. Maybe it happened and they've both regretted it ever since."

"So?"

"I'm just saying that maybe your mom didn't consciously cheat on your dad. Maybe she never meant to. Or…" He hesitated, then plunged on. "Or maybe she just did it in a moment of rage to get even."

Joni shook her head, disgust written all over her face. "Saying no isn't that difficult, Hardy. I've said no plenty of times."

"Yeah? Maybe you just haven't met the right guy under the right circumstances."

You know, he found himself thinking as his words cast the room into utter silence, at his age he ought to have better control of his tongue than that. Now how the hell could he apologize for his remark in a way that would undo it?

But before he could think of anything, Joni was glaring at him. "Just need the right man? Jeez, Hardy, you sound like one of those jerks in a bar! It's not about raging hormones, it's about love and caring."

He knew better, but he supposed that, given her history, she was going to be inclined to feel that way. "Sure," he said, trying to smooth it over. But she was not so easy to placate.

"You men are all like my dad. You want something, you take it, and never mind who it hurts."

"Now wait—"

"It was probably all Witt's fault," she said, charging forward without regard to his interruption. "*All* his fault. He probably seduced my mother."

"Whoa. Are you saying Hannah was a helpless pawn? Because I'll tell you, Joni, I really don't think she'd like that description. What's more, she's not the type to be a helpless pawn. You're just going to have to get used to the idea that your mother and your uncle, for whatever reason, had a passionate affair, albeit probably a brief one. They're human.

And like all the rest of the damn human race, they make mistakes.''

"Yeah? Then how come you weren't allowed to make a mistake? How come I wasn't? Where the hell does Witt get off being so damn judgmental?''

"He's hurting."

She made a disgusted sound. "Yeah. That's a great excuse. He's hurting, so he spends twelve years lashing out at other people.''

"Only at me, Joni. Only at me.''

She waved her arm almost wildly. "What right does he have to do that? What *right?*''

Hardy looked down at his hands, still holding carefully shaped pieces of wood hardly bigger than toothpicks. He should never, ever, have allowed Joni into his life again, he thought. Never. His chest was so tight he could hardly breathe, and she was bound and determined to keep raking at the past until all the wounds were open again. Witt evidently couldn't handle bleeding all over again, and Hardy wasn't sure he could, either.

"Look, Joni," he said, trying to keep his voice level. "I've spent years trying to get past that night. I may not have done a perfect job of it, but I spend every day of my life trying to look forward and not back. And I really don't want to rake this all up again.''

"Sure." She put her hand on her hip and looked at him with disappointment and disgust. "We'll all go back to living in our glass cages, crippled by feelings we can't deal with.''

"I've dealt with it. I've been dealing with it for twelve goddamn years!'' He didn't mean to shout the words, but they came out that way. And she shouted right back.

"Right. Dealing with it. And you can't even date! God almighty, Hardy, we're all of us messes and we won't even admit it.''

"You...?''

"Me. Yeah, me. I've been feeling guilty every day since Karen died. Guilty I'm still alive. Guilty I can still have fun. Guilty that I wanted her boyfriend, and I find myself wondering if those jealous thoughts had something...something...''

She broke off, turning her back to him and hunching her shoulders. Her words struck him like bricks, awakening all the guilt he'd been carrying, leaving him feeling almost sick.

"Joni...Joni, being jealous doesn't kill people. Not unless you pick up a weapon and do it yourself.'' She had wanted him, too. He'd guessed it. And he'd been about to ditch Karen.... Oh, God, he hated himself.

He couldn't say any more. Couldn't bring himself to talk about this with her another minute. All the things he'd thought he'd buried were clawing their way out of the graveyard of his soul and shrieking at him.

It was far from over, he realized as lead settled in

his heart. Far from over. Joni was bound and determined to rock the precarious balance they'd all managed to find. She was determined to claw her way out of the past, no matter what the cost.

And he didn't know if he was for her or against her. He didn't know if he could survive it.

Getting to his feet, he walked out of his office, grateful to see that his mother had come back from her lunch date. "Joni's in my office," he said abruptly. "Keep an eye on her. She's terribly upset."

Barbara's face creased with concern. "Where are you going?"

"Out. Anywhere."

"Hardy…" But Barbara stopped herself and, with the wisdom of a mother, let him go.

But there was something she *could* do. Squaring her shoulders, she marched into the office to deal with *one* problem she could attack. It was time for tough love.

Joni was sitting slumped at the table, such a picture of dejection that Barbara unwillingly felt a twinge of sympathy. Then she thought of the look on her son's face as he'd stormed past her, and she hardened her heart.

"Why are you doing this to Hardy?" she demanded.

"I'm not doing anything to him," Joni said, looking up with red-rimmed eyes. "He's the one who dragged me back here."

"Only to help you. Well, why don't you climb out

of that pit of self-pity you seem so determined to sink into, and look around you at what you're doing to other people.''

''What *I'm* doing?''

''What *you're* doing. You're hurting my son. He's spent twelve years paying for an accident he couldn't prevent. Paying for a crime that was committed by someone else. Hardy's spent twelve years beating himself up, twelve years being haunted by one single night that wasn't his fault. Where the hell do you get off rubbing his nose in it all over again? Why in God's name can't you just leave him in peace?''

Joni's face was as white as the snow outside the window. Her blue eyes were dark, so dark they were like windows on a grave. ''Peace?'' she repeated thickly. ''What peace? None of us have had any peace since that night.''

''You're not helping.''

''Maybe not.'' Joni's head sank again, as if it were being weighed down. ''But if we don't ever face it, Mrs. Wingate, we're never going to get past it.''

''And you're the self-appointed catalyst for all this healing you think everyone needs, huh?''

Joni shrugged but didn't answer.

Barbara, who had seen the pain written clear on Hardy's face, wanted to stay angry with Joni. Wanted to tell the young woman to get out of her house and never come back.

But as she stood there glaring at Joni's bowed

head, her anger began to soften and her kinder side to come to the fore.

As difficult as it had been on Hardy, he'd at least been able to get away from memories of Karen occasionally. To forget it for a few days or even weeks at a time as he became involved in a project. Or took a trip. But Joni…Joni dealt with it every day because she saw Witt every day. Even if he didn't say anything about it, how could Joni see Witt without remembering Karen? God knew, Hardy couldn't.

A sigh escaped her, and she sagged into a chair at the table. Hardy must have been sitting in it when he decided to depart in a hurry, because it hadn't been pushed back under the table, but sat askew. It was a silent testament to his agitation, because Hardy *always* put things back in their proper places. Even chairs.

"I'm exhausted," Barbara said after a while. "I'm not coming back from that pneumonia as fast as I'd like."

"I'm sorry," Joni said quietly. "You were very ill. And I shouldn't be here."

"No, you stay. I don't mind you being here."

Joni lifted her head. "How can you say that?"

"After getting so angry, you mean?" Barbara shrugged. "Getting angry isn't usually a permanent state of affairs. Not for me, anyway. I said what I needed to, and now I'll put it behind me."

"I wish I could be like you."

Barbara smiled faintly. "I think you have a bit of your uncle in you."

Apparently that was the wrong thing to say, because much to Barbara's horror, tears began to roll down Joni's face.

"He's going to be all right, you know," she said reassuringly. "It was just a little heart attack. He might not like giving up his bacon and eggs at the café three mornings a week, but he'll get used to it."

"It's not that," Joni said, tears still flowing, her voice thick with them. "It's not that. It's…it's that I just found out…Witt is my father."

Barbara was shocked. It wasn't that such things were unknown to her. It was that it seemed so unlike Hannah Matlock. And Hardy… Her first, numb thought was, why had *that* made Hardy so angry?

"That…must have been quite a shock for you, Joni."

Joni nodded.

And difficult in so many *other* ways, Barbara realized. Karen was Joni's sister. Witt was her father. Her mother had kept a terrible secret from her for years. So many, many things must be running through Joni's mind and heart right now.

Barbara felt a wave of forgiveness fill her. Never having been in the position, she couldn't fully comprehend what Joni must be thinking. But she *could* comprehend how confused and hurt she must be feeling.

"Let's go make some tea," Barbara suggested. It

was her panacea for everything. A cup of tea, a couple of shortbread cookies...the warm coziness of it made nearly anything look a little better.

Joni followed her mutely, breaking her silence only once to offer to help. Barbara handed her the box of cookies and asked her to put a few on a plate.

Water boiled fast at this altitude and never quite reached the uncomfortable temperatures of lower places. The tea steeped slowly because of that, but when it was ready it was exactly drinking temperature. Barbara heated a little milk in the microwave, but she was the only one who used it.

She poured the tea into the pretty Blue Willow-patterned cups that matched the teapot—an heirloom from her grandmother, one of the few her late husband hadn't managed to destroy—then sat near Joni, waiting.

She couldn't have said what she was waiting for, only that she knew somehow that Joni would have to start it.

But for a long time Joni sipped her tea in silence. She didn't even reach for a cookie. Barbara thought of all the reassuring, comforting things she could say but realized they wouldn't really help at all.

But at last, into their second cup of tea, Joni sighed and spoke. "Am I overreacting?"

"Overreacting?" Barbara repeated the word with surprise. "I hardly think so. This has to be a terrible shock for you. It has to make you wonder what else

you've always believed about yourself might be un-
true.''

"Exactly. Exactly." She repeated the word, drawing it out almost wearily. "I mean, part of me says
it was a long time ago and doesn't make any real
difference. Witt has been like a father to me ever
since my da—ever since Lewis died." She stole a
glance at Barbara. "I'm sorry. After the way Witt
has treated Hardy, you probably don't want to hear
about it.''

"I'm sitting here, aren't I? I can separate the Witt
you know from the idiot who's been unkind to my
son.''

"Then you're better than I am. Because I can't. If
my dad knew—I wonder if he knew?—then Witt hurt
him. He certainly hurt Hardy. And he hurt me when
he disowned me.''

"Well, yes." Barbara had never been one to deny
the obvious. "You know, before Karen's death, I believed Witt Matlock was a good and kind man.''

"And now?''

Barbara shook her head. "I don't know. Maybe
he's...crazy with grief. Crazy with...guilt?" She
said the word tentatively, as if trying out the concept.

"Grief? After twelve years? I don't know, Mrs.
Wingate.''

"Barbara, please. I agree, twelve years seems like
a long time. But...I've never lost my only child. Or
what I believed was my only child. That might be
very different.''

"Maybe. I don't know. I still miss Karen. Sometimes I ache just to hear her laugh. Sometimes I close my eyes and remember the way we used to stay up half the night talking. But to stay so angry, to let it consume you so much…"

"But *is* he really letting it consume him? Hon, I know he's been angry at Hardy ever since. But he never liked Hardy to begin with. And I can't say that I'd have felt any different in his shoes."

"Why not?"

"Because if I had a daughter who wanted to hang out with the slightly wild son of an abysmal alcoholic, I'd have my doubts. Especially when she was so young."

"That still doesn't excuse the way he's treated Hardy all these years."

Barbara's gaze was wise and very steady as she looked at Joni. "Is that what precipitated all this?"

Joni started to nod, then moved her head in an indecisive shake. "I'm not really sure what got me going. Except that it was like something inside me started screaming, 'enough of this.' And it started when Witt decided to look for bids to build a hotel. All I could think was that Hardy deserved that job. That and the fact that I was sick of not being able to talk to Hardy for fear of upsetting Witt. I'm not sure exactly. I mean…when I did it I thought I knew why. But it's like I told Hardy earlier…" She trailed off.

Finally Barbara prompted her. "Go on."

"I don't know. Every time I say it, I feel so stupid.

But it's like Witt's anger has kept us all emotionally frozen in time. We can't move on because *he* won't move on. Stupid. Anyway, it doesn't matter anymore. He disowned me. I hurt him so much that he had a heart attack. And now…now I don't even care if I ever speak to my mother again.''

"Joni…''

"No, I'm serious. She kept this secret for all my life, then she dumps it on me the day after Witt has a heart attack. Why? So I can feel *really* awful? As if I didn't already?''

"Maybe she's trying to hang on to you. To give you a reason to stick around even though Witt's angry.''

"Well, that isn't going to do it.'' Joni's chin set even as her eyes moistened again. "I'm feeling used, Mrs. Matlock. I'm feeling like Witt matters more than I ever will. To anyone. Including my mother. Everyone's been tiptoeing around him for years. *Years!* When you were so sick in the hospital, I talked to Hardy for a few minutes in the cafeteria. He could barely hold still. Why? Because Witt wouldn't approve. When I went home and mentioned to my mother that I'd talked to him because I was concerned about you, the first thing she told me was to remember how Witt felt about Hardy. What's wrong with this?''

"Plenty.'' Barbara wasn't going to lie, even to soothe the younger woman's upset. But it seemed to her that Joni was barely scraping the core of what was bothering her so much. Witt, after all, couldn't be so angry every second of the day that it was making Joni's life hell. Over these past years, his anger had seemed to become something quieter, anyway, as long as he and Hardy avoided each other.

No, there had to be something more there. And Barbara wondered what it was.

11

"Let's get the hell out of here," Hardy said to Joni three days later. She hadn't left his house except to go to work. All the rest of the time, except when Barbara made her come down to dinner, Joni hid in the guest room.

It wasn't healthy, and sitting around brooding wasn't going to help her solve any of her problems. Besides, he was getting cabin fever just *thinking* about how cooped up she was, despite the fact that he'd been going about his daily affairs as usual.

She was standing at the kitchen sink, rinsing her oatmeal bowl before putting it in the dishwasher. "Where?" she asked. Snow was falling outside, and the day was dark and leaden, the clouds so thick that it felt like dusk rather than morning. "We're getting a blizzard."

"So what's new?" he asked impatiently. "It's winter. We get two hundred inches of snow every year. If I let that stop me, I'd never get out the front door."

"True."

But her answer was listless, almost lifeless. And he was more worried about her than he wanted to admit, even to himself. "Let's just get out. But first come help me clear the driveway."

She shrugged. "Okay." Indifferent.

He had a snowblower, so most of the work was relatively easy, but there were a few places that needed the shovel. Joni took care of those for him while he wielded his monster machine.

Then, because he was already out and the physical exertion was feeling good, he cleared the driveways of a couple of his neighbors who didn't have snow-blowers. When they finished, Joni at least had some color in her cheeks, even if it did come from the cold.

Inside again, they made hot drinks.

"I figure," he said, "we could go shopping in Vail."

"Expensive."

"Well, we don't have to buy anything. Or we could go into Denver."

"Maybe Barbara would like to come along."

But Hardy didn't want her along. He wanted to get Joni out of here and away from things for a while. "She's not up to a major expedition yet," he replied. It was true; she wasn't. It was also a good excuse.

"Okay."

"Or would you rather go to the Springs? It's probably a lot warmer."

"I don't care. You're driving."

He wished she would summon at least a little interest in the project. But hell, that was the whole problem. Joni didn't seem to be interested in anything at all anymore—other than her problems. Last night he'd tried to get her to join him and Barbara in a game of dominoes, or cards, but she'd merely shaken her head, finished the dinner dishes and disappeared upstairs. She was way too withdrawn, and something inside him demanded he find a way to get her out of this pit.

It was with no plan at all that they finally climbed into his sport utility vehicle, and he supposed that was okay, because the snow was flying thickly now, and the day getting even darker.

"Feels like it should be around four o'clock," he remarked.

"Mmm."

He had to suppress an urge to shake her, just to get something out of her besides indifference. Instead of heading toward Vail or Denver, though, he decided to head south into the dryer, warmer part of the state. The snow might let up, and an opportunity to do something interesting might turn up.

"You still don't downhill ski, do you?" he asked.

"No."

He'd been on the downhill-skiing team in high school. He and Karen had enjoyed a lot of trips to a nearby slope where the lift tickets didn't cost an arm and a leg, mainly because there were no resort facilities around. Witt's hotel could change all that, he found himself thinking. A good place for people to stay near the slopes could be the first chink to turn this town into something besides a mining company town.

Regardless, it had been a bad question to ask her, because it led directly back to Karen, and through Karen to Witt.

"I prefer cross-country," she said as if making an effort.

A little spark of hope ignited in his breast. "Yeah? I like that, too. In fact, the older I get the less addicted I feel to rushing downhill at sixty miles an hour."

She gave him a fleeting smile.

He returned his attention to driving. A narrow, twisty road, parts of it once a stagecoach road, wound its way through the canyon, demanding all his attention as they made hairpin turns on slick pavement that perched on a ledge above a shallow river. "Can you imagine what it must have been like to get to Whisper Creek in the old days?"

"Yeah." She sighed, then made another effort. "It's hard enough now."

"Yeah, but back then…" He shook his head. "I guess a lot of people did it, though. Have you ever walked the old coach road? Those ruts are so deep, even after all these years. And you can see places that must have been really dangerous, where rocks stick up at the edge of the track, or where the angle is really steep. Walk a little of that and you can imagine how your bones would have jolted running over it. Or how many broken wheels they must have had.''

The road was getting even slicker, and he gave up on conversation as he devoted all his attention to driving. This was stupid, he thought finally. Stupid. Yes, they had blizzards all the time, and snowfall sometimes seemed almost constant, but in this kind of weather he shouldn't have gotten the insane idea to take a trip. He should have just taken her out somewhere in town, and to hell with the gossip.

"Witt's home."

The sound of her voice startled him, and his hand jerked a little on the wheel. He felt the tires lose traction for an instant, then grip again. No, he should never have suggested this insanity. "Out so soon?" he managed to ask.

"Hannah took him home last night."

He nodded, wondering what he should say, if anything. "I'm glad he's okay. How'd you hear about it?" Maybe...maybe she was talking to her mother again. He hoped so.

But she dashed his hope. "I work in a hospital, remember? Everyone I know mentioned it."

He felt stupid. Then he felt irritated with himself. It was none of his business whether she ever spoke to her mother again or not. But in his way of viewing the world, he felt very strongly that family was important, and that you owed your mother a great deal for raising you. He couldn't imagine any situation that would cause him to cut his ties with Barbara.

But maybe that wasn't what Joni was doing. For all that she talked about leaving town and never seeing any of them again, maybe all she really needed was some time to adjust to all the shocks.

But she wasn't talking much anymore about anything, and that gave him serious cause for concern. At least talking about things meant you were still connected to the world. And sometimes saying things out loud made you see how crazy you were being. He certainly had enough experience with that.

"So..." He hesitated, then decided to take the bull by the horns. "Are you going to visit him?"

"No! What, are you kidding? He disowned me."

"I'm sure he didn't mean it to be permanent."

"I'm sure I don't care. You don't do that to someone you love."

He agreed with her. But Witt had always been a hardass, at least about some things. Totally unreasonable.

"Well," he said presently, "I'm kind of reluctant to comment on Witt. He's always been something of a mystery to me. I mean, there I was in high school. Yeah, my dad was a drunk. But my mom wasn't. She was a hardworking woman. And I was getting decent grades, participating in sports, keeping my nose pretty much clean—and he hated me. I know I got a little wild at times. But even in retrospect, all these years later, I don't think I got *that* wild. It was mostly the kind of hijinks you expect from kids that age.''

''I thought you were a pretty good guy,'' Joni said. ''And you sure took good care of Karen.''

Did her voice waver a little on that? He wasn't sure, and, at that moment, he didn't want to know. He had some things roiling around inside him, especially after she said that she thought he took good care of Karen. ''I don't know about that. Taking her out behind her dad's back could be regarded as reckless. And sneaky. I'm none too proud of that. Or of the fact that if I hadn't done it, she'd probably still be alive.'' Or of the fact that he'd been getting ready to break things off with her. Christ, he wished he didn't have to remember that along with everything else.

''I know.''

He wished she had disagreed with him, even though it wouldn't have convinced him otherwise. He knew his responsibility in this mess; but it would have been nice if someone, anyone, had disagreed with him.

''I mean,'' she said a little while later, ''I know you feel responsible. But you didn't make that guy get drunk. And Karen being out with you...Hardy, if it was her time, it was her time. She could have been in the car with Witt.''

He glanced toward her. ''You really believe that?''

Her eyes met his briefly. "I'm trying to," she finally said.

Trying to. Yeah. Maybe he needed to get his butt into therapy. Soon. Figure out just exactly what he was responsible for and how to deal with it. Because he sure as hell wasn't dealing with it real well.

"I'm sorry," she said. "I really don't think it's your fault that Karen died. I really don't. It's just that...well..." She trailed off, then muttered a sharp word under her breath. "Forget it. I guess we're all guilty. You for seeing her over Witt's protests, me for being jealous of her, Witt for being overprotective, because if he hadn't been, you'd have been able to see Karen at her house, and you wouldn't have had to be in the car that night at all. Did Witt ever think of that? Did he?"

"Joni..."

She waved a hand, silencing him. "If anyone's responsible for anything, maybe it's Witt. He drove her to date you secretly. And ever since, he's been blaming you for something you couldn't prevent— and blaming me for being alive!"

Her last words came out as a near shout, filling the car, then leaving in their wake a silence so profound that Hardy could hear his own heartbeat in his ears. Blaming her for being alive? Had Witt been doing that?

Christ! If he could have gotten to Witt Matlock in that moment, he probably would have come close to killing him. How could that son of a bitch have spent the last twelve years making Joni feel that way? How could he have been so cruel?

"Joni…"

"It doesn't matter. But I just figured out something."

"What?"

"Another reason why my mother told me Witt is my dad. All these years, I've been feeling that he wished I'd died instead. I guess she sensed that. Maybe she even guessed it was true."

"So what difference does telling you make?"

"So I'd know that if I'd died, Witt would have lost a daughter anyway."

"Jesus." He breathed the word and had to prevent himself from closing his eyes against the strength of the pain he was suddenly feeling for Joni. He didn't dare give in to it, though. The snow was getting worse, and getting deep on the road.

He spoke. "When we get to Wetrock, I'm going to pull in someplace for a meal. Then we can decide if we want to try to get home tonight."

"I need to. I have to work tomorrow."

"It'll probably clear up. But I'll tell you something, Joni. I'm not killing another one of Witt's daughters by doing something stupid."

The words appeared to hit her forcefully. From the corner of his eye he saw her stiffen a bit, then, after a bit, relax again. "Fair enough," she said finally. "Fair enough. But keep in mind, I'm not really his daughter. He disowned me."

Like that was going to make any big difference to *him*. She was *still* Witt's daughter. And all he wanted to do was get her safely home so he didn't have to go through any part of that nightmare ever again.

He concentrated on his driving after that, letting the miles pass in silence. Only the tall reflectors along the shoulder were telling him where the road was now. His hope that they would escape the storm by heading south had apparently been misguided. It seemed to be getting worse.

"I should have checked the weather report," he muttered as snow suddenly whirled before him, completely blinding him for a moment.

"I told you we were having a blizzard."

"You did. But I wasn't expecting one this big."

"It's hitting three states."

"Great. No end in sight."

"Not unless you want to drive to southern New Mexico."

He realized she wasn't criticizing him. In fact, it almost sounded as if she was teasing him. Hardly daring to believe it, he glanced at her and saw that she was smiling. A faint smile, but a real one nonetheless.

"And all I wanted," he remarked, "was a cup of coffee and maybe some lunch away from all the prying eyes, flapping ears and wagging tongues in Whisper Creek."

A brief laugh escaped her. "It feels more like the Donner expedition."

He dared another glance her way. "What made you feel better?"

"Realizing what's been wrong all these years. Realizing Witt resented me, even though he didn't say so. It wasn't me, Hardy. It was Witt."

What a hell of a condemnation.

"Man, that guy's got his head screwed on all wrong." It was all he could say, because he couldn't imagine resenting someone because they hadn't died in a car wreck. Christ almighty!

They reached Wetrock at last, and he pulled in to the first passable restaurant they could find. The parking lot was nearly empty, because sensible people—unlike him—had listened to the weather forecast. There was a waitress, though, and a lot of empty tables, so they could have privacy while they watched the snow blow outside.

The waitress came immediately with cups and a pot of coffee. "You folks are lucky," she said. "We're only open because we're family owned and operated. Everybody else is closing."

Hardy looked at her with a sinking sensation in the pit of his stomach. "It's that bad?" Very little stopped traffic in these mountains for long. People were used to this kind of weather.

"Gonna be," she said as she filled their cups. "Take your time ordering. No rush. And if you need it, there's a motel a little ways up that still has some vacancies."

"Maybe I should call and reserve a couple of

rooms," Hardy said, looking uneasily at Joni. She shrugged, then nodded.

"I'll call 'em," the waitress said. "Fred'll do it for me. Two rooms?"

"Please."

"I'll let you know what he says." She handed them some plastic menus, then disappeared into the kitchen.

"I'm sorry, Joni," Hardy said.

"Don't be. I watched the weather, but I had no idea it was going to be *this* bad. I figured it'd be the usual."

Which was nice of her to say. "Did I ever tell you about the time I got caught in Deer Lodge, Montana? Well, actually, I got caught in Missoula, too."

She shook her head. "What happened?"

"I was coming back from a trip to Boise. Late May. Anyway, it started to snow heavily as I was coming down out of the mountains, so I decided to spend the night in Missoula. By morning it looked pretty good, so I set out again. Big mistake. By the time I got to Deer Lodge, I figured I was lucky to still be alive, so I pulled in to this little motel. Talk about rustic." He smiled reminiscently. "Got so bad I had to share the room with two truckers who couldn't get any farther. We wound up cooking one hell of a dinner together with stuff we got from the grocery across the way."

"Sounds like it turned out to be fun."

"It did, actually. I heard some pretty tall stories, especially after those guys started drinking the beer."

She smiled at that, making him feel a bit better.

They ordered, burgers and fries, since nothing else on the menu looked very tempting. The waitress was bored and spent more time chatting with them than Hardy would have liked, since it effectively prevented him from conversing privately with Joni. Although they would have plenty of time later, he reminded himself. They were going to be staying at the motel down the road. The waitress, who finally got around to telling them her name was Sally, had managed to get them two rooms.

Half an hour later they headed down an empty road to the motel. The cars parked in lots and along the street were drifting over with snow.

"I feel like such a jerk," Hardy said.

"You're not. If I'd known it was going to be like this, I'd have said so. It'll let up soon."

Maybe, maybe not. He wasn't betting on anything until he had a chance to watch the weather report.

The motel turned out to be nice enough, though. Not exactly a Holiday Inn or a Courtyard by Marriott, but clean enough and new enough that he didn't feel like the walls would be sticky. Their rooms adjoined, with a door between them, which was either good or bad, depending on how you looked at it. Good because neither of them would have to go out in this weather just to pass a few words, bad because...

Well, it was a temptation. He might as well do himself the courtesy of admitting it. Joni Matlock tempted him. Something about her drew him the way a flower drew a bee. He could almost imagine himself buzzing around her, dipping in for quick, sweet tastes.

But that could never be, so he wasn't doing himself any favors by thinking about it. He would just have to watch it and remember that he was supposed to be wearing the white hat this time. No more corrupting Witt's daughters.

Hell, that set him back on his heels. Still. Even after three days to think about it. Witt's daughter. What the hell was he doing hanging out with another of Witt's daughters?

Joni disappeared into her room, so he disappeared into his and figured it had better stay that way. Except he thought of something.

He knocked on the adjoining door. After a minute she unlocked her side and opened it.

"I need to go out and see if I can get us some food for tonight and tomorrow morning," he told her. "There was a Safeway around the corner, I think. I'll be back in a bit."

She nodded. "Okay. Thanks."

The door closed again, the lock turned.

Good, he told himself. But the truth was, he really didn't feel it was good at all.

He took the car. The supermarket was a block and a half away, and he gave thanks for four-wheel drive by the time he got there. The snow was getting very deep, and if the plows were working, they sure weren't bothering with the side streets.

The store was still open, though there was almost no one inside except a bored cashier and an unhappy-looking manager. Hardy grabbed a cart and started along the aisles, grabbing canned foods that could be eaten without cooking, a selection that he hoped was broad enough for Joni to find something she liked. Peanut butter, jelly, a loaf of bread, paper plates, napkins, plastic utensils, a can opener, some chips and pretzels.

He paused, looking down at his stock, and realized he'd bought a lot more than two people would need for one night. But he wanted variety. He didn't want them to be stuck with peanut butter or cold baked beans. Whatever they didn't eat, he could take home.

Milk and soda, which he could keep cold in a little snow in the ice bucket, or in the sink. Well, heck, why not get one of those small foam ice chests to keep it in? If he did that, he could get cold cuts, too....

He realized he was distracting himself, trying not to think about Joni, about Witt, about the mess everything seemed to be turning into all over again. About how he was hiding out with Witt's daughter, which felt like a reprise of twelve years ago. Damn, he wished Joni hadn't told him that.

Rounding a corner, he came upon some T-shirts. Touristy stuff, ballyhooing Colorado, the Rockies and skiing. Still, neither of them had a change of clothes, so he grabbed a couple of the biggest ones he could find. Socks, too, he realized. They would both be glad of some fresh socks. Hell, he'd be glad of some fresh Jockey shorts, but there weren't any here.

He was stalling again. Forcing himself to face that fact, he headed for the checkout. Then he remembered reading material. Heading back, he picked up a couple of magazines, a thriller and a romance novel. It was appalling to realize that he had no idea if Joni liked to read, or, if so, what she enjoyed.

It seemed crazy to buy a bag of ice in the middle of a snowstorm, but he needed it for the cooler. Ten minutes later he was parked in front of his room again.

He was surprised, when he entered with the plastic bags hooked over his fingers, to find the adjoining door open and Joni standing there.

"I was beginning to worry," she said.

He held up the bags. "I went overboard."

"You planning to feed an army?" She looked wary.

"Nope. Just wanted to give us some choices."

Next he brought in the ice chest and stuffed it with soda cans and milk. "No hot drinks, I'm afraid."

"I already took care of that. I called the office and Fred offered us a hot plate and drip coffeemaker he keeps around."

"Hell. I didn't buy any coffee or tea."

She leaned back into the room, grabbed something from the dresser, and held up a box and a can, going, "Ta-da!"

He laughed. "Fred?"

"Yup. He's a real sweetie. Apparently we rate because we're friends of Sally's."

"I need to meet more waitresses."

"It might smooth the road a bit."

He finished unpacking the groceries, setting things on the top of the dresser against the wall.

"A T-shirt," he said, holding up the two he'd bought. "I figured they could double as nightwear. Take your pick."

"How thoughtful!"

She wanted the teal one, and he was happy to settle for the navy blue one. She seemed equally pleased by the thick, warm socks he offered her. "Sorry, no undies."

"I can just wash mine in the sink and hang them over the heater to dry."

The thought of her tiny panties spread out on the heater made his mouth grow dry. It occurred to him that even though the adjoining door was open, he would be wise not to cross the threshold.

The fact was, he thought as he passed her the magazines and books, he'd been trying not to think about Joni Matlock for an awful lot of years. And all of that not thinking seemed to be bubbling up inside him suddenly, reminding him of what he'd wanted for so long but could never have.

And that was indeed the simple truth of it: he could never have her. Witt would blow a fuse, would make her life even more miserable, would make Hannah's life miserable, maybe would even make Barbara's life miserable. So no matter what the opportunity, he had to keep a reasonable distance from Joni. And that meant not having any sexy, yearning thoughts about her.

It also meant not getting himself into stupid fixes like this one. Christ, what had he been thinking this morning, taking off in the car with her? Did he have some kind of self-destructive urge? Did he want things to get worse instead of better?

"You'd better call your mother," he said to Joni. The suggestion came more from his need to have a few minutes away from her than because he was really worried about Hannah. If Hannah cared for Joni, she should have called some time over the last three days. But she hadn't. And he found it hard to believe that Hannah didn't know where her daughter was staying.

On the other hand, maybe Hannah knew but figured Joni needed time by herself. Maybe she was just giving her daughter some space. Could be. It still unsettled him.

"No, I'm not going to call her," Joni said. "Why would she even be worried?"

"Oh, I don't know. But she might."

"Forget it. I'm not talking to her right now."

At least she wasn't saying she wasn't going to talk

to her mother ever again. "Okay. I need to call Barbara."

Joni disappeared into her room, carrying her clothing and the reading material. She closed the adjoining door behind her, giving him privacy. He found himself wondering why he suddenly felt so cut off. And how long that door would stay closed.

But for the moment, at least, he was glad it was closed. It gave *him* some mental space. It made a visible barrier, which he needed. And it would also allow him to talk privately to Barbara.

She answered on the third ring. "Where have you gone?" she asked, first thing. "Do you know how bad this storm is going to be? They're calling it the storm of the century."

Great. Absolutely great. More of his karma, he supposed. "Joni and I are down in Wetrock. I thought I'd get her out for some lunch, a change of scene, only we got stranded."

"How lovely." Barbara's voice implied that he was insane.

"I know, I know. I should have paid closer attention to the weather. But it's too late now."

"Maybe you never should have invited her to stay with us. You know, Witt is a powerful man in this town. He's a supervisor at the mine, and an awful lot of people look up to him. Now this. You know what he's going to think!"

"He's not going to think anything, because he's

not going to know. Nobody knows we're here together. And besides, he's disowned her.''

''Right. And pigs fly. He got angry. He's not going
to stay angry, not with his own niece.''

''You sure about that? He's managed to stay angry
with me for twelve years. The man doesn't seem to
have a forgiving bone in his body.''

Barbara sniffed and fell silent. ''I'm sorry,'' she
said after a moment. ''I'm glad you invited Joni to
stay with us. She needs someone right now. As for
Witt…well, his whole problem is that his mother
died when he was sixteen. He never got over having
to grow up too soon, and he could have used a little
more parenting. An extra spanking or two. Well…''
She paused. ''All right. I suppose you want me to
call Hannah?''

''It crossed my mind.''

''All right. But I'm not going to tell her Joni's with
you. She can dot the i's and cross the t's however
she wants.''

''That's fine by me, Mom.''

''As for you,'' she said sternly, ''have the good
sense *not* to do something you might regret.''

''Trust me, I've learned that lesson.''

Maybe. Maybe, if he said it often enough, it would
actually penetrate his lame brain. Maybe he could
hypnotize himself into believing it. But all he could
think right now was that he was on the verge of
making the worst mistake of his life.

12

Joni turned on the TV and was glad to see they had cable. Immediately she hunted for the Weather Channel, and what she saw didn't make her feel any better. The predictions were far worse than they had been that morning. A major storm was stalled over five states, dumping record amounts of snow, and it wasn't expected to budge for at least another twenty-four hours. That meant they might be stuck in this motel yet another night.

The idea made her uneasy for a lot of reasons. The first and foremost was that she really didn't want to be cooped up with nothing to do but think for two days. It hadn't been so bad at Hardy's house, because she had her job to distract her, and if it had gotten really bad, she could have gone out for a walk. But after three days of basically running on automatic and thinking the same thoughts over again, she didn't know if she could stand two whole days of her own company.

Then there was Hardy. He could certainly distract her. But she was afraid of the ways he could do that. Afraid of the barely acknowledged longings in her own heart and body. Well aware that giving in to them might be the biggest mistake of her life.

He wouldn't want her, of course. Being with her must be like rubbing salt in a wound. She was rather surprised that he could stand it at all.

Sighing, she went to pull the curtains back and look out at the· snow. It was really blowing hard, looking like a dense, white whirlwind. Even if it stopped overnight, there was a chance the plows wouldn't be able to clear all the roads until late tomorrow.

She ought to use the time to take a nap. Since her mother had dropped the bomb, she hadn't slept well at all, tossing and turning for much of the night, and having nightmares when she *did* sleep. Too much stress, too much anxiety, too many shocks.

She turned to look at the double bed, thinking how good it would feel to just stretch out. Maybe, with the TV on, she could keep herself distracted until sleep managed to catch up with her.

She propped herself up against some pillows and stared at the TV, flipping through channels, hoping to find something that would hold her interest just enough to keep her from thinking, but not so much that she couldn't fall asleep.

Of course she was out of luck. It was the middle of the day. The movies were all old and too familiar to appeal to her, the soaps had never really engaged her, and the other programming didn't catch her eye. Finally she returned to the Weather Channel, telling herself that she might as well get ten-minute updates on the storm.

Which reminded her that she needed to call her boss and warn him that she probably wouldn't be in tomorrow. He was understanding, and three minutes later she was staring at the tube and trying not to think.

But she thought anyway. Much to her own dismay, she remembered a fantasy that she'd had in high school. She and Hardy got stranded in a snowstorm. The way in which Karen was removed from the picture varied. Sometimes they'd been going to pick her up at the airport. Sometimes they'd just gone on an errand together, while Karen stayed at home to do something.

And then they got caught in a blizzard. The car went off the road. Nearby was an old cabin, where they went for shelter and found enough wood to build a fire in the fireplace, and some canned goods that looked safe to eat. And while they were stranded, Hardy always discovered that he was crazy about Joni and wanted to be with her instead of Karen.

Those fantasies had seemed harmless back then, simply because she knew she would never act on them. Drawn as she was to Hardy, Karen was her best friend and cousin. She would never, ever, have done anything to hurt Karen.

But since Karen's death, those fantasies had come back to haunt her in the most awful way, making her feel like a terrible person. Making her wonder if her wishing Karen out of the way in all those secret fantasies hadn't had something to do with what happened.

That was magical thinking, and she knew it. But she couldn't escape the guilt.

Then there was Witt. She sometimes wondered if she imagined that look in his eye, that look that seemed to say, "Why are you here and not Karen?" He'd never said anything like that, but she'd felt it. Felt it so strongly it hurt.

And now he'd disowned her. God. The man who had grieved unstoppably for twelve years for his daughter had tossed *her* away as if she mattered no more than a used paper napkin.

That hurt. And she didn't want to think about it. Not at all.

There was a knock on the adjoining door. For an instant she considered pretending to be asleep, then decided that was childish. What could it hurt to talk with Hardy for a while? He'd never expressed any interest in her at all, other than as a friend.

Rising, she went to unlock the door and open it.

"Sorry to bother you," he said, "but I'm bored. Nothing on TV. So I thought if you wouldn't mind sharing one of the magazines or books...?"

She felt herself color. "I'm sorry! I forgot all about them." Forgot that she had taken them with her into her room. "Come on in. They're on the table."

"I wish I'd gotten a deck of cards," he said as he followed her in. "But I didn't run across any, and it never occurred to me to look."

"That's okay."

He went to the table and picked up an entertainment magazine. But he didn't walk out immediately. Instead, he stood there holding it, looking at her. "The weather's going to be bad for a while."

"I saw." Talking about the weather. After all they'd been through together, one way or the other. It seemed…strained.

"Yeah." He stood there, looking uncertain in a way that seemed to touch her past all the feelings that had been swamping her for days. "You know…"

"Yes?"

But he hesitated a few moments longer. "Why don't we just make some coffee or tea and kibbitz our way through one of the movies that are on or a soap opera."

She had to admit that TV didn't sound so boring when she thought about watching it with him. "Sure." And she smiled, the first really easy smile she had given in days.

He seemed to catch his breath, then nodded. "Let's go."

She wondered what had made him catch his breath that way, but his face offered no clue and for some reason she was afraid to ask. Maybe he'd just had a twinge of some kind. After all, he must have gotten very tense while they were driving through the storm.

They decided on tea, then fluffed the pillows on his bed so they could sit up with a bag of chips between them. It was, Joni thought, almost like a pajama party.

Except no pajama party with Hardy Wingate could ever be innocent. Not in her mind, which seemed bound and determined to play nasty little tricks on her, by making her notice how long his legs looked encased in those worn denim jeans. How soft the denim looked.

She dragged her gaze away and tried to focus on the soap—she didn't even know which one of the daytime programs they had tuned in to—where one of the characters was having a major crisis over whether his wife was really having an affair with a guy she used to be in love with but had ditched because he was a ne'er-do-well. Or at least that was the impression she was getting.

Then the scene switched to the wife—or she assumed it was the wife, anyway—who was indeed meeting secretly with her former lover, but not to have sex, or so she said. It was just to help him with some personal angst he was having with another ex-girlfriend....

Joni looked at Hardy. "Why does this remind me of my own life?"

He laughed, and his eyes sparkled. "Maybe because it really does resemble real life. We all go through periods that would make good fodder for these shows."

"We do?" Joni didn't know if she wanted to believe that. She supposed it was true. "Well, I guess my problems are trivial by comparison."

"Comparison to what? This show? That's not a good comparison to make, Joni. Your problems are real, and they hurt. If you want to pace the room, rubbing your arms and dumping all over me, be my guest. You're entitled."

But she didn't want to do that. "I've been doing enough of that," she said. "I'm sick of myself."

He nodded. "Been there. It's an awful feeling, isn't it? The problems won't go away, but you can't stop thinking about them until all you can do is feel disgusted with yourself."

"You've done that, too?"

"I sure as hell have. There've been times when I've wanted to run to the far ends of the earth. Trouble is, all your problems just go with you."

She shook her head. "I don't know about that. I'll just stay away from Hannah and Witt. If I don't have to be around them, I don't have to think of how... duplicitous they are. I mean...I still can't get over it. If they'd been total strangers, I could understand it better."

"Yeah." He sighed and slouched down lower on the pillows. Apparently he wasn't even going to pretend to watch the show anymore. "You know, I can't imagine how it happened. You know I'm not real fond of Witt. I sometimes think he's one of the biggest jackasses in creation. But only about how he's treated me. Otherwise, I've always figured him for a real straight arrow."

"Me too. He goes to church twice a week and teaches Sunday school every spring."

"That doesn't mean he isn't human."

"True." She sighed and looked down at her hands, which were twisting in her lap.

"It just kind of boggles my mind," Hardy continued. "Witt worked hard to put Lewis through med school. I mean, he practically gave up his own life from the time he turned sixteen. A guy who'd do that wouldn't be really keen on committing adultery with that same brother's wife."

"You wouldn't think so." Joni's tone was almost bitter.

"No, I wouldn't. And Witt's never been one to hang around married women, either. At least, not in my memory. Mainly he hangs around your mom, since his wife and Lewis died."

"Yeah. Probably hoping for another sip of honey."

She must have shocked Hardy a bit, because both his eyebrows lifted. But he didn't say anything about it, just went on with what he'd been discussing.

"So anyway," he continued, "I can't see Witt doing something like that carelessly. Casually. I can't see your mom doing it, either. She's had guys drooling after her since she moved up here, and she's indifferent. Doesn't even go out. So she's not given to fooling around, either."

"But all this is since Lewis died," Joni pointed out. "Neither of us knew them before I was born."

"But I've heard enough about Witt. He gets a lot of respect in Whisper Creek. A lot. He's one of those guys everybody is sure walks on water. Well, everybody except me. So…"

"Yeah. So? Neither one of them has casual affairs. But they still created me."

Hardy nodded. "Exactly. And I would sure love to know what precipitated it. I think the circumstances must have been extraordinary in some way."

Joni hadn't thought of it that way. She'd been so focused on how sordid it was, how icky it made her feel somehow to learn that her uncle was her father. "The whole idea makes me want to take a bath."

"Really? But…what would you think if the two of them wanted to get married now?"

"I wouldn't have a problem with it. Frankly, I've been wondering for years why they didn't. Maybe this is why. Maybe they feel too guilty. Or maybe Mom doesn't want to tell him the truth about me after keeping it secret for so long. I don't know. Either way, it doesn't make me feel any better. It was

different back then. They were cheating on somebody they were supposed to love.''

He nodded. ''Yeah. They were. They were also
younger.''

''And they've also managed to keep their hands
off each other for twenty-six years now. So what was
the problem back then?''

''Maybe you should ask.''

Joni shook her head immediately. ''No way. I
don't want to know. I don't want to see either one
of them ever again.''

If Hardy didn't believe her, he at least had the
sense to keep the feeling to himself. Joni scrunched
down on her pillows and pretended to stare at the
TV screen. Ask her mother? Hell would have to
freeze over first. She didn't want to know the sordid
details. She didn't want to know anything about it at
all.

Because the whole damn thing just hurt too much.
It hurt to be Witt's daughter.

''Hardy?''

''Hmm?''

''What did Karen think of Witt?''

He hesitated, and reluctantly she looked at him.

''Well,'' he said finally, ''you were closer to
Karen than anyone. What did she say about him to
you?''

''Very little. Probably because he was my uncle.
What did she say to you?''

''Well...she said he clung to her too much after

her mother died. She said she felt like he was suffocating her sometimes. I think that's part of the reason she ran around with me instead of listening to him.''

Joni thought back over the years, trying to remember. ''I think he *did* suffocate her a little. But probably not as badly as she thought. He'd lost his wife and brother. I think he was terrified he'd lose her, too.''

''Maybe so. I was too young to think of it in those terms back then.'' He scooted farther down on his pillows. The TV show was forgotten. ''I thought he was being overbearing and unreasonable. I'm not sure anymore if I wouldn't be the same in his shoes.''

She looked at him curiously. ''Are you always so generous?''

He shrugged. ''I try to be fair.''

''Fair? He hasn't been fair to *you*.''

''Doesn't mean *I* can't be.''

Which, thought Joni, was actually a profound statement, one she'd been losing sight of lately. One she needed to keep in mind. ''You've grown up to be a very nice man, Hardy.''

Much to her amazement, he reddened. The sight tickled some deep place inside her, making her smile. And teaching her that he wasn't used to personal compliments, which struck her as a bit sad.

Then he seemed to get interested in the TV again, so she turned her attention in that direction, pretend-

ing to watch. Giving him space to get over his embarrassment.

A few moments later, hardly aware of what was
happening, she sank into deep slumber for the first
time in days.

Hardy dozed off, too. It wasn't that he was short
on sleep, but it was the kind of day where a nap
seemed inevitable, and there really wasn't anything
to hold his attention. Soap operas slid into talk
shows, and he slipped into sleep.

When he awoke, the first thing he noticed was the
howl of the wind outside. It *sounded* cold. Then he
realized there was a weight on him. Turning his head,
he found Joni curled up against him, her head tucked
comfortably on his shoulder. Even in the dim light,
he could see the dreams racing behind her eyelids,
and he hoped they were happy.

Oprah was talking to a middle-aged woman with
a strong southern accent about her childhood in Mis-
sissippi. Another Oprah book, he thought. At the moment, he wasn't interested.

He was more interested in trying to figure out how
to disengage himself from Joni without waking her.
She needed the sleep desperately, and he needed the
bathroom desperately. He also needed to move before his arm became paralyzed.

Then, of course, there was the fact that Joni was
sleeping against him, which was awakening other
kinds of needs, needs he couldn't afford to satisfy.

He was old enough to control those urges, but that didn't keep him from feeling a deep ache that tried to convince him otherwise.

It was, he thought, a bittersweet agony to lie beside a woman he had wanted for years and know that he could never touch her. Witt's daughter. Man, if there hadn't been enough shit between them before, that was the crowning piece. There'd been no way to get close to her before, but now it felt as if the cage bars had just turned into a wall of solid steel. As if even glancing her way was apt to get him into trouble.

Part of him figured that was damn unfair. The rest of him knew that life wasn't fair, and there was no point in whining. Joni Matlock might as well live on another planet.

Deciding there were limits to the torture he had to endure, he eased out from beneath Joni's head and was relieved when all she did was sigh and turn onto her back. Dreams still chased behind her eyelids.

Rising, taking care not to bounce the bed much, he went to peek out the window. The early winter night was settling in, but in the motel's outdoor lighting, the whiteout was visible. The motel office, cattycorner to their room, was invisible beyond the swirling snow, and all he could see of his car, parked right out front, was a hazy view of the grill.

Visibility zero. A silent chuckle rose in him as he realized those words could also describe his life.

"Why'd you come back to Whisper Creek?"

The sleepy question, in a voice so sexy it felt as if he had been physically stroked, came from behind him. He turned and saw that Joni's eyes were open. She still looked sleepy, and amazingly huggable.

"Sorry," he said. "I didn't mean to wake you."

"You didn't. Are you going to answer my question?"

He shrugged. "I don't know. It's home."

She shook her head and pushed herself higher on the pillows. "I'm serious, Hardy. The way Witt has treated you…why didn't you take a job with some architectural firm in Denver or Chicago? Why'd you come back? You could have made more money, probably built more of your designs.…"

"Is that what you think I should be doing? Making more money?"

The question seemed to startle her. "No. God, no! It's just that I wondered why. You had a way out."

"So did you."

"True." She sighed and closed her eyes. "I came back because…" She hesitated. "You know, I don't really know why. I told myself it was because of Mom."

"Yeah, me too. I didn't want Barbara to be all alone, and I didn't want to uproot her. At least, that's what I told myself."

"Yeah. Exactly." She opened her eyes again, and pushed her hair back from her face. "It's all about Karen, you know. It's all about this feeling of unfinished business. At least for me. But I guess Witt finished it, didn't he?''

She bounded up from the bed then. ''I'm going to wash up. Then I guess we ought to make some kind of dinner.''

Before he could say another word, she'd disappeared into her room. He turned back to the window, this time using the cord to pull the curtains wide open. Staring out into the teeth of the blizzard, he thought about what she'd said.

Yes, it was unfinished business that had brought him back. But not Karen. Not Witt. His mother.

And Joni.

13

Hannah felt a draft snake around her ankles and wished she could put more wood on the fire. But she knew Witt, knew how he hated to be hot, and right now he wasn't feeling too spunky.

In fact, she thought, standing in the doorway of his living room, he was downright depressed. Since she'd brought him home from the hospital the other day, he hadn't done much except sit and brood. And when he wasn't sitting, he was moving gingerly, as if he feared every step he took might bring on another heart attack.

Right now he was sitting in his easy chair, looking out the window at the storm.

"Looks pretty bad, doesn't it?" she said, trying to keep her tone normal. She had always hated fake sickroom cheer, and as a nurse had refused to let herself slip into the pattern.

He moved one shoulder, a halfhearted shrug, but didn't even turn his head to look at her.

"They say it's the worst storm in at least fifty years."

He didn't answer that, either, and she felt a chill in her heart. Witt could always find something to say in response to a remark like that. Could always remember a worse storm or a worse time. Sometimes that habit irritated her, but the lack of it frightened her. "Nothing's moving in the mountains," she continued as if she was sure he must be interested. "It's supposed to keep on through tomorrow."

No response again. Part of her wanted to shake him. Hannah was a calm woman, accustomed to facing things with a steady eye and without a whole lot of emotional hoopla. But right now she was so frightened for Witt, and so angry with him, that she had the worst urge to just shout at him until he finally said something, anything other than an indifferent grunt.

Fat chance. God. She raised her gaze over his head and looked out into the storm. *Joni.* Concern for her daughter filled her, overwhelming her fear for Witt. Where was she? What was she doing? Was she safe? Would she ever forgive her mother?

And Witt...Witt. Hannah found herself wondering if *she* would ever be able to forgive *him* for disowning Joni that way. Witt could be a hard man, but that was unforgivable. Or damn near it, anyway.

All these things were roiling around in her heart, and it felt terrible that she couldn't talk them over with Witt. For twelve years now they'd been as close as any two people could be, sharing everything. Talking over everything. They'd been family in the best sense of the word.

Now, she supposed, they were family in the worst sense. With a huge rift and no ready way to fix it, at least not as long as Witt was ill and refusing to talk.

But years of love weren't that easy to relinquish. Her heart filled with sorrow and concern over Witt and Joni, she went to stand at his side. She put her hand on his shoulder, offering silent comfort and commiseration, and wished with all her heart that Joni would call.

But of course Joni wouldn't. She knew her daughter's temperament all too well, and Joni could be every bit as hardheaded as Witt.

Lewis hadn't been that way. Lewis had had other faults. Serious ones. But he'd never been hardheaded. Lewis's inclination to philander had, in the long run, been a lot harder to deal with than Witt's stubbornness, and it was good to remind herself of that fact.

The phone rang, and she went to answer it. To her surprise, it was Barbara Wingate.

"I figured you might be there," Barbara said. "I've been trying to reach you all afternoon at home."

Fear grabbed Hannah's heart. "Joni?"

"Joni's fine. But that's why I called. She and Hardy got stranded down in Wetrock by the storm. They're holed up in a motel. Hardy wanted me to let you know."

"Thank you." Relief flowed through her, a warm, springlike breeze. The fact that Hardy had asked Barbara to call, though, was as plain as a nasty-gram.

Barbara spoke hesitantly. "Joni told me what happened."

Hannah closed her eyes against a flood of humiliation. "Yes?"

"I just want you to know...I'll do what I can to get her to talk to you."

"That's very generous of you." Very generous from a woman whose son had been the recipient of unending anger from Joni's uncle. No, her father.

"Not generous," Barbara said warmly. "I'm a mother, too. Anyway, Joni's staying with us for the meantime, so you don't have to worry. I'll look after her. I just hope Witt doesn't find out."

Me too, thought Hannah as she hung up after thanking Barbara. Me too.

And she resented the hell out of that.

Witt hadn't moved a muscle. If he was interested in who had called, he didn't express it. Until the storm had started to get really bad, they'd had a stream of well-wishers stopping by, and even then Witt hadn't said much, had barely managed a polite smile.

Hanna wondered how long this was going to go on. And what she might do to ease his depression. It was a normal enough feeling after a heart attack, that and fear, but rarely had she seen as profound a depression as Witt seemed to be going through.

Maybe she should call his doctor.

Not that that would do any good today. As bad as it was, she didn't want to attempt to get to the pharmacy. She would probably wreck the car or break her neck just trying to get down the hill.

And the drugstore was probably closed, anyway. Everything was closed. Besides, she reminded herself, reaching into the depths of her memory for the nurse she had once been, antidepressants took weeks to work. Nothing she could get today would help Witt right now.

It was nearing suppertime, so she went to make him a bowl of soup and a sandwich. He wasn't going to like it very much. No mayonnaise on the turkey, only a little bit of mustard. A can of low-fat minestrone, when he preferred chowder.

Then, of course, there was the challenge of getting him to eat it. He didn't want to eat anymore, either.

For an instant, just an instant, Hannah felt a surge of frustration that nearly blinded her. Then she tamped it down, because it wasn't going to do her a lick of good, not her nor anyone else.

Since Witt seemed glued to his recliner, she opened a wooden TV table in front of him and laid out his soup and sandwich, along with a spoon and napkin. Then she went back to the kitchen to get him a glass of water. Later she would make a pot of tea; it was one of the few things he seemed willing to touch.

When she returned to the living room, he still

hadn't moved a muscle. The food sat untouched, and he continued to stare out the bay window at the swirling snow.

"Witt. You have to eat."

Finally a response. "I'm not hungry."

"Too bad. Unless you want to be back in the hospital by nightfall, you *have* to eat."

"What's the point?"

She was so relieved to have him talking again that she considered finding some conciliatory answer. Then she decided to speak her mind. "Oh, I don't know. How about that I've had enough of sitting in the hospital worrying about you? How about that you'll never get better if you don't start taking care of yourself?"

"I'm not going to get better."

"Not at this rate." She went to stand in front of the window, putting herself right in his line of sight. "Look. You had a relatively minor heart attack. You suffered some injury to the heart muscle, but not enough to get worried about. You can live another twenty or thirty years, so maybe you'd better decide if you want to spend them all in that chair. Or if you want your life back."

Once again he didn't answer. But he *did* sit up and look at his lunch. "What the hell's that?" he asked, pointing at the soup.

"Minestrone."

"You know I only like New England clam chowder."

"Too much fat."

He made a disgusted sound and settled back in his chair. "I'm not hungry."

"Eat the damn sandwich, Witt."

She walked out of the living room, her head high, her shoulders square, daring him to argue with her. A couple of minutes later she peered around the corner and saw he was eating the sandwich.

Thank God.

One hurdle down. For the moment. Of course, that could change in an instant. Returning to the kitchen, she put water on to boil for tea. Maybe she needed to get a part-time nurse to help out with this. Because she wasn't as young as she used to be. Because she was too emotionally close to Witt to brush off his depression and irritability easily. Because after only three days she was beginning to feel worn to a nub. Not so much physically as emotionally.

But she didn't want to do that. She *ought* to be able to care for him. It wasn't as if he were running her in circles, or demanding constant critical care. He was just depressed and cranky. That shouldn't be too much to deal with.

And maybe she wouldn't have felt it was, except for her problems with Joni. Awful as it sounded, she felt Witt was a big impediment to her working them out. If he hadn't disowned her, maybe Joni would find it easier to accept the truth.

Even though the truth was awful. Hannah knew that and had been carrying a heavy, dark burden of guilt for twenty-six years. Ever since the one night of madness that had created Joni. Ever since she had faced the fact that she was no better than Lewis.

And she really wasn't. She might have succumbed only once, and Lewis might have done it multiple times, but that was only a matter of degree. She had been unfaithful to her husband, and, worse, she had been unfaithful with his brother.

That bitter knowledge had lain buried in her soul for nearly three decades, but it had never stopped hurting her. She supposed it had been hurting Witt, too, although they had never mentioned it, not even when they could have, freely, after they were both widowed.

Witt was an upright man. Sometimes wrong-headed, but very upright. He always made the choices that he believed to be correct, even if the rest of the world could see how wrong he was, as in the case of Joni. It must have tried him sorely to remember he'd been unfaithful with his brother's wife.

Which was why neither of them had mentioned it. Which was why neither of them had pursued a closer relationship when they had been free to do so. She had no doubt that Witt would have thought of it as enjoying the fruits of his sin. And frankly, so did she. A little. Nothing changed the fact that at the time they had come together, they had been sinning against their marriages.

Then there was Joni. She sometimes wondered if Witt guessed that Joni was his. Probably not. Joni had kindly cooperated in the coverup by being born several weeks early. And Witt had no reason to know that Hannah hadn't had sex with Lewis in over two months. Lewis had known that, of course, but he'd never said a word about Joni's surprising arrival. Never asked a question.

Maybe because he'd felt too damn guilty to do so. When she'd finally screwed up the nerve to tell him she was pregnant, he'd merely nodded and said, "Nice." He hadn't asked a single one of the questions she'd been dreading.

Probably because it set him free. Whatever, he'd been a good enough father to Joni, treating her with every bit as much love, attention and concern as if she'd sprung from his loins. He'd certainly been a far better father than he'd ever been a husband.

She supposed it was because he really liked children. Lewis had, at one time, talked about a big family. Then he'd seemed to become content with just Joni.

Hannah sometimes thought about that, and wondered whether, if she hadn't gotten pregnant with Joni, they could eventually have mended their marriage and had that big family.

She had no way of knowing now, because she still didn't know what had gone wrong in the first place. She didn't know if it was her fault, or his fault, or both their faults that he'd started playing around. It was easy to blame herself, though. She'd been doing that for a long, long time.

Now she had to wonder if she'd made another really big mistake by telling Joni the truth. The problem was, Joni was more flexible than Witt. Not by much, sometimes, but even a little was better than none.

Hannah was watching her family get torn apart by one man's hardheadedness and grief. Why shouldn't she use every weapon in her arsenal to keep either of them from doing something irrevocable?

She only wished she could tell Witt. But it was too dangerous. Yes, he was past the heart attack, but if she upset him, his blood pressure could go up, so for a while, at least, she had to keep him calm. Keep him away from major upsets.

And for the present that seemed to mean ignoring her daughter.

For the moment that made her almost hate Witt.

But she couldn't really hate him, much as she might want to. She could be angry with him, call him names and tell him he was a stubborn old cuss and she washed her hands of him—she'd done that a few times—but she couldn't really hate him. Nor could she abandon him.

She had to trust that Joni would work her way to a point that she was willing to talk to her mother again.

But looking at Joni's father, the dictionary definition of intractable, she began to wonder if her daughter had it in her.

* * *

Joni had a crackbrained notion. At least, that was what she called it. The storm tad taken out the cable TV, which wasn't all that entertaining anyway—

"Saves us from having to watch the news," Hardy had said when it went out.

—so she found some cheap motel stationery, wrote the alphabet on it and cut out all the letters.

"What are you doing?" Hardy finally asked.

"Making a Ouija board."

"You're kidding."

"No. It's crackbrained, I admit, but it's fun."

"Hmm."

She looked up from the round table that sat near the window. "Am I scaring you?"

"Hell no! I just think it's ridiculous."

"Of course it is. But it's still fun."

"I don't believe you can communicate with ghosts." But he was enjoying seeing her look almost happy. Well, maybe *amused* was a better word. Happiness was beyond reach for the two of them at this time.

"Neither do I." She leaned back, her blue eyes sparkling in the lamplight. He could hear snow crystals beating on the window behind her. "But it's fun anyway. It's silly, it makes you laugh, and that's all it is."

He still felt uneasy. Maybe he was a little more superstitious than he thought. He glanced around, noting the antiseptic motel room, thinking it was hardly the place for a ghostly visitation, then asking himself why the hell such a thought was even crossing his mind. Because he *never* thought about things like that.

Still, Joni was smiling and looking content, humming quietly under her breath, the happiest he'd seen her in twelve years. If this was going to make her happy, even for an hour, he would bite the bullet and do it—superstitions aside.

The squares on which the letters were written were ragged, because she'd had to fold and tear the paper without scissors. But she laid them carefully out on the table in a circle, along with squares that said *yes* and *no*. Then she put an upended water glass in the middle.

"This is it?" he asked. Why was the back of his neck prickling?

"Yup."

It looked harmless enough.

"I know," she said, misreading his uncertainty. "This is a girls' game. I promise I won't tell anybody you played it."

That put him on his mettle. "I'm not even thinking of that."

"No? Then why are you looking ready to bolt?"

He pulled out the chair and sat. "I'll play."

"Great. The alternative seems to be sitting around trying to tell each other tall tales."

He had to laugh at that. "You mean the one about the spruce tree that grew so tall the top got burned off by the sun?"

"Sounds like a combination of Icarus and Jack and the Beanstalk to me."

"I confess. So what do we do?"

"Just rest your fingers lightly on the glass, like this." She demonstrated. "They should barely be touching it. Not enough to create any pressure."

"Okay." He felt like a jerk siting there with his hands hovering over the glass. "Now what?"

"Ask a question. Anything."

Now he really felt foolish. Ask a question of the empty air? What kind of question? What did you ask an empty, upside-down water glass?

"Don't be shy."

He lifted his gaze to her face and found she was teasing him. "I'm not shy. But I *am* feeling totally ridiculous."

"That's part of the fun."

"Maybe in your book." He frowned at the glass and his fingertips, which were barely touching it. His fingertips, which were perilously near to brushing hers. Hmm.

"Okay," he said finally, deciding to be a man about it and just plunge in. "Will the storm stop?"

"That's a dumb question," Joni said. "Of *course* it's going to stop."

"I'm testing whether it works."

"Fair enough."

They waited. Nothing happened.

"Ask again," Joni prompted.

"Okay. Is the storm going to stop?"

Then the absolute weirdest thing happened. He felt almost as if there was a pressure on his hand, pushing it. And the glass zipped over to the *yes* square.

Joni laughed. "Did you feel it?"

"Uh..." He was reluctant to admit what he'd felt. "It's subconscious," he said. "Like when you're hypnotized. This is autohypnosis."

"Probably," she agreed, undeterred. "That's what I always figured. It's still fun."

He wasn't so sure of that, but he decided he could do this a while longer just to keep her smiling. No...he could do this all night if she would just keep smiling.

He guessed that made him lamebrained. And he didn't care. "Okay, you ask," he said, unwilling to talk to the glass again.

She closed her eyes for a moment. "Will the storm stop tonight?"

The glass moved again, this time to *no*. And Joni giggled.

"Hey," said Hardy, trying to enter the spirit of the game. "Ask something better. Like, 'Will we be able to get home tomorrow?'"

After a few seconds the glass slid around the table, describing a big circle, and came back to the *no*.

"It's feeling contrary," Hardy said.

"It's probably true, anyway. We know the weather says the storm is slow moving. Let's try something we *don't* know."

He figured they would just get a lot of garbage.

Alphabet soup or nonsense words. "Do we stick to yes-or-no questions?"

She shook her head. "Anything at all. It just takes longer to spell out answers than to get the yes or no."

He figured they had plenty of time. It was only seven-thirty, and when you were snowbound, those evening hours could get long. "I'm not in any rush."

"So ask."

"Hmm." He had to think about that. It wasn't as if he had any burning questions—at least, none he would feel comfortable asking in front of Joni. "Well, okay. Who's going to get the contract for Witt's hotel?"

Joni drew a sharp breath, as if the question surprised her. Or worried her. Not that it really mattered, Hardy thought a few moments later as the glass remained stubbornly still. He opened his mouth to make a humorous remark, but then the glass started sliding rapidly around, touching letters one after another. Joni had a pad beside her elbow, and after each letter, she wrote it on the paper.

THEBESTMAN. The glass stopped moving.

"The best man," Joni read aloud.

"That's suitably opaque and general."

"Yup." Her eyes sparkled. "We've got a smart subconscious operating here."

"Or a very cagey one. I wonder if we'd get the same answer if we asked about the outcome of the next election?"

"Probably. Sexist board."

He had to laugh. "Wanna try? Maybe it'll have the sense to answer 'the best man or woman.'"

"After my remark, it probably will."

They took a break to get some soft drinks, and Hardy broke out a bag of chips. "You know," he said as he sat munching, "this would be a better game if we had a list of questions. I'm having trouble thinking them up."

"Me too," she admitted.

"What did you girls do when you played it?"

"It was always at a slumber party, and there were at least six of us. And we always used to ask questions like 'Does so-and-so like me?' 'Who will I marry?' 'Will so-and-so take me to the prom?' Girl stuff."

"Well, it's too late to ask who's going to take you to the prom."

"And I'm *not* going to ask it who I'm going to marry."

"Me neither." He didn't want his subconscious tipping his hand on that one. "So we need grown-up-type questions."

She reached for a chip and chewed it thoughtfully. "I don't want to ask any serious questions."

"Me neither."

"Just silly things that make us laugh."

"I agree." But neither of them seemed in a real hurry to get back to the game, he realized, even Joni, who'd conceived it and spent all that time making up the letters. The wind was getting more persistent, too, rattling the window now. He pulled back the curtain and peeked out, only to see nothing but white haze.

"It looks really bad," Joni said. "I can't remember one ever looking this bad."

"Maybe we're in some kind of pocket that's catching the snow and making it look worse."

"Could be." But she pulled back the curtain and looked, too. "I wish I'd brought all my snow clothes. It might be fun to go stand outside for a few minutes."

"I'm afraid it's too badly drifted."

She nodded. "It'd be up to my hips. Makes you wonder if we'll be able to get out of this room at all tomorrow."

She dropped the curtain and looked at him. And Hardy, who'd been resolutely avoiding all such thoughts and feelings, felt the air thicken with something hot and heavy.

For an instant or two he couldn't even breathe. But then she looked away, and the world came back to normal.

"Shoot," she said. "This game isn't anywhere near as fun as I remember."

"It's probably more fun with a whole group of people."

"Maybe. Or maybe you and I have just gotten too old and stodgy to be silly."

"No way."

Her eyes leaped to his; then she smiled. "Okay, we're not. But this game still isn't any real fun."

She turned from him then and pulled back the curtains so she could look out at the swirling snow that seemed to light up the dark night. Her face fell into a thoughtful expression, then slipped in to one of pain.

Anger filled him. It was so damn unfair, he found himself thinking. So damn unfair. Both of them had been caught up in the repercussions of Karen's death to the point that they had virtually wasted more than a decade of their lives. Survivor's guilt? This was far worse. This was a trap built of grief and guilt, and one man's unforgiving nature.

But as he watched Joni's face tighten and sadden even more, his anger eased and became empathy. He watched as a tear rolled down her cheek and felt his own chest tighten in response. "Joni?"

She shook her head but didn't look at him. "I can't stop thinking of them."

"Who? Witt and your mom?"

"Yeah." She swallowed hard. "I keep feeling like there's something I should do. But I can't fix any of it."

He thought about that for a minute or so, trying to figure out how to tell her that she *could* fix at least some of it without setting her off. Joni had always had a bit of a temper. It wasn't that he was afraid of it, but he just couldn't see making her angry when she was so upset already.

Finally he got up and went to turn off all the lights. Then he used the cord to open the curtains fully. Outside the night was thick with blowing snow, and the world glowed a pinkish yellow from streetlights and the motel lights.

"It's breathtaking, isn't it?" she murmured.

"Yeah. I love it when you get away from lights, though. You can't even really see the snow at all except as a faint shimmer—until it's right in your face. Surprising."

She barely spared him a glance. "You like surprises?"

"Good ones."

"I could do with one of those."

So could he, but he didn't say so, because she might ask him what kind of surprise he would like, and he already knew that the one he wanted was out of reach.

She sighed again. Finally he told her what he thought as gently as he could.

"I really think you ought to talk to Witt and your mom."

"In the first place," she said bitterly, "I can't talk to him, because he's just had a heart attack and I can't upset him. Anyway, if he'd blamed you for twelve years for something that wasn't your fault, why do you think he'd be any more forgiving of me?"

"Because he's your father?"

"He doesn't know that. And there's probably a

damn good reason why my mother didn't tell him. Something like that would have infuriated him."

Hardy shook his head, resisting an urge to go hug her. "You can't know that. Nobody can. Because nobody's given him the chance to respond."

"I know how he'll respond?" She laughed bitterly.

Part of him wanted very much to argue with her; it seemed she was leaping to conclusions. Another part of him recognized unhappily that he couldn't. Witt had given him no reason to assume that he was a man who could ever forgive and forget. While he could tell himself that Witt would feel differently about Joni, since she was a member of his family, he couldn't guarantee that.

And since he couldn't guarantee anything, he would be wisest to keep his mouth shut.

He really wished he could make things better for her somehow, but without a magic wand tucked in his boot, he figured there wasn't a hell of a lot he could do except listen. And maybe nudge her a little.

"You can talk to your mom," he reminded her. "She's probably sick at heart at the way you cut her off."

Joni hunched one shoulder, a childish gesture, but he ignored it and waited for her to say something.

"Maybe," she said finally. "But what's the point? I'm not going to forgive her. She cheated on my father. With his brother."

"That *is* a big pill to swallow. But...didn't you tell me that he had cheated on her?"

"He cheated on her constantly. Maybe because he found out she cheated on him. How would I know? And what difference does it make, anyway? Two wrongs don't make a right."

"I guess not." He could sense the dead end coming, but he didn't put on the brakes just yet. "But it was a long time ago, Joni. A *long* time ago. You need to forgive her."

She turned and looked at him from red-rimmed eyes. "A long time ago? You forget. I just learned about it, Hardy. For me it's *right now*."

He couldn't deny that. He supposed he wasn't keeping his sights on that fact well enough. It was too easy to slip into a "Witt has always been this way" mode of thinking, because *to him* Witt *had* always been this way. But he hadn't always been this way to Joni, and Joni's mother's indiscretion might be more than a quarter century old, but it was new to Joni. "I'm sorry."

She shook her head and returned her attention to the snow outside. "Don't be sorry. You're being reasonable and I'm not. I hurt too much to be reasonable right now."

"Fair enough." Didn't mean he didn't still want to find some way to ease her pain or make her feel more optimistic about the whole mess.

"You know," she said, "part of me just wants to walk out into that blizzard and disappear."

His heart nearly stopped. "No."

"Oh, I won't. I won't give them the satisfaction." She sighed, and another tear trickled down her cheek. "I'm sorry, Hardy. I wanted to have fun this evening instead of being such a drag. That's all I am anymore, a big drag."

"That's not true. You're having a rough time is all."

"So? Doesn't mean I can't still try to be pleasant. Doesn't mean I have to spend all my time moaning about what's happened."

But even as she spoke the last word, her voice broke, and her tears began to roll with a vengeance. She put her hands to her face. "Oh, God, it hurts so bad. I feel like I've lost everything that matters in life. Witt. My mom... Even the memory of my dad."

Well, it was just too damn bad that she was Witt's daughter, and too damn bad that touching her was dangerous. Rising, he rounded the table and drew her up into his arms, hugging her snugly and letting her cry into his shoulder.

She felt so good against him that for a few minutes all he could do was swallow and hang on to his self-control. And feel like a beast that it was even a problem when she was so distraught.

It seemed so wrong to be aware of her curves pressed firmly against him, of the fullness of her breasts and the tininess of her waist, when she was weeping. But the desire he was feeling had been thwarted for years by circumstances out of his con-

trol. By his feelings of guilt. But now, in these moments, it was a raging monster that refused to be
tamed.

But he tamed it finally and found a few words to
offer in comfort. "You haven't lost your dad," he
said gently. "No way. Whether he was your biological father or not, he loved you and raised you. He
was your dad in every way that counts, and no one
can take that away. No one."

That seemed to make her cry harder, and he started
to feel truly helpless. Maybe he should just shut his
damn yap. Maybe it would be best to just let her cry
it out and work her own way through her problems.
What the hell did he know, anyway? His life was
hardly a sterling example of having it all together.

But holding her felt too good to let go, so he stood
there, stroking her hair and feeling her hot tears soak
his shirt.

It didn't last all that long. Maybe fifteen minutes.
Then she was drying her puffy eyes and mumbling
apologies for being a baby.

"Hey," he said, catching her chin in his hand and
making her look at him. "It's okay to cry. Always."

She gave a raspy, short laugh. "But not all the
time. I feel like I'm drowning in self-pity."

"Maybe you are. So what? You're entitled."

"But you're not required to listen to it."

He shrugged. "I don't mind."

Her eyes met his then. Such a bright, clear, strong
blue, like the Colorado sky. Red from crying, so

puffy they couldn't open all the way, yet still the
most beautiful eyes he'd ever seen, bar none.

In an instant, the planets halted, the earth stopped
revolving around the sun, and the last bit of air was
sucked out of the room.

Oh, God, he thought, I knew it was a mistake.

But it was too late now.

14

Hardy was going to kiss her. There was a look in his eyes right now that was stealing her breath away. Locking her in a web of longing and aching that drove nearly everything else from her mind.

She didn't deserve this. She wasn't entitled to this. Guilt from years past slipped into her mind and slithered along nerve endings, reminding her that Hardy had belonged to Karen.

But it wasn't enough to make her pull away. Not enough to yank her out of the longing that was weighting her limbs with need. Then and now seemed to be merging, fusing her long-ago fantasy with the reality of these moments with Hardy.

She was pressed so closely to him that she could feel his hard angles and firm muscles, could feel his heat…and his growing desire. So close that she felt it when he stiffened infinitesimally, as if he was having second thoughts.

He was going to pull away. Her heart sounded a

sad note and began to sink, but she had enough control not to grip his shirt and hold him. *This couldn't be...this couldn't be....* The reminder whispered in her mind, a background chorus to all the needs and yearnings that filled her.

It would be wrong for so many reasons, and he must know it as well as she did. Wisdom told her to step back. Hunger kept her rooted.

A soft breath escaped his lips. His eyes narrowed, then, almost reluctantly, his head lowered.

Their lips touched. Light as the kiss of a snowflake, but hot as the tropical sun. His breath was scented faintly of chips and cola, or maybe it was hers; she didn't know. She only knew that her soul hushed, as if it had been waiting aeons for this moment. This touch. This kiss.

His lips were like velvet, so soft and warm, and they caressed hers lightly, enthralling her the way no deep, hard kiss could have done. It was a coaxing, questing kiss, seeking her response but never demanding it. It was like riding a gentle river while knowing all the while that rapids lay ahead.

Her heart began to thud heavily, pumping liquid desire through her, bringing every nerve ending to life, making her sparkle and glow. Oh, she had never imagined that such a light touch could make her feel so much. Or maybe she was wrapped up in a fantasy from long ago, swept away on imaginings rather than reality.

She didn't know, and soon she didn't care, because

his arms tightened around her, drawing her closer still in a way that told her how much he wanted her. His kiss deepened, grew firmer, while his tongue tasted her lips, almost tickling, but undeniably sending rockets to her very center.

She wanted him. And suddenly it didn't seem important anymore that this could only bring grief and disappointment. Could only bring anger and make things worse for both of them with Witt.

Why was she even thinking of Witt? He'd disowned her, and what he thought didn't matter anymore at all.

There would be a price for this. She knew it with every cell in her being. There would be a terrible price. But right then she couldn't care about that. This was something she'd been dreaming of for so many long years, and while it could never be more than these moments and this night, she couldn't pass it by.

Her arms lifted, signaling her decision, and wrapped around his waist, feeling muscle and sinew and strength. Hardy was a rock, both physically and emotionally, she thought dreamily. He was a man you could depend on.

His kiss teased her, tormented her, teaching her how to duel with her tongue in a way that drew her mind inexorably to the delights that lay ahead. *Yes!* The thought was unequivocal.

He shifted against her, and for an instant she feared he was going to leave her, but then his hand closed over her breast, squeezing and cupping gently, causing her head to reel in delight. Through layers of tricot and wool, that touch seemed as intimate as if he had cradled her very soul in his hand.

Unnoticed by either of them, a tear squeezed beneath her eyelid and trickled slowly down her cheek. It was a tear of joy and release, of fulfillment and escape. For a little while the shadows were gone.

Each touch of his hand stoked her desire even more. When she at last felt him tugging her shirt up, she thought she couldn't stand the anticipation. Why was he moving so slowly?

But then, with a twist, he released the clasp of her bra, and his hand, slightly chilly, closed over her warm, bare skin, claiming her breast.

Delighted shivers ran through her, filling her with a heady sense of glee, hunger, joy and need. Emotions tumbled through her as wildly as water through rapids and mingled with physical sensations that were as close as a body could ever come to physically feeling a pure emotion.

His mouth left hers, and both of them gasped for breath. He muttered, ''You don't know...''

Yes, she did know. She remembered all the lonely nights she had filled with dreams of him. Dreams of doing exactly what they were doing now. Dreams of feeling his skin on hers, hearing his voice husky in her ear, of curling up with him and feeling safe, so safe....

In all her life she had never felt quite as safe as

she did right this instant, tumbling over a precipice of desire. It was suddenly the easiest thing in the world to fall.

She fell, light as feather down. He tugged the curtains closed with an impatient hand, though no one at all would venture out in the midst of this storm. Then he tugged at her clothes impatiently, and she was glad of his impatience, because at that moment, if he had hesitated or drawn it out too long, she might have had a thought, a qualm, an unwelcome remembrance.

He spared her that. Her clothes fell away, landing somewhere across the room. Even her socks were tugged away, at last leaving her naked for him. Naked and shivering with desire more than cold.

He looked at her, his eyes hot and hungry, his gaze painting her with fire.

"You're beautiful," he said hoarsely. "So beautiful…"

Then, before she could try to respond, he scooped her up and carried her to the bed, tucking her beneath the warm covers.

Standing over her, he stripped. He showed no modesty or fear, as if he, like she, was well past such thoughts. His nudity filled her with wonder, seeming as perfect as a statue. And he was offering it all to her.

Her hands reached for him eagerly, drawing him down to her, and when he slipped beneath the covers beside her, she felt such an incredible sense of satisfaction that a long, joyous sigh escaped her.

This was meant. This had to be. And nothing else at all mattered. Nothing.

Bodies, lips, hands met and melded, striving to learn, to know, to capture, to possess. Untutored though she was, Joni felt as comfortable as if she had been here a million times. Nothing had ever seemed so right.

He kissed her breast, sucking gently, his mouth hot but leaving behind patches that grew shivery cold in moments. She loved the contrast, loved the sensations, loved the intimacy. She loved being with Hardy.

Because not for one minute did she think this was merely a matter of physical sensations. The sensations with other men had never been enough to carry her to this point.

This was all about Hardy, and her hands tried to tell him so as they caressed him and learned how to please him.

His nipples proved to be as sensitive as hers, and she reveled in playing with them, drawing deep groans from him. When his hand slipped between her legs, touching the aching petals of her flesh, answering her need while fueling it even more, she responded in kind, delighting in his delight.

But all of those things, wondrous though they were, were merely a backdrop for the earthquake taking place in her heart.

This was Hardy. She was with him at last, and she didn't know if she could ever bear to let him go.

Her body accepted him, drawing him in with only the merest twinge of discomfort. He filled her as she had dreamed of being filled, and her soul overflowed. This had always been meant to be. She had been created just for him.

Higher they rose, reaching for the elusive peak, bodies straining together to create the physical replica of all that was in their hearts.

When they crested, they did so together. Then they tumbled down the other side.

Into the abyss.

Reality didn't leave them alone for long. When had it ever? Reality crept back on the tendrils of cold air that whispered through the room, on the tick-tick of the snowy claws that scratched at the window. It came back and slipped into the bed with them.

Between them.

"Joni, I..." Hardy trailed off. His eyes were still closed. His hands on her back seemed to be saying how much he enjoyed her. But his words never said so.

Before he could say what she assumed he was about to, she said it for him, because she didn't want to feel stupid. "We never should have done this."

His eyes opened then, and there was no mistaking the pain in them. It never occurred to her that she had caused that pain.

Instead, she climbed out of the bed and grabbed up her clothes, too wounded now to even feel tears. Moments ago, or so it seemed, he had been deep within her, and nothing had ever felt so right.

At this moment, however, nothing had ever felt so wrong.

"I'll see you tomorrow," she said, her clothes bundled awkwardly in her arms. Then she closed the adjoining door between them.

And locked it.

Karen, she thought bitterly as she threw her clothes into a heap on the bed. *Karen.* Always Karen. She and her cousin—sister!—had looked somewhat alike. Maybe enough alike that Hardy had thought he was making love to Karen. Maybe he'd slipped into that fantasy, while she'd slipped into hers.

Or maybe he was just feeling guilty. Why the hell not? Because Joni suddenly felt that she had done something truly awful to Karen's memory.

She tried to tell herself that was stupid as she took a hot shower to wash the last of Hardy off her, to erase even his scent. Karen had been dead for so long now. She no longer mattered. Anything Joni did now couldn't hurt Karen. People died, and normal people moved on and forged new relationships. Hardy was entitled to that, and so was she.

But she feared Hardy wasn't doing that. And she feared what Witt would think, too. Because even though he'd disowned her, he wasn't above giving her a piece of his mind.

And the truth was, she really had no desire to wound Witt. None whatever. She loved him.

Even if he didn't love her.

Slowly she sank to the floor of the shower, and as the hot water beat on her head, she cried soundlessly.

Oh, God, what had she done?

Hardy felt as if he'd been hit by a Mack truck. He stared at the closed door between the rooms and heard the snick of the lock turning like a death knell in his heart.

Christ, what had happened? He'd been lying there feeling the most incredible afterglow and had opened his mouth to tell her how wonderful he was feeling when she'd turned on him.

He should have kept his mouth shut. Until the instant that his speech had shattered the silence, she had seemed as content and comfortable as he. He must have surprised her.

But that was still no excuse. No excuse to hop out of bed saying, "We never should have done this."

What had he done wrong? Had he hurt her? Moment by moment he reviewed their lovemaking in his mind, trying to penetrate the hazy glow that lay over it to get to the kernel of what had really been going on.

No, he hadn't hurt her, of that he was sure. Nor did he believe her orgasm had been faked. So what the hell had gotten into her?

He *knew* they shouldn't have done this. He didn't

need her to tell him that it would have been wiser
not to take a bite of the apple. God, he knew that.
He *knew* that. There were too many problems, too
many memories, too much guilt.

Except that he wasn't feeling especially guilty.
Much to his own amazement, he didn't feel as if he'd
betrayed Karen. Not this time. How could he? Karen
hadn't been around for a long time. He owed her
nothing anymore. At least, not in this regard.

He was a thirty-year-old man who had every right
to love any willing woman he chose. Never mind that
he felt guilty about what had happened to Karen. He
did, and he would probably carry that guilt to his
grave. But that absolutely did not mean he couldn't
have a life.

So what was going on in Joni's head? He knew
her well enough to know that she responded to impulse, and some impulse, poorly thought out, must
have struck her. He wondered if he should try to
speak to her about it, then decided it was probably
too soon for that.

Whatever had happened, he hoped to heaven it
hadn't been something about him that had sent her
into flight.

He was no Don Juan, but he tried to be a consid-
erate lover. He tried to be sure his partner enjoyed
herself.

Maybe that was the problem. Maybe Joni felt
guilty for enjoying herself. Maybe with all that was
on her plate she felt awful about it.

Could be.

He stared at the closed door and wondered how he was going to stand the awful silence for another day.

As it turned out, he didn't have long to wonder. He awoke in the morning to a dying storm, with only light flurries falling. By ten the motel owner told them he'd heard that the roads were pretty well cleared between Wetrock and Whisper Creek.

Hardy took the opportunity to knock on the adjoining door and tell Joni they could go home now. Not that that would make it any better, he thought irritably. She would still be under his roof once they got there. Unless she decided to move in with one of her girlfriends.

But he knew why she hadn't done that to begin with. They all had children and families, and very little room. Besides, he reminded himself, he'd practically insisted on her staying with him.

Now he wished he hadn't done that. The frost was bad enough when emanating from the far side of a closed door. It would be intolerable at home.

Ten minutes later she joined him, looking as redeyed and sleep-deprived as he felt. Before they went out to get in the car, he tried to ease the atmosphere.

"Sorry if I hurt you last night," he said tentatively.

"You didn't hurt me." She didn't even look at him, just brushed past him and headed for the car.

What the hell. Giving up, he followed. The motel

had cleared the parking lot as best it could with a snowblower, but he still had to brush a foot of the stuff off the windows and hood, and use his emergency shovel to clear out the drifts around the tires. Joni waited, saying nothing.

Great. Wonderful. Life could be such a bitch sometimes. He almost snapped something at her, then bit his tongue. What was the point?

At last they climbed into the car and roared out of the parking lot.

"You know," he said as they made their way up a hill that had been plowed recently, "it would be nice if you would at least tell me what you're mad at me about."

"I'm not mad at you." But she didn't offer anything else, leaving him in the same state of limbo.

A mile passed, then another and another. The silence was getting so thick he considered turning on the radio just to dispel it. That was about when he noticed that the snow was getting thicker, too. The road was still well plowed, though, and the driving wasn't bad as long as he kept to a reasonable speed.

He considered dropping her at her mother's house when they got back to town. It would at least make a point.

But somewhere over the next few miles he started to feel guilty for being irritated and angry with her. Something serious was obviously troubling her. It didn't matter whether she was right or wrong about whatever it was, just that she was upset. But without knowing what she thought the problem was, he couldn't do a damn thing to help.

This was unlike Joni, he found himself thinking. Oh, not the taking of some notion or the acting impulsively on it. But the silence... He couldn't remember Joni ever having been silent when something bothered her. Take this whole hotel mess. She'd made plenty of ruckus for no better reason than that she was bothered by the situation.

And leopards didn't change their spots overnight.

Well, when she had gotten pissed at Witt, she hadn't told Witt so. No, she had gone and set up a situation that was supposed to precipitate the outcome she wanted. She had come to *Hardy*. Which meant that if she wasn't talking to him, she must be angry at *him*.

Cripes.

"Joni? What's wrong?"

For an instant he thought she was just going to ignore him. But then she said, "Everything."

"Hmm. What did I do?" As if he didn't know. Making love to her last night had been an act of stupidity. There was too much between them, not the least of it Witt. But he wanted to hear it from *her*.

"I told you," she said. "We shouldn't have... shouldn't have..."

"Shouldn't have made love. I know. You said so. Was it awful for you?"

Her head whipped around. "No!"

"Then what? Witt might not approve? Hell, Witt

won't approve. So what? We're grown-ups.'' Which was something he needed to remind *himself* of, he realized suddenly. Man, he'd been reacting to Witt as if he were still eighteen. Maybe it was time to take the bull by the horns.

''Okay,'' he said when she didn't answer. ''Why don't you just tell me the truth? I'm feeling like shit here. I thought we made beautiful love. Instead, you took flight as if I'd hurt you terribly.''

''No…no.'' She shook her head.

He waited, wondering if he needed to prod her some more. Because, he was discovering, he couldn't stand to have Joni upset and not know why. He couldn't stand being unable to help her in some way. It was a new and unexpected feeling. And if he'd had an ounce of common sense, he would have realized that feeling was even more dangerous than their lovemaking had been.

''I'm sorry,'' she said, her voice small. ''I'm sorry. Last night was… Well, it was everything I'd ever dreamed of. More than what I'd dreamed.''

Did she mean that she'd dreamed of him? His heart seemed to slam, and he cast his mind back over the years, trying to discover if there'd been any indication back in high school.

But he couldn't remember any. She'd always treated him like her cousin's boyfriend, somebody to tease or be pleasant to as the mood or moment required. He couldn't remember any longing looks or any hints, however faint, that she was interested in him.

Part of him thought it was egotistical to even consider such a possibility. But a deeper part of him wondered anyway. Hoped, even, that he hadn't been alone in the yearning that had made him decide to break up with Karen.

Although even then he'd known that if he ditched Karen, Joni wasn't going to go out with him. She would have been too loyal to do that. Even so, he felt like a sleaze for dating one girl when he was wanting another. So the gentlemanly thing was to break up with Karen, even if it meant being alone.

But Joni... Nah, he told himself. If she'd dreamed of him, it had probably been recently. Not while he and Karen had been an item. Not that he thought she would have been a bad person if she had—no, a bad person would have acted on those urges. Like him.

God, he hated himself. Then he wondered how he'd gotten all tangled up. He'd been going steady with Karen, but they'd been kids, and going steady wasn't a lifelong commitment. Which meant there was nothing wrong with him for wanting to break it off. That was natural and normal at that age. At any age, actually, when you weren't married.

So he hadn't been doing anything wrong. Wrong would have been dating some other girl behind Karen's back. He hadn't done that. He hadn't *acted* on his yearning in a dishonorable way.

But man, he sure wished he'd broken up with her

sooner. Wished he'd done anything to keep them off the road that night.

"What did you dream of?" he heard himself ask.

There was a silence. Long. Heavy. Pregnant with possibilities that had him feeling like he was on tenterhooks.

"You," she said finally, her voice almost atonal. "I was jealous."

He considered a number of different ways to respond. Considered telling her that he'd been about to break off with Karen. But, he asked himself, was that going to make her feel any better?

"Do you feel guilty about that?" he asked.

"Constantly."

He could identify with that. "Yeah," he said. "Me too."

She looked at him as if she was about to ask a question, but just then an oncoming car lost control.

It began to spin out on some ice, and for an instant he froze, remembering that night so long ago....

But then his reflexes kicked in. Letting up on the gas, he started to take an evasive maneuver, one that would keep them from colliding with the oncoming car, which was spinning wildly and still coming straight at them, too fast.

The river. He didn't want to go into the river. Gauging the snowbank beside the road, he tried to figure what angle to hit it, an angle that wouldn't flip the car.

He hit the brakes, feeling the antilocks kick in with

rapid jolts. God, the road was pure ice. The tail of the other car was swinging right toward him. The snowbank was too close. No room...

At the last instant he saw his opening and steered right toward it. A moment later he felt the impact as they hit the snowbank.

Hannah was trying to talk Witt into eating a turkey sandwich on whole wheat when the call came. Witt didn't like whole-wheat bread. She had also discovered he wouldn't eat oatmeal for breakfast, that he wouldn't eat *anything* for breakfast except bacon and eggs, and he wasn't going to spend the rest of his life eating spinach pasta—which she hadn't offered him—just because some idiot doctor thought it would be good for him.

In fact, she'd discovered that as far as he was concerned, he would rather sit in that chair and die than live anything but his normal life.

She told herself the anger was a good sign, better than the silent, motionless depression of the last few days. At least he was reacting. But when the turkey sandwich hit the floor, she had had enough.

"Damn it, Witt," she said, she who never swore. "I will not be treated this way."

"Then get the hell out. I'll make myself some decent food."

She was tempted, sorely tempted. He had worn her out more than any obstreperous patient ever had. Possibly because she didn't get a break after every eight hours. More likely because she cared too much about Witt. "No," she told him, reverting to her more usual calm demeanor. "I wouldn't give you the satisfaction."

He got out of the chair. "Then stay out of my way. I'm going to make myself a *real* sandwich."

"That might be difficult. I threw out the white bread, the roast beef, the mayonnaise…"

"Who the hell gave you the right to do that?" he thundered.

She didn't even bother to answer. She could see he was fuming mad, and she felt a pang of fear, given what he'd been through. Then she reminded herself that there was no way to keep Witt from getting angry forever. Nor was his condition so bad that he couldn't survive it. A serious shock might cause him a problem, but this kind of anger? Not likely.

"Get out of my way, woman."

"Don't you talk to me like that, Witt Matlock. I've had enough of your attitude."

"Attitude? I'll give you attitude." He shouldered past her and stomped into his kitchen, flinging open the refrigerator to reveal exactly what she'd promised. No bacon, no eggs, nothing fatty at all. "What the hell have you done to me?"

"I'm taking care of you."

"What's the point? I don't want to live if I have to give up everything I enjoy."

"You don't. Just the foods that are bad for you."

He glared at her, but she refused to glare back.

"I," he said, "am going to keep on living the way I've always lived."

"You know, Witt, you're a tiresome man." As soon as she spoke the words, she realized something: Witt reacted to everything that was beyond his control with anger. Yes, he *was* tiresome, but only because he seemed to have one emotional tone when he was unhappy about anything. And right now he wasn't really angry about food. He was *frightened*.

"Then leave me alone," he said.

"Don't be a jackass. You're scared, I know you're scared, and you'll only be *more* scared if I leave you alone."

He glared at her but didn't hurl any more nasty words her way. The silence that suddenly stretched between them was profound. Hannah felt herself holding her breath, waiting...but for what she couldn't say.

Into that silence came the ringing of the phone. It was an old phone, and the ringer was jarring, loud. Witt jerked, and Hannah jumped. For an instant she considered ignoring it, but its clamor wouldn't silence. Turning, she snatched it from the hook.

"Hello?"

"Hannah? Hannah this is Sam Canfield. You might want to come to the emergency room."

"Joni?" Fear clutched her heart, drove everything else from her mind.

"She's been in a car accident. There don't appear to be any major injuries, but she's unconscious."

Hannah didn't wait to hear any more. She dropped the phone in the cradle and headed for the mud porch.

"Hannah?" Witt asked. "What's wrong with Joni?"

"I have to go to the hospital. She's been in an accident."

"I'm going with you."

She turned on him then. "Are you, Witt? Are you? You disowned her, remember? You don't have any rights at all anymore."

"I'm going anyway."

She didn't argue this time, just grimly started pulling on her boots and parka. It didn't do any good to argue, anyway, she told herself miserably. Witt was as hardheaded as a concrete block. And Joni seemed to be the same way.

All she knew right then was that her heart felt as chilly as the January day.

15

"**G**od, I hate emergency rooms," Sam Canfield said. He was sitting in one of the uncomfortable chairs in the waiting room, across from Hardy. "Ever since the night my wife died, I can't sit here without remembering."

Hardy nodded, although he was so worried about Joni he didn't have much room for feeling anything else. "You don't have to sit with me, Sam. I just got a few bruises. I'll live."

"Maybe. If Witt doesn't show up with Hannah. And what do you think the likelihood of that is?"

Hardy didn't want to think about it. Bad enough about Karen. He could just imagine how Witt would react this time. Not that it mattered what Witt might say or do. At this point Hardy was beating himself up with a mental baseball bat, beginning with bashing himself for even considering taking a relative of Witt Matlock's in his car again. Good God almighty, he needed his head examined.

And Joni. God. He felt bad about keeping Sam here, but Sam was the only way he could find out about Joni's condition. Doctors were weird that way. If you weren't family, you could kiss off getting any news.

"It wasn't your fault, Hardy," Sam said for probably the fifteenth time.

"It *was* my fault she was in my car."

"Since when is that a crime?" Sam snorted. "It's not like you caused the accident. I could see plain as day what happened out there. What you did was keep the two of you from getting killed. That damn boat of a car was going too fast. Even in that skid he'd've killed you if he'd hit you head-on."

Hardy just shook his head. He'd heard all this stuff when Karen had been killed. Wasn't his fault. The other driver was drunk and came straight for him. Sure. That was what had happened. But Hardy had hardly passed a day without wondering what he could have done differently. Now he was going to do the same thing about today.

God, if he ever took another Matlock in his car, he was going to cut his own throat.

"It's karma," he heard himself say.

Sam lifted his eyebrows. "You believe in that?"

"I'm beginning to."

Sam bobbed his head a little, a maybe-so agreement. "Or just some really rotten luck."

"Same thing."

"Maybe." Sam sighed and leaned back, closing his eyes. "It doesn't do any good, you know."

"What?"

"Second-guessing. Doesn't do a damn bit of good. I've second-guessed that day Bonnie was killed until I'm not sure I even remember it right anymore. Anyway, hindsight's always twenty-twenty. Problem is, all those things you think you should have done just plain don't occur to you beforehand."

"I guess not." But that didn't help the feeling of guilt any.

Sam checked his watch. "Time to go bug the nurses for information," he said. "Sit tight."

As if Hardy was going to do anything else, except maybe bust into the treatment rooms and demand to see Joni. Which would probably get him thrown out of the hospital.

Smothering a groan of despair, he leaned forward and put his head in his hands. He'd been luckier than Joni, just a few bruises and a huge headache. It should have been him lying in the bed in there, unconscious. Not Joni.

Joni. Her name kept echoing inside him, bouncing off the walls he'd tried to build around his heart. Remembering how she'd looked only last night when they'd made love. Remembering how her every sigh had seemed to send tendrils of warmth to the farthest reaches of his soul.

Remembering how she'd fled from him.

He lifted his head and told himself to get a magazine from one of the tables. Read something distracting. Stop whipping himself over things he shouldn't have done and would never forget.

Christ. The only two accidents in his entire driving life, and one of Witt's girls had been involved in each. It *had* to be karma.

"Hardy?" Sam entered the waiting room from the corridor. "She's awake. I twisted some arms, and you can go in and see her. Three doors down on the left."

Hardy started to dart from the room, then caught himself. "How is she?"

"She appears to be fine. They're going to keep her overnight for observation, because of the concussion, but they don't see anything significant wrong."

He didn't wait any longer. Walking as fast as he could, he left the waiting room, traveled down the short corridor and through the swinging doors of the E.R. treatment area. Three doors down and on the left, he found her.

The head of the bed was cranked up a little, and she was lying on a pillow. An IV was hooked to her arm, but he guessed that didn't mean much. It was probably standard procedure.

She didn't even look especially pale, although her color wasn't as high as it usually was. Her lips were still pink, though, and slightly parted. Her long dark hair needed combing, but that didn't keep it from looking beautiful splashed across the pillow. In fact, he thought she had never looked more beautiful.

He approached the bed hesitantly, reluctant to disturb her if she was asleep, yet needing to hear her voice. Desperate to hear her voice. Karen hadn't said a word ever again after the accident, and he couldn't help feeling that he would believe Joni was okay only if he heard her voice.

She must have sensed his presence, because her eyes opened and fixed on him. "Hardy?"

Relief and joy filled him in equal measures. He crossed the space between them in two long strides and took her hand gently. "How are you feeling?"

"Not too bad. I have a headache, and a big goosebump where my head hit the window. At least that's what they think happened. I don't remember. How are you?"

"A few bruises. No biggie."

"Good." She sighed and squeezed his hand, closing her eyes for a few seconds. "I remember that other car skidding toward us, but I don't remember much else."

"Probably just as well. Some things don't need to be remembered, like moments of sheer terror."

She managed a weak laugh. "Yeah."

Giving in to an impulse he'd been trying to curb since he set eyes on her lying in the bed, he bent over and gently kissed her forehead. "God, I'm glad you're okay. I've been scared to death."

"It's just a concussion." She sighed and turned toward him, bringing their faces to within a couple of inches. "They won't let me go home until to-morrow. Not that I've got a home."

"You'll always have a home with me, Joni. Always." It was a rash promise, but every cell in his body compelled him to say it. He thought she caught her breath, but the sound was so slight he wasn't sure. What difference did it make? He'd probably just surprised her.

"Thanks, Hardy. But I won't impose forever."

"You can impose for two forevers and I won't mind."

Her blue eyes opened a little wider, searching his face as if for some kind of confirmation.

"Thank you," she said again. But he could hear the hesitation in her voice.

Hell, he thought, it wasn't what she wanted to hear from him. Of course not. Last night had been a big mistake. She'd said so.

Feeling as if he were horning in where he wasn't wanted, he backed off until he was standing straight beside her bed. Just in time, as it happened, because at that moment Witt and Hannah came bursting into the room.

Witt glared at him. "You!"

It was not an auspicious greeting. Hardy felt something inside him wilting, curling up into a protective knot as both his mind and his emotions tried to fling him back into that night so long ago when Karen had died.

But he was not eighteen years old anymore. He

wasn't the same person. Joni wasn't dead. And Witt, he suddenly realized, was nothing but a scared, sick old man.

"Yeah, me," he said to Witt, trying to keep his tone nonconfrontational. He wasn't sure he succeeded, especially when he felt his jaw harden.

"Witt, please," Hannah said sternly. "Joni."

Then Hannah brushed past Witt and approached the bed across from Hardy. "Honey," she said, her voice unsteady. "How are you feeling?"

"Pretty good, except for a headache. And except for having to spend the night here." Joni's voice, unlike her mother's, was cool, detached. As if she were talking to a stranger. Hardy hated the sound of it.

Hannah flinched. "That's a good thing, actually."

But Witt was not to be silenced for long. "You're lucky you're not dead," he said harshly. "What were you thinking, getting into a car with that man?"

Joni's face set in hard lines. "What the hell difference does it make to you?" she demanded. "You disowned me, remember? And anyway, the accident wasn't Hardy's fault. He's probably the only reason I'm still alive!"

Witt opened his mouth, his face reddening, but before he could speak, Hannah's voice cut through the room like a whiplash. "Witt, enough!"

"Oh, just get out of here, you two," Joni said. "I'm ashamed of both of you!"

Great reconciliation scene, Hardy thought uneasily. He wished he knew what to say or do to help all of them past this, but he was acutely aware that he had no right to intervene. And acutely aware that Witt would object to anything he said. Anything. God, what a mess.

A nurse came into the room. "Who's shouting? All visitors out of here now."

"No," Joni said. "I want Hardy to stay. Those two can go. Now."

Witt barely glanced at Joni as Hannah took his arm and began to lead him from the room. But he *did* glare at Hardy, a look that said he had plenty more to say and was going to say it at a later time.

Which, Hardy suddenly realized, was something he was going to look forward to. The last time he'd really faced Witt was when he was eighteen and frightened and hurting. The meeting at the hardware store a few days ago didn't really count. No, he had plenty he wanted to go toe-to-toe with Witt about, and this was as good a time as any.

"Hardy?"

He looked down at Joni. "What?"

"Don't let him get to you. He's a mean old man."

There was a time when Hardy would have agreed with her, but at that moment he couldn't bring himself to. "He's not mean, Joni. He's terrified."

"Of what?" She started to shake her head, then winced. "God, this headache."

He took her hand again, squeezing gently. "He's

scared of losing everything he cares about, including you.''

''Me? He disowned me!''

''He was angry. And scared.''

''Scared of what?''

''That you might get so mad at him over his reaction to my bid that you'd stop talking to him. Scared because what you did showed your major disapproval of him. So he preempted you.''

Joni mulled that over for a few minutes, then finally sighed. ''My head hurts too much to think about it.''

''So think about it another time. I do have one word of advice for you, though. Talk to your mom.''

''I can't.''

He sighed and leaned closer to her, fixing her with his gaze. ''You know, Joni, you're a wonderful woman. But there's part of you that's still very much a spoiled child. Don't you think it's time to grow up?''

Then, before she could say another word, he leaned over and kissed her lightly on the lips. ''I'll check on you tomorrow. Right now, you need your mother.''

Then, as if it wasn't one of the hardest things he'd ever done, he walked out of the room.

God, he couldn't believe he'd said that to her. Now he would probably be on her list of people she was never going to speak to again. And for some weird reason, he didn't think he could stand that.

* * *

Hardy found Hannah in the waiting room. Witt was nowhere in sight. "Where's Witt?" he asked.

"I sent him home. Why? Do you want to have it out with him?" There was no challenge in her tone, merely curiosity.

"No, I was just surprised not to see him. Anyway, I'm leaving now. Why don't you go see Joni?"

Hannah patted the chair beside her. After a moment's hesitation, he sat.

Hannah spoke quietly. "Did she tell you why she's so angry with me?"

Part of him wanted to lie to her to spare her embarrassment, but he'd never been very good at lying and rarely was inclined to, anyway. "Yes."

She nodded, looking down briefly. "How do you feel about that?"

"Me? What does it matter what I think?"

"Because you might be influencing her opinion."

He hadn't thought of that. "Well, I don't give a damn, if you want the truth." Which wasn't strictly true. The idea that he was tangled up with another one of Witt's daughters gave him serious heartburn when he thought about it. But that didn't mean he thought any less of Hannah. "I mean, human beings are human beings. We all do things that later we don't feel too proud of. Things that other people can't understand. But what I think doesn't really matter."

"It could," she said enigmatically. But before he

could pursue that assertion, she continued. "I wish Joni would let me explain. I suppose I don't have any excuses, but I certainly have some reasons."

"Which are better than excuses any day. I told her she ought to talk to you. Why don't you go in there now? Maybe she's finally ready to listen."

Hannah nodded. "I'll do that. And you stay clear of Witt until I can talk sense to him."

Hardy couldn't help it. He might be aching all over from bruises and muscle strains, and his heart might feel as heavy as lead over Joni, but he couldn't prevent himself from seeing the humor in that statement. "Nobody can talk sense *into* Witt."

A smile flickered over Hannah's face. "You might be surprised. Take care, Hardy."

Then she squared her shoulders and left the waiting room. And he realized he hadn't asked if she had a way home. Sighing, he went to call his mother and tell her he was going to be late. He couldn't leave Hannah here to fend for herself.

That was when he remembered that Barbara didn't even know there'd been an accident. He'd been able to prevent Sam and the medical personnel from calling anyone except Hannah. So there Barbara sat, thinking her son was safely in some motel in Wetrock. Hah! Maybe he shouldn't call her at all.

Then he thought how mad she would be when she found out that he'd kept this from her. Hell, he didn't know who was going to give him a worse tongue-lashing: Barbara or Joni.

Probably Barbara, he decided. She loved him. And Joni didn't give a damn.

Hannah discovered that Joni had been moved up-stairs to a regular room. It took her a few minutes to get the number out of the admitting clerk, then she headed upstairs, hoping Joni would still be awake.

She wanted to talk to her daughter. *Needed* to talk to her daughter. They had a lot of things to clear the air about, and she was getting rather tired of living with this emotional pain and emptiness. If Joni didn't feel up to it tonight, that was fine, but she was going to make it clear to her daughter that they were going to discuss this *soon*.

However, when she reached the second floor and was on her way down the hushed corridor toward Joni's room, doubt began to gnaw at her. Maybe she shouldn't confront Joni. Not just at this time, but ever.

What could she possibly offer in her own defense? The weak excuse that Lewis was doing it, too? That wasn't going to hold much water with a daughter who had been raised to believe that "everybody's doing it" was no excuse to lower herself.

Hannah paused and leaned against the cool wall, closing her eyes. This past week had worn her out. Age must be catching up with her, she told herself, but she didn't quite believe it. At no time in her past had she had to deal with so much in such a brief time. Witt disowning Joni, Witt's heart attack…and now Joni apparently disowning *her*. She'd felt emotionally battered and bruised before in her life, but never quite like this. Never.

What did she hope to accomplish by confronting Joni, anyway? Surely she wasn't hoping that Joni would give her some kind of absolution that would allow her to shed her disgrace and guilt? Because if so, she had no business talking to her daughter about this at all.

But no, there was Joni's relationship with Witt to consider. That was what had prompted her to tell the story in the first place. If she'd had her druthers, she would have told Witt first, but…but not when he was so sick. Although after tonight, she figured he might be able to handle the shock.

Now she didn't feel she could tell Witt without Joni's permission. So what good had she accomplished? Her intent had been to encourage Joni not to accept Witt's rejection as final. But all she'd achieved was to create another split.

Dear God. It was all her fault. She should have told Witt the truth years ago and withstood his anger at her deception. Back when Joni was small, it never would have come to this. Everything might have been different.

"Hannah?" A woman's soft voice reached her, and she opened her eyes to see Martina Escobar, a nurse she'd known for years. "Are you all right?"

"I'm fine," Hannah lied. "Just exhausted."

Martina smiled. "After taking care of Witt Matlock? I should think so. He's a handful and a half. But your daughter's fine.''

"I know." Except for the remote possibility she might still have some brain swelling. It had been a bad concussion, and Joni had been unconscious a long while. But Martina was probably right. At this point, with Joni fully awake, they were almost certainly out of the woods.

Smiling back at Martina, she straightened. "I can see her, right?"

"If you'll help me keep her awake all night, you can stay."

The teasing way Martina said it brought a small laugh to Hannah's lips, the first in what seemed like forever. "I'll help."

Moments later she was standing on the threshold of Joni's room. It was a private room, possibly because Joni was a hospital employee. Joni's face was turned toward the dark window, split by horizontal blinds set between the panes of thermal glass.

Hannah's heart squeezed with such pain that she stayed on the threshold, paralyzed by feelings too strong to bear. The reality of what had happened gripped her fully for the first time. Joni could have been killed in the accident. She could have died without ever smiling again.

Hannah would have given anything to see that happy smile again. Anything. Unfortunately, she didn't know how to accomplish it. And even if she'd had an idea, she didn't think she would trust it. All her other attempts to protect those she loved seemed to have turned into disasters.

Finally, acknowledging that hovering in the doorway wouldn't accomplish anything at all, she entered the room.

If Joni heard her, she gave no sign. She continued to stare blindly at the window. Hannah felt a sharp pang of fear.

"Joni?"

"What?"

It was an irritable, truculent question, not so very different from the way Joni had said it when she was little and feeling cranky. "How's your headache?"

"Better." But she still didn't turn to look at her mother.

"Good." Hannah approached the foot of the bed, unwilling to step into Joni's field of view until she got some sign that it was okay. "You're just like Witt," she said, trying to keep her voice light. "He's been grousing at me and throwing things since he got out of the hospital."

No response. The tide of sorrow and fear began to rise in Hannah's heart again.

"Well," she said, trying to sound brisk, "they told me I could stay here with you tonight and help keep you awake."

"I don't see why I have to stay awake." Crabby, petulant.

"Because you've had a severe concussion. They

need to keep an eye on you. If they let you just fall asleep, you might wake up dead.''

She had chosen her words with care and felt a brief surge of relief as she saw one corner of her daughter's mouth lift slightly.

"No one wakes up dead," Joni said. But not quite as irritably.

"Depends on your point of view, doesn't it?"

At last Joni turned and looked at her. "Will you please not make me laugh?"

Hannah knew such a wave of relief then that she couldn't help smiling. "Why not? Are you allergic?"

"Lately I seem to be."

"Hmm. Laughter's the best medicine, you know. If you weren't so bruised, I'd tickle you."

"Jeez, Mom!" But the frown wasn't quite convincing. And Joni had called her Mom.

"I suppose you don't want me to sit where you can actually see me, so how about I hang from the ceiling like the old bat I am?"

"Oh, cut it out." Grumpy, but not so much. Joni pointed to a chair beneath the window. "Sit there, okay? This is the only position I can get comfortable in."

Good, Hannah thought. She hadn't been thrown out, and Joni had told her to sit where she could be seen without effort. A marked improvement. The sting of tears bit at her eyes again, this time from welcome relief. She held them in, though. It was far too soon to be claiming a victory.

Slipping her jacket off, she hung it on the back of the chair. Her purse she dropped to the floor beside it. Then she sat, facing her daughter.

Joni didn't say anything, just continued to stare out the window.

Finally Hannah asked, "Can you see something out there?"

"UFOs."

Shocked, Hannah started to vault from her seat to go look for help, but Joni's voice stopped her before she fully stood.

"Take a chill pill, Mom. I'm just joking."

Not a very good joke, under the circumstances, but Hannah was willing to accept it as an olive branch. "Oh. I got scared."

"Sorry. Where's Witt?"

"I sent him home."

Joni's eyes widened. "*You* sent *him* home?"

"Yes. Why not? He was only upsetting you."

"But, Mom…" Her voice trailed off.

"But what?"

"You and Witt have been joined at the hip ever since we moved up here. We hardly ever did anything without him. He might as well have been living with us."

Hannah took a moment to look out the window and gather her thoughts. She hadn't seen it that way before. "I suppose you're right," she said finally.

"Of course I'm right. He spent almost as much

time with us as Dad did. Maybe more, because Dad
was always working.''

Or screwing around, Hannah thought with the old
resignation. She'd never told Joni about that, although Joni had figured out some of it. Not knowing
quite what to say, she asked, ''Did that bother you?''

It was Joni's turn to look thoughtful. ''I don't
think so. Well, maybe that's not true.''

When she didn't speak again, Hannah prompted
her. ''Why isn't it true?''

Joni bit her lip, then sighed. ''I don't know. I
guess there were times when I resented him, especially right after Dad died. I wanted you all to myself.''

''Oh, honey, I'm sorry!''

Joni shrugged. ''I was just being selfish, and I
knew it. I mean, I figured Dad had died, and you
needed someone, too. It was just every now and then
that I got angry. I think Karen resented it a little, too.
She'd had Witt all to herself for a few years before
we moved up here. But then we became really close
friends and it didn't seem so bad anymore.''

Hannah compressed her lips, holding in a whole
bunch of emotions, not wanting to inflict her feelings
on her daughter. ''I feel bad about that. Witt and I
thought we were replacing missing parts in your
lives. Building a family for you two.''

''I guess you were,'' Joni agreed. ''But sometimes
it didn't feel that way. But we were just kids. You
know how cockeyed kids can get.''

"Sometimes they aren't cockeyed, Joni. They're just seeing truth from a different perspective."

"Well, it doesn't matter anymore."

"Yes, I think it does," Hannah said firmly. "Especially since you were surprised that I could send Witt away. Do you think he's running my life? *Our* lives?"

Joni didn't even hesitate. "In some ways he is. Like this thing with Hardy. It's fine if he wants to hate and blame Hardy for the rest of his days. But there's no reason why *I* should be expected to."

"You're right."

"So why did we put up with it for so long?"

"I guess because we didn't want to hurt him." Which was true. Witt had always been good to them. Always. It seemed so ungrateful to fly in the face of his wishes or do something that might hurt him.

Joni stirred restlessly, then winced as something hurt. "I think I got a few more bruises than I thought."

Hannah wanted to go to her and comfort her, but she didn't feel Joni was ready for that yet. "Bruises can be so painful, can't they? Especially deep ones."

"More painful than I would have thought. Man, the seat belt must have made me black-and-blue."

"Probably."

"Hardy saved us, Mom."

Hannah nodded encouragingly.

"I'm not kidding. That car skidded, and it was going so fast, and it started to fishtail right toward us…. We'd have been dead if it had hit us. Or if Hardy had hit that snowbank at the wrong angle and we'd flipped.''

"I know.''

"Are you going to tell Witt that?''

Hannah tilted her head a little to one side. "If I don't, I suspect Hardy will. Tonight he had the look of a man who is determined to finish something. But yes, I suppose I *will* tell Witt. I've been trying to tell him for years that Hardy didn't kill Karen, so I don't suppose he's going to listen to me, but I'll try.''

"Witt feels guilty.''

Hannah acknowledged that with a nod. "We *all* feel guilty when someone we love dies. We think about what we could have done differently that might have changed the way things worked out. We wish we'd died in their place.''

Joni surprised her with the tack she took. Instead of continuing to discuss Witt, she moved to Hannah. "Did you feel that way when Dad died?''

16

Hannah had to draw a long breath and take a moment to compose herself before she could speak. She had anticipated that the conversation would move in this general direction, but she hadn't realized just how difficult and frightening it was going to be.

She was grateful when Martina came in to take Joni's vital signs and check her pupil reactions. "Looks good," Martina said, giving them each a smile. "You getting hungry, Joni? I could bring you some Jell-O."

"Jell-O? Hah."

"I know it's not much, but at least it tastes good."

"You wouldn't happen to have ginger ale or a cola, would you?"

"Sure. I'll get you some from the lounge."

"Jell-O," Joni said, wrinkling her nose after Martina had left. "Every time someone mentions that, I remember you feeding it to me when I was sick."

"You loved it!"

"That was back then."

Hannah shook her head, smiling, glad of the reprieve. Apparently Joni had forgotten the question she had asked. But the reprieve wouldn't be forever, she reminded herself. Sooner or later Joni would ask again.

So maybe she should just go ahead and answer the question. It was...

"Mom? Did you feel guilty when Dad died?"

Not much of a reprieve after all. "Yes, I suppose I did. But you have to remember, honey, that was a long time ago. I'm not very clear on exactly what I felt then."

"Hedging?"

"No, I'm not hedging. I'm just not clear. I was upset. So upset that...well, I don't remember everything that went through my head. I remember the shock when the police told me. I'll never forget that feeling. It was as if my body went numb, and my shoulders started to melt...."

She shook her head, trying to dismiss that part of the memory, because it was still so vivid. Her body was responding to it even now. "Then...well, I stayed numb for a while, at least until after the funeral. It was like a fog settled over my brain. Or maybe as if my brain had gone somewhere else and was watching from a distance while my body went through the motions. None of it seemed real."

Joni gave a very slight nod. Apparently she could remember how *she* had felt. The younger woman's face shadowed, and she said softly, "I couldn't believe it."

"I couldn't either," Hannah agreed. "I really couldn't. And it must have been so much harder for you."

"Why?"

"Because I hadn't really loved Lewis in years."

The words dropped into the stillness of the room, and Hannah could feel the ripples spreading. She wondered where they would carry her and Joni, but she was past lying anymore. Those words, which she had never said out loud before, *needed* saying. For the good of her own soul, if no one else's.

"Why not, Mom?"

"Because he'd been cheating on me since before we were married."

Joni pushed herself up against her pillow, her eyes widening. *"Before?"*

"Before," Hannah repeated flatly. "It started while we were engaged. Of course, I didn't know it until *after* we were married."

"Why in the world did he marry you, then?"

Hannah shrugged. The shrug was more to conceal her pain at the question than because she was really indifferent. "I've often wondered. I suspect it had to do with the fact that I was a nurse and held a decent job so he could live a whole lot better. The other woman didn't work at all. She came from a wealthy family and didn't need to."

Joni's expression saddened even more. "When did you find out?"

And just like that it came around to the situation surrounding Joni's conception. Hannah hesitated. "Are you sure you want to hear this? Do you feel well enough?"

"I'm supposed to stay awake all night, Mom. This discussion is more likely to accomplish that than TV is."

One corner of Hannah's mouth lifted. "Fair enough. But it's not pretty. I'm still ashamed."

Joni didn't say anything, which, Hannah supposed, meant she was keeping her judgments in reserve until she heard the whole story. It was the best she could hope for.

"We'd been married a couple of years," she began, hoping she could hang on to her calm until she finished the whole sordid thing. "Your father was in his third year of medical school. We were at a New Year's party on campus, a really big one. Most of the med students were there, plus all their dates. Witt was in town because he was having some marital problems and wanted time to think about things before he went home, so we took him with us."

"What kind of marital problems?"

"I don't really know. He never told me. He said it was private, and he just needed some time away."

"Okay." Joni sighed and closed her eyes for a moment. "Oops. I'm not allowed to do that."

"Not for a while, honey."

"So go on. You went to the party."

"Yes. I had a couple of drinks. Witt had more than a couple, I think. He pretty much kept to himself, brooding in a corner. At some point I realized I hadn't seen Lewis in a while. So I went looking for him. And I found him."

Joni sat up. "That was when…?"

"That was when. I walked in on him in the middle of making love to this woman. I stood there, shocked and angry and confused and hurt, while they scrambled to cover themselves. I didn't say a word.

"Then the woman said to me, 'Get used to it, honey. He loved me before he even met you.'"

"Oh my God," Joni breathed.

"I looked at Lewis and…" Hannah's voice broke, then steadied. "And he didn't deny it. I ran. I had a couple of drinks, trying to drown the pain. I don't exactly remember the rest too clearly, except that I told Witt all about it, and he got upset, and somehow we wound up in another building. He held me while I cried, swearing he was going to teach Lewis a lesson and… There's no excuse, Joni. No excuse. I don't know if I was too drunk, if Witt was too drunk, if we were just angry and hurt and wanting to get even or what. But we made love. And conceived you. And afterward…afterward we swore we'd never tell anyone what we'd done because we both felt… ashamed of ourselves."

Joni nodded, wincing as her headache reminded

her of the concussion. "I've got to stop doing that. So what happened then?"

"We went back to the party. Witt rounded up Lewis and insisted we go home. Nobody said a word, not that night or the next day. It was as if we were all robots. Then, a couple of days later, Lewis told me he'd made a huge mistake, that he was getting rid of the bimbo, and it would never happen again."

"But it did."

"Well, I didn't find out about it immediately. I spent the next month trying to believe what he said, partly, I guess, because of what I'd done with Witt. I mean, who was I to criticize?"

"Come off it, Mom. It wasn't exactly the same thing as a long-term affair."

"I was still unfaithful. I had to deal with that. Anyway, things with Lewis seemed to be improving. We even started having sex again. And I was pregnant. I knew that. I knew it within a week. And I knew it wasn't Lewis's baby."

Hannah sighed and looked away, casting her mind back as best she could to that discovery. "I agonized for days about whether to tell Lewis. Then, finally, I realized that if I told him, I'd do something worse than destroy our marriage. I'd destroy his and Witt's relationship. I couldn't bring myself to do that. Witt doted on Lewis, and Lewis worshiped Witt. I couldn't do anything to mess that up. So I never told either of them. It was better just to let everyone believe you were Lewis's."

Joni didn't say anything for a while. She lay back on her pillow and stared out the window. Presently she said, "How long before Dad cheated again?"

"I don't really know. I didn't find out about it until a few years later. I think you were four at the time."

"Why didn't you leave?"

"Because I felt so guilty. Because you loved your daddy. Because, frankly, I'd gotten to the point where Lewis couldn't hurt me anymore. I just plain didn't care. Something…something inside me was dead, Joni. That's the only way I can explain it."

"You have no idea," Joni said, "how often I wondered why you put up with his cheating like that."

Hannah drew a sharp breath. "You knew?"

"Sure. I didn't say anything, because I had the feeling you didn't want me to know. But I knew. From the time I was eleven, I knew. It was obvious. And I just couldn't figure out why you didn't tell him to get lost. On the other hand, I lived in terror that you would. Because I *did* love him."

"I know you did." A tear rolled down Hannah's cheek. "I know you did."

Silence fell over the room. The early winter night seemed to creep inside with them, and Hannah felt the chill in her heart. She'd made so many mistakes, apparently more than she'd even realized. And she could no longer figure out which was the worst one. Maybe they were all equally heinous. Certainly they all had caused enough pain.

Right now, healing all those wounds looked like an insurmountable task. She might, with time, persuade Joni to forgive her, but then there was Witt. He was such a hardheaded man, and she could anticipate his anger. And his refusal to ever forgive her. But for his sake and Joni's, she had to confess as soon as it seemed safe.

But not yet. Deep inside she felt she had to settle things with Joni first, to be sure that Joni stood on a firm base from which to meet the uproar with Witt. Never mind what it did to Hannah; she needed to be sure Joni was going to be okay.

"Mom?"

"Yes?"

"Why didn't you and Witt ever marry? Really."

Hannah didn't know how to answer that. "I'm not sure we have that kind of relationship."

"The spark was there once."

"A long time ago."

"But you love each other. I can see it in everything about you two."

Hannah sighed. "I don't know. Maybe we both feel guilty for what happened. Maybe that settled the whole thing forever."

Joni sighed and turned her head a little, so that she was looking away. "People are so stupid."

"People make mistakes. It's how we learn. I wouldn't call it stupidity."

"You're probably right. I think I have a tendency to see things too much in black and white."

"We all do when we're young. The curse of getting old seems to be that everything starts to look dingy shades of gray."

"You're not old."

Hannah smiled at her daughter but said quite honestly, "Sometimes I feel older than those mountains out there."

Joni remained quiet for a few minutes. Just as Hannah began to wonder if she'd fallen asleep, Joni spoke.

"Have you ever been happy, Mom? Ever?"

"I'm content."

"That isn't what I asked. I asked if you've ever been *happy*. It's not the same thing as contentment."

Hannah didn't quite know how to answer that. Happy? She'd always equated it with being content. But Joni didn't, and thinking about it, she realized there *was* a difference. "I've been happy at times," she finally said slowly."

"But not in my memory. I can't remember when you ever seemed to feel on top of the world."

"That's a hard place to reach."

"Maybe." Joni frowned. "I want to be happy. I don't mean deliriously happy. But I want more than contentment. I'd like a little joy, too."

Hannah nodded. She didn't have the heart to tell her daughter that she was looking for the end of the rainbow. Life didn't let people feel that way for long, or often.

But as soon as she had the thought, she realized

that there was something wrong with thinking that way. Had she really allowed the disappointments in her life to skew her so much? It wasn't as if there had been that many.

"Mom? What was your childhood like? You never talk about it."

"There isn't much to tell. I was born on the reservation. You know that. And my mom died when I was four, so I don't remember much about her. A cousin who lived in Pueblo took me in."

"Was she nice?"

"Nice enough. I had no complaints." Which wasn't exactly true. The cousin had taken care of the basics, but grudgingly, never failing to remind Hannah that she was a charity case. "She was an old woman. It wasn't easy for her. But I never did without anything." Except, maybe, love.

"What about your father? Why didn't he keep you?"

"He was long gone, I guess. I don't even know who he was, and my cousin would never speak of him."

"Oh." Joni's gaze moved to the window again, and it seemed to Hannah that her face had saddened.

"It doesn't matter," Hannah said. "I never knew him, so I couldn't really miss him. Oh, I suppose I missed the idea of having a father, but I couldn't miss *him,* if you understand."

Joni nodded. "And this cousin never spoke a word?"

"Not about him. She talked about my mother some, usually saying she was a good-for-nothing, but I never knew why. I asked her once, and she'd say, 'It don't matter, just don't you turn out like her.'"

"Ouch."

Hannah smiled faintly. "It was a good enough answer to keep me from asking again."

"I bet. So basically you had a hard childhood."

"Not really. I was never abused."

"But you were lonely."

Joni's perspicacity surprised her. With that surprise came the realization that she was accustomed to thinking her daughter was utterly self-centered. Maybe some of that was starting to wear off with increasing maturity. "I suppose I was. I pretty much kept to myself until I went to nursing school. I made some good friends there."

"And then you met Dad. Lewis."

"Yes." Hannah smiled softly as she remembered. "He was exciting. He made me feel dizzy and high and special. I'd never felt like that before." Then she grimaced. "I suppose I should have been leery. It should have dawned on me that I couldn't be the only one he charmed out of her socks."

"But even then, why would you think he was taking advantage of everyone he charmed?"

"I don't know." Hannah sighed. "It never occurred to me. I just assumed he was showering me with all that attention because he thought I was special. And I guess he did. For a while."

She twisted her hands together and watched her fingers grip each other. "You know, Joni, I know what that woman said, and that Lewis never denied it. But...I sometimes wonder what *I* did wrong. He married *me,* after all, and I'm sure he could have taken his pick of nurses. So there must have been something else about me that drew him. And somewhere along the way, I must have ruined it."

Moving cautiously, Joni sat up and swung her legs over the side of the bed. Just then Martina returned with a cold can of 7UP. "Sorry, she said breezily. "No ginger ale. Hope this will do."

"That's great, thanks," Joni said with pleasure. "I don't know how I can be so thirsty when I'm on an IV."

"An IV doesn't do much for the cotton in your mouth, especially when you're talking. And what the heck are you doing getting out of bed?"

"I wanted to hug my mother."

Hannah's cheeks warmed with pleasure.

Martina put her hands on her hips. "So tell her to come over here."

"And I wanted to go to the bathroom."

"You know you're supposed to have somebody with you. Right beside you. So..."

"I'll do it," Hannah said. "I haven't forgotten all my nursing skills."

Martina relaxed. "Fine. But if I find out she's been cheating, I'm gonna sit on her."

When Martina was gone, Joni pulled the tab of the soft drink and drank thirstily.

"That's going to leave an aftertaste," Hannah said.

"I don't care. I can have water then. Right now I just want to clean out my mouth."

After Hannah had escorted her to the bathroom and back to bed, Joni used the switch to put the head of the bed up higher.

"You're feeling better," Hannah noted.

"The headache's letting up a little bit. And I've got more questions I want to ask."

Hannah realized she'd been hoping that Joni was done for now. She had been feeling emotionally worn-out even before she'd learned of the accident, just from dealing with Witt and the rupture with Joni. Since then, she'd drained her reserves even lower, until now she didn't know if she had an ounce left to run on.

But she didn't want to postpone this talk, either. They were rolling, and it felt as if they were actually moving forward *together,* as if Joni was beginning to understand. It would be a mistake to halt this now.

Joni spoke. "Maybe you're being too hard on yourself. Maybe you didn't do anything to ruin it, Mom. Maybe he was just the kind of guy who couldn't be content for long."

"But why did he pick *me?*" It was a question that had plagued Hannah for a long, long time, but even as she said it, she knew it was unfair to ask it of Joni.

How could Joni possibly know any more about it than Hannah did?

"I don't know, Mom. Any more than you do. But you're a beautiful, exotic-looking woman. Maybe he found some kind of thrill in that. Or maybe he felt he could take advantage of you more than the others. Or maybe he just thought he really loved you. Only he wasn't the kind of guy who could love any one person for long."

Hannah sighed. "I'm sorry. I shouldn't have asked you that question."

Joni shrugged. "Why not? It's helping me understand some of what happened. The point is, I don't think you should take responsibility for *his* failings. At least that's what they taught me in psych class," she qualified almost ruefully.

Hannah smiled back at her. "That's what I heard, too. Funny how we do it anyway."

"Yeah." Joni wiggled on the bed and took another sip of her 7UP. "You don't have to stay with me all night, Mom. It's going to be long."

"Only because you can't sleep. And I *want* to be here."

"Thanks."

Silence fell again, but this time not as chilling as it had felt earlier. Hannah, who was willing to hug even slender hopes to her breast, hugged the awareness that Joni wasn't getting angry with her but instead was actually trying to make her feel better. But something else needed saying, and she said it.

"Honey, I'm sorry I hurt you."

Joni nodded and for a little while looked out the window. "I was hurt," she said finally. "Not in the way people usually mean when they say they're hurt. It's not as if you did something intended to wound me. But...I was hurt. Because things were different. It was like an earthquake. Afterward so much is tilted and askew. My whole world looked that way."

"I imagine so."

"Then there was doubt. Namely, how much of what I thought I knew was true? I felt almost like I didn't have any foundation at all."

Hannah nodded. "Yes. I understand that."

"But, I guess...well, it's not as if some stranger is my father. It's Uncle Witt. Of course, right now, I don't like him very much."

"Right now *I* don't like him very much."

Joni's eyebrows lifted. "Really?"

"Really," Hannah said frankly. "He's being a pain in the ass."

Hannah rarely talked that way, and a startled laugh escaped Joni.

"Well, it's true," Hannah said. "He disowned you over a little thing like passing the bid to Hardy."

"I thought you didn't approve of my doing that."

"Well, I didn't, because I felt your first loyalty should have been to Witt. But what harm was done? He could still turn down the bid. It certainly wasn't worth disowning you."

"I don't know, Mom. I was impulsive. Angry at

the way...well, don't think me harsh and uncaring, but Karen's been shadowing our lives for a long time now. Even Dad's death didn't shadow my life the way Karen's has. At least, not for as long. There's something...not right about it.''

Hannah sighed. ''I think we've had this discussion, honey, but you need to understand that losing a child is far, far worse than losing a wife or friend. It's as if the whole soul rebels, because it seems so unnatural.''

''Maybe. But that doesn't justify the amount of anger and hate Witt is carrying around, or the fact that he's using it to control me.''

''He's not controlling you. He just didn't want you to associate with Hardy.''

''But Hardy used to be my friend, Mom. And Witt never took that into account, did he? Anyway, it's not his fault I feel shadowed. Not completely, anyway.''

Hannah wanted to pursue that, but before she could, Joni asked another question. ''So Witt's really been bugging you since he got out of the hospital, huh?''

''Oh, yeah. He's been impossible, but I think he's more scared than anything.''

''Maybe. Although it's hard to imagine Witt scared.''

''That's because he always gets angry.''

''Sheesh. Men.'' Joni sighed in disgust.

Hannah shrugged. ''They're different.''

"Sometimes. Hardy isn't. Well, Hardy's just special in a lot of ways."

"Oh?"

"Yeah. He actually listens to me." Joni's face darkened a little. "Of course, he told me it was time for me to grow up."

Hannah wisely kept silent. She suspected that whether she agreed or disagreed with Hardy's assessment, Joni was going to get angry with her. Although part of her agreed with Hardy. Joni was only twenty-six, young still. Certainly young enough to tend to see things in black and white. Young enough to charge full tilt into situations she didn't totally understand. Young enough to be unwilling to compromise.

Yet, even from the vantage of Hannah's greater years, that didn't look like such a bad thing. She envied Joni's passion and commitment, even if it *did* need to be tempered a little with experience.

But her comments about Hardy were interesting in and of themselves. Back when Joni had been in high school, Hannah had suspected that Joni was sweet on Hardy, even though he was dating Karen. Hannah had never mentioned it, and Joni had never acted on those feelings, but it had still been apparent, to Hannah at least, that Joni felt something other than friendship when she looked at Hardy.

She wondered if Joni was feeling guilty about that, if that was the reason she'd chosen in such a startling way to stand up to Witt over Hardy. Maybe. But she didn't know how to ask without upsetting Joni all over again.

The idea, though, that Karen had shadowed all their lives—well, Joni was right about that. Karen had, if only because of Witt. And she really couldn't blame Joni for trying to break free. Although she wondered why Joni hadn't taken the easy route and simply moved away.

That thought brought her right back to Hardy. Apparently Joni still felt some of that longing for him. Maybe was feeling a fresh case of it. It wouldn't be surprising.

But, God, what a tempest that would raise with Witt. And Hannah, feeling extraordinarily worn-out emotionally, honestly didn't know if she could handle it.

But it wasn't her decision. Joni was going to do what Joni chose to do. Time to buckle her mental seat belt.

Instead of pursuing the potentially disastrous subject of Hardy, she returned to her first concern. "Do you understand better now, honey? Do you think you might be able to forgive me?"

"It's not my place to forgive you," Joni said. "But…I'll have to think about it, Mom. I'm still not sure."

Hannah's heart went tumbling down another rocky slope. "Why?"

"Because…because I'm still not sure how I feel about it. It's…I don't know. It's like everything I believed just came crashing down around my head and I'm standing in the rubble trying to figure out what I can salvage.''

Hannah was past tears. She asked herself what she had expected. All the explanations in the world didn't make her feel any less guilty or ashamed, so why should she expect them to change Joni's mind? It was a ridiculous hope.

''I'm sorry,'' Joni said. ''I…need time to absorb all this.''

At least the door wasn't closed. And for that, Hannah would have to settle.

17

Hardy couldn't wait for morning to check on Joni. The longer he stayed away, the more concerned he grew. Hell, she'd had a serious concussion. Enough to knock her out for almost two hours. That was nothing to treat lightly. In fact, it was serious enough that the hospital was keeping her overnight. What if her brain started to swell?

Barbara tried to soothe him, but she wasn't a doctor, and nothing she said made much of an impact, not even when she pointed out that Joni had her family and didn't need miscellaneous friends showing up.

The idea of her family merely made him snort. Some family. Moreover, he didn't think of himself as a miscellaneous friend. Not anymore. Not after the past week.

Finally Barbara cocked her head to one side. "Okay, okay. Finish your tea and go. But don't blame me if you and Witt get into it again."

"Witt's not there. Hannah sent him home."

"Really?" Barbara looked curious. "I wonder why?"

"I suspect it had something to do with the fact that he confronted me, and Joni told him to get out."

Barbara's mouth curved in a smile. "I like that young woman more with each passing day."

"Of course you do. She's taking *my* side."

"No." Barbara shook her head. "She's standing up to Witt. And it's high time *somebody* did."

"You're not suggesting I do that, are you?"

"No." Her brief laugh was rueful. "It'll come in its own good time, I suppose, but I don't want you seeking it out."

"I don't go looking for trouble, Mom. You know that. I don't need to. Trouble enough seems to find *me.*"

And it was all too true, he thought as he drove back toward the hospital through the frigid night, his tires crunching on snow and ice. All too true. Look at the accident with Joni. He just couldn't seem to avoid the stuff.

It was as if he was carrying a private curse around with him, fating him to terrible experience with the Matlock family. But as soon as he had that thought, he dismissed it as lunacy. Curses didn't exist. He'd just had one of those runs of bad luck that happened sometimes to people, the kind that when you read about them in the newspaper, all you could do was shake your head.

He did, however, scan the parking lot to be sure that Witt's battered old pickup wasn't anywhere in sight. It wasn't. Relieved, he pulled up near the entrance, parked and stepped out into the icy night.

Snow crunched beneath his boots; he loved that sound. Sometimes he got sick of shoveling and blowing the nearly two hundred inches of it they got each year, but he still loved it. He loved to ski, especially cross-country, which could take him out into the wilderness away from everyone. He liked the way the cold invigorated him, making him feel truly alive and awake.

The minute he stepped through the automatic door, the cold was gone and the heat was on, making his nose and cheeks feel hot. Oh, well. Everything had a downside.

Because the hospital was small and he was well-known to everyone who worked there, he had no difficulty learning where they'd stashed Joni. He hesitated on the threshold of her room, though, when he saw that Hannah was talking.

But almost instantly she looked his way and smiled. "Come in," she said warmly. "I think Joni's getting sick of my company. She'll be glad of a fresh face. Besides, I need to go find a vending machine. I haven't eaten since breakfast."

"Downstairs, Mom," Joni said as Hardy stepped into the room. "Behind the door marked Staff Lounge. They have dried-up sandwiches, candy bars, chips, cookies…and there might even be some fresh coffee in the pot.''

Hannah rolled her eyes. ''Doesn't she make those sandwiches sound tempting?''

Joni blew a raspberry. ''The guy only gets up here once a week to restock them. Draw your own conclusions.''

Hardy stepped aside to let Hannah pass, then looked at Joni, feeling strangely diffident. ''I hope it was okay to come by?''

''Sure. Why wouldn't it be?''

''I don't know. Maybe because I was driving the car when you got hurt.''

She shook her head. ''It wasn't your fault. If you hadn't handled your car so well, we'd probably both be dead.''

He sighed and went to stand at the window, seeing nothing but his own reflection against the night and the opened blinds. Shoving his hands into his pockets, he said, ''I've been rehearsing that maneuver for twelve years.''

Joni drew a sharp breath. He didn't want to look at her for fear of what he might see.

''Ever since the night Karen was killed, I've wondered what I could have done differently. It's been…haunting me.''

''It's haunted us all. Don't tell me you think the accident was your fault.''

''No.'' He shook his head, shifting his attention from his own reflection to hers. It seemed safer than looking at her. "No, I don't think it was my fault. But I haven't been able to stop wondering what I might have done differently. I practiced maneuvers in my mind until I felt as if they were engraved on my muscles. And sometimes I'd go out on an empty road and try them out."

"Oh, Hardy!"

"Anyway, now I know. If I'd had more experience, I might have been able to save Karen's life."

Silence answered him. It was a deep silence. He couldn't hear Joni breathe or stir against the sheets. The silence went on so long that he grew concerned. He turned at last, afraid she might be unconscious, and found her looking at him with tears running down her cheeks.

"What's wrong?" he asked, his heart suddenly pounding. "Does your head hurt?"

"You're still in love with Karen, aren't you?" Then she turned her face away.

His instinct was to answer no. He hadn't been in love with Karen when she died; why would he be in love with her now?

But he didn't answer quickly. Instead, he forced himself to consider her accusation, to weigh it carefully against everything in his heart.

"No," he said minutes later. "No. I'm in *guilt* with Karen."

"It's not much different, is it?" she said in a muffled voice, keeping her face averted. "You and Witt both. You're stuck to her memory and living in the past. And you're never going to be free.''

There was a certain justice in what she said, much as it stung. But because it stung, he couldn't ignore it.

"What do you want me to do, Joni? Pretend it never happened? Slough off my guilt as if I don't care? It's not that easy!''

"No, it isn't," she shot back. "I know it isn't. I've been living with guilt, too. But you couldn't have saved Karen's life back then, no matter what you say now, because you didn't have the *experience* when you were eighteen!''

"I know that. Do you think I don't feel that every day?''

"Then what is the point, Hardy?" she asked sadly. "What is the point? To find new ways to beat yourself up so you can keep it all fresh?''

The words hit him like a slap. He didn't like seeing himself as someone who kept picking at an old wound to keep it fresh. But then he realized something else, and it drove him to say, "Is that what *you're* doing, Joni?''

"I guess so," she said weakly, and turned her face away again. "I guess so.''

"But why? You didn't have anything to do with Karen's death. Nothing at all. There's nothing for you to feel guilty about?''

"No?'' She sniffled and wiped at her eyes. "I coveted you. I used to imagine taking you away from her. I feel guilty, all right.''

''Surely you don't think that had anything to with Karen dying....'' But even as he spoke, the words trailed off. He knew that was part of the reason he felt so guilty himself.

''I wasn't a good friend,'' she said, wiping away more tears. ''I wasn't a good friend to her.''

He stood there, trying to decide whether to reveal the darkest secret in his heart. Which really wasn't so much worse than hers. But he knew the guilt it was causing him. Maybe she wouldn't feel so bad if she knew....

So he spoke, putting his trust in her understanding. ''I was...going to break up with Karen that night.''

At first he thought she didn't hear him. She kept right on sniffling and watching her tears fall on the sheet. Just as he was about to repeat himself, she looked up.

''What?'' she said. It wasn't a confused question. It held the ring of disbelief.

''I said, I was going to break up with her that night.''

Her eyes widened, then closed, and she breathed a strained, ''My God.''

''Yeah. It really messed things up, frankly.''

''Had you told her yet?''

''No.'' He shook his head firmly. ''I was going to save it until I dropped her off. I didn't want her to be stuck somewhere with me, with no place to go hide if she wanted to.''

"So she never knew." Joni started to shake her head, then winced. "My God."

"It makes me a real slimeball, doesn't it? I had a lot of fun with Karen, but…" He couldn't bring himself to tell the whole truth. "I knew it wasn't love."

"She was certainly in love with you!"

"She thought she was. Hell, for a while I thought I was in love with her. But it was puppy love, Joni. It wasn't ready for reality. It was based on having a great time together on weekends. Having fun hanging out. Not on anything real. And quite frankly, looking back at it, I think half the reason Karen hung around with me was because it angered her father."

Joni picked at the blanket that covered her, pulling little balls of fuzz off it. "Maybe," she said after a while. "It's possible. I know she seemed angry with Witt a lot, but I thought it was because of you."

"Probably was. I don't claim to be a mind reader. And it was a long time ago. Maybe I've amended my memories."

She lifted her gaze to him. "It's possible. I don't know how much of what I remember is real anymore. I've played it all over in my head so many times. How do I know I haven't rationalized a whole bunch of things? But if she was angry with Witt over something other than you, she never told me what it was."

"She used to complain that he watched her like a hawk, as if she might go up in smoke at any moment.'' As soon as he said the words, he felt a shiver run down his spine. Had Witt had a premonition?

''Well,'' said Joni, ''that was understandable. He'd lost his wife and brother. Naturally he was scared he might lose Karen.''

It sounded reasonable. But Hardy still couldn't quite shake the chill that had come over him. He told himself it was a crazy feeling, that there was no way Witt could have known or even guessed that Karen was going to die.

But then he found himself remembering his craziness in those last few weeks before the accident. That feeling of almost suffocating under a dark cloud. Of the need to get away and get away fast. He'd thought it was because it was time to move on, but what if...?

What if? So what *if?* If he'd been able to read the future in tea leaves, he would have broken off with her sooner. He never would have taken her out that night. But the impending sense of doom had been so amorphous that he'd put it down to a mood. Teenagers had moods all the time. He'd managed to realize that by the age of eighteen and had stopped putting a whole lot of stock in them.

But what if Witt had...no. Witt had believed from the outset that Hardy was bad for Karen. That, combined with two grievous personal losses, would have been enough to make Witt paranoid.

''Hardy?'' Joni's voice interrupted his thoughts. ''What's wrong?''

He almost groused, "What isn't?" but caught himself in time. Joni didn't deserve that. "Just remembering. Wondering about things. But there'll never be any answers, so what's the point?"

"No, there won't be." She shifted against her pillow and sighed. "Somehow we all need to just let go of this. We all made mistakes. We all did things we're not proud of. But…we all must feel that when someone we love dies. I think everyone must sit around wishing they hadn't done this or wishing they *had* done that."

"Probably."

"So we're not all that weird."

He pulled the chair away from the wall and dragged it around to where he could see her better. "Except for hanging on to this thing for so long."

"So how do we let go?"

"I don't know." He rubbed his chin and sighed heavily. "I don't know, Joni. Everything that's happened since you gave me that bid package has only seemed to make it all fresh again. As fresh as it ever was."

"God. That wasn't what I wanted to do at all."

"I know." He felt his mouth trying to smile at her, but he wasn't ready to smile at anyone. About anything. He felt as if he were sitting on a psychic minefield, waiting for the next explosion. But he couldn't be the only one feeling that way. Joni probably did, too, to judge by the things she'd been say-

ing. And maybe even Witt. Although Witt had always been a great big minefield.

"Listen," he said abruptly, suddenly needing to
get away for a few minutes. "I'm going to go see
what's taking your mom so long. Maybe she needs
a chain saw for that sandwich. I'll be right back."

Joni obligingly laughed, but her eyes were haunted
as they followed him from the room.

Haunted. The word fit them all, Hardy thought as
he went looking for the staff break room.

But he couldn't blame Karen for that. She had
been a sweet girl, with a genuinely kind heart. And
while she'd also had a wild streak that led her to fly
in the face of her father's dictates, that wasn't so
weird for anyone that age.

But she had had a good heart. A kind and decent
heart. The kind of heart that he sometimes thought
had made her date him just because he was something of an outcast in school because of his father.
Well, that and the fact that it was guaranteed to turn
Witt livid.

The thought almost succeeded in drawing a reluctant smile out of him. He hadn't thought of Karen as
being particularly rebellious back then, but she must
have been. He'd probably been blind to it, involved
as he had been in his own problems. Teenage ego-
tism at its best. The most real thing in any teen's life
were his own internal emotional storms.

And if that had been true of him, it had also been
true of Karen. And Joni.

Joni. Christ, imagine her having a crush on him back then. He'd thought of her primarily as Karen's younger cousin, too young to consider as serious date material. Heck, even when he'd begun noticing he was drawn to her, he'd managed to convince himself she was too young and he shouldn't even be noticing her that way. And most especially he shouldn't be noticing her that way because she was so close to Karen.

But he'd noticed anyway. Well, hell, she'd been fifteen toward the end there, and that certainly wasn't too young for an eighteen-year-old to at least notice.

But he'd never guessed she was noticing him, too. Now, looking back on it, he wondered if it would have made any difference if he *had* realized she was attracted. Maybe he would have broken off with Karen sooner?

But he doubted it. Because the things he'd started feeling about Joni back then had made him feel sleazy. Doubly so because of Karen. So he wouldn't have acted on his attraction anyway.

Then a bitter thought struck him. That high school crush of Joni's might explain why she'd made love with him last night, then leaped out of bed so convinced it was a mistake. She might have acted on the memory of the crush, then realized there was nothing left of it. Nothing to justify sleeping with him.

God, that made him feel awful. Just awful. And not simply because Joni might be disgusted with herself, but because the closeness he'd been feeling with her might have been an illusion. An illusion born of something that had been little more than illusory twelve years ago: a girl's crush.

Man, that thought hurt.

It also made him a fool, and he was never happy to discover he was a fool, especially when his foolishness hurt someone else. Then, too, he was a proud man, one who preferred never to do anything he was ashamed of. Right now, he felt ashamed.

He found Hannah in the break room, eating a plastic cup full of fruit salad and a small bag of chips. Coffee in a disposable cup steamed beside her.

She looked up when he entered. "Do I need to go back?"

He shook his head. "She seems okay, Mrs. Matlock. Really. I'll go back in a minute. I just needed…a moment to myself."

She lifted an eyebrow, then gestured for him to make himself comfortable. He could have sprawled on the now-empty couch, but instead he chose to sit facing her at the small table.

Finally he said, "What do you think of this whole mess?"

She dabbed her mouth with a paper towel and met his gaze. "Which mess?"

"The whole mess. All the way back to Karen."

"Ah." Her dark eyes grew gentler. "It's a mess, all right."

"Do you think I killed Karen?"

"No. Nobody but Witt thinks that."

Hardy sighed and rubbed his chin. Two days' growth of stubble rasped noisily, and he stopped, looking rueful. "That's nice to hear. I still blame myself."

"Of course you do. Survivors tend to do that."

He nodded. "Doesn't make me feel any better. So...do you mind me hanging out with Joni?"

"Not at all. I think she's missed your friendship."

Hardy realized he'd missed Joni's, too. All these years... "But what about Witt?"

"Witt is an ass," Hannah said bluntly. "A lovable, redeemable ass, but still an ass."

Hardy had to laugh. The smile that accompanied it seemed to ease all the terrible tension in his face, neck and soul. "Yeah. He is."

"But only about this," Hannah cautioned. "Don't ever mistake the man for a fool. He's just got this one awful blind spot." She sighed and stirred some half-and-half into her coffee. "I don't know what in the world to do about it. I've certainly argued with him more than once. All he hears is his own pain."

Hardy drummed his fingers once, quickly, on the table. "I can understand that."

"So can I. I love the man dearly, but this is...well, it's been a big problem for a long time. He's clinging to his grief past reason. And I'm still trying to figure out why. There *has* to be a reason."

"Maybe. Or maybe it just hurts that bad."

Hannah shook her head. "No. He's nursed that

pain and anger. He's tended it like a fire he's afraid to let go out. I just wish I could figure out why.''

Hardy shrugged. ''Beats me. I know Karen thought he was too strict, but what teen doesn't feel that way about their parents? I still wonder sometimes if she dated me just to make him mad.''

''It wouldn't surprise me. Joni had some spells of that, too. And Karen was far more rebellious than Joni. At least back then.'' Her expression turned wry. ''She's done quite a bit of catching up over the years.''

''She sure has.'' A kind of admiration filled him. ''But she was always impulsive and stubborn.''

''True. But not to this degree.''

''Well, I don't think she ever stood up to Witt before. Has she?''

''Never. Maybe it was high time.'' Hannah sipped her coffee, then set the cup down. ''Witt's autocratic. Always has been. Maybe it comes from having so much responsibility thrust on him. I know there were times when I resented it. Lewis was married, I was working, and Witt still insisted on paying for Lewis's medical school. That was generous and kind, of course, and I'm not knocking it, but the fact that he kept slaving to earn all that extra money when he had a wife and child of his own…it made me feel bad. Made us both feel indebted. And gave him a shoe in the door to comment on everything.''

Hardy nodded slowly. ''But you still love him.''

''Yes, I do. You see, his intentions were good,

Hardy. The best. He didn't want Lewis living off me. Felt it was a bad setup for both of us." She shrugged. "It ended up that way anyway. We just lived better than a lot of other students." She looked down, staring into her cup as if she might find answers there. "After…after things went south with Lewis and me, I found myself wondering if Witt hadn't suspected that Lewis was just using me. I never did reach a conclusion about that. Most likely it was a mixture of motivations. Anyway, Witt was just trying to prevent Lewis from taking advantage of me."

"I can understand that." Hardy felt a sharp, unexpected pang of sympathy for the woman. Given what Joni had told him, he suspected her marriage had been no bed of roses.

Hannah glanced up. "Witt didn't succeed, but it wasn't his fault. It was mine. I let myself be used."

Hardy didn't know how to respond to that. He couldn't argue with her, because he didn't know all that she knew. But agreeing seemed cruel and pointless.

"Anyway," Hannah said after a few seconds, "Witt meant well. He usually means well. There's just this one problem, and I don't know what to do about it. He's being irrational."

"Maybe…" Hardy hesitated and cleared his throat. This was a stupid idea. Crazy. But he said it anyway. "Maybe I should talk to him."

Both of Hannah's dark eyebrows lifted. "He'll just get furious."

"Well, I can get as loud as he can. Maybe if you're there... I don't know. It's just been bugging me that the two of us have never really had it out. It's like unfinished business, and maybe he feels the same. But then...well, he's sick. I guess it's not a good idea."

Hannah sat thoughtfully for a few minutes. Although he hadn't seen a whole lot of her over the intervening years, because of Witt, he still remembered that thoughtfulness of hers. Back in their teen years, she'd been something of a mother to Karen, and both he and Karen had come to trust Hannah's thoughtful, quiet, composed way of looking at the universe. Karen had often said she could talk to Hannah about anything and never get fireworks, not even little sparklers, the way she always did from her dad.

Joni had felt the same way, he recalled. For his own part, he'd used Hannah as a sounding board when needed. She'd always seemed like the calm in the middle of a storm at a time when life had seemed to be a series of typhoons.

"You know," Hannah said, "I'm not sure we need to protect Witt that much. He's had a couple of angry eruptions that haven't seemed to affect his health. In fact, I'd say he's pretty much recovered. Except for his attitude."

"Attitude? What's wrong?"

"He's terribly depressed. And he's refusing to change his eating habits to something healthier."

Hardy nodded. He could understand the eating

habits part. He would find it pretty hard himself to part with thick, rare steaks. "But wasn't anger what caused the attack?"

"It appeared to be. But in the final analysis, no one can really say. There was no serious damage to his heart muscle, no evidence of a clot…basically, they think he had a serious arrhythmia. They're treating that."

"Still…" Hardy had enough on his conscience. He did *not* need to risk causing Witt another heart attack.

Hannah nodded. "Still. Well, I'm going to speak to him. If he starts to get too irate, I'll shut up. But he rarely blows up that way with me, Hardy."

"But what good will it do for you to talk to him? You've talked to him about this before, haven't you?"

"Yes. But this time I'm going to make the old fool hear reason. And I'm going to make sure he'll sit down and talk with you. Joni was right about that. It's high time."

18

Joni was released from the hospital around noon the next day. Hardy picked her up.

"Where's my mom?" she asked when he walked into the room.

"The vet had an emergency and needed her." He looked pained. "Afraid to drive with me again?"

"No!" Joni was appalled that he should think such a thing. Then she realized that asking where her mom was could have implied a whole lot of things to him, none of them flattering. "I'm sorry. It's just that last night she said she'd be picking me up."

"I'm a poor second, I know. But I rode here on my brand-new trusty charger...."

That piqued her curiosity. "You got a new car? Already?"

"Didn't have much choice. I can't get much work done if I can't get around when I need to. Come on, I think you'll like it."

It was at least something different to think about.

Most of the night, with Hardy sitting beside her, trying to keep her awake, her mind had gone on worrying about the same old problems, round and round like a carousel she couldn't get off.

"Maybe I need to see a shrink," she announced as they crunched across the icy, snowy parking lot.

"Why?"

"Oh, well, how about the fact that my mind keeps running in circles over the same stuff all the time?"

"Obsess much?"

He said it lightly, and she couldn't resist smiling back. "It's never quite gone out of my mind, but lately...lately this whole thing with Witt is driving me nuts."

"You know what your problem is? You're a problem solver. You can't let go of things until you think you've found a way to solve them. And the closer you think you might be to a solution, the more you worry the problem. No big deal. You don't need a shrink."

She looked up at him, her cheeks already pinkening from the cold. "You don't think so?"

"Hell no. Look at Witt and me. Why would *you* be exempt?"

Another smile helped lift her spirits as he made her feel better. Hardy, she thought, was so good to her. So understanding. So kind. A flicker of dismay went through her as she remembered how she had acted only the night before last, running from him like some crazy kid after they made love.

Then her eyes fell on a cherry-red Suburban, so new it had hardly picked up any dirt from the snowy roads. "Is that it? *That?*"

"Yup. I kinda went hog-wild."

"Red? Oh, Hardy, you always wanted a red car. Always!" She couldn't help clapping her mittened hands together with delight.

He laughed. "Well, yeah. Except that I originally envisioned different lines, you know? Something lower, more aerodynamic, with twin chrome exhaust pipes and an engine that rumbled with power…. You know. A Corvette. Or a Mustang. Or…"

She laughed with him. "Our priorities change."

He half shrugged. "I guess. I have to carry a lot of junk with me to job sites these days. The gas mileage ain't nothin' to write home about, but this baby can handle just about anything."

She approached the vehicle, admiring it. But the instant he opened the passenger door for her, all thoughts of the cherry-red Suburban went out of her mind. On the gray cloth seat was a florist's box.

Her heart fluttering, she turned slowly and looked at him.

"That's for you," he said offhandedly.

Her hands were suddenly shaking, and her knees felt like rubber. It was just flowers, she told herself. Just flowers. It didn't mean anything….

But she lifted the top of the box and wondered how it could possibly be meaningless. A dozen long-stemmed roses looked back at her, a dozen *red* roses.

Not yellow or pink or white, but *red*. Her heart thumped so hard it seemed about to leap out of her breast. "Hardy?" She spoke his name almost tentatively. Afraid of anything he might say. Anything at all.

"I hope you like them," he said, sounding awkward.

"Like them? I love them! But you didn't have to."

"I *wanted* to."

She faced him then, her heart beating a rapid tattoo, her body suddenly remembering the night they had spent together. Why was she remembering that now? She tried to quell the gooey warm feeling that seemed to be spreading through her, but failed. Her body seemed to be reaching out to him, as did her heart, but her mind was screaming, *No, this is not right!* "But...*red* roses...." She wanted to believe they really meant something but was terrified of believing it all at the same time.

He looked down. "I never felt like giving anybody red roses before."

Her heart slammed again, then climbed up into her throat. Her mind shrieked warnings to get out of there now, because only trouble could lie ahead, but her feet remained glued to the parking lot.

He sighed almost inaudibly, then said, "I'm sorry I upset you at the motel. But I don't regret it. I'll never regret it."

Then, before her scattered thoughts could come up

with a single thing to say, he leaned toward her and kissed her.

He probably meant it to be a light, brotherly kiss, but her body and heart weren't going to settle for that. She melted into him, every cell and fiber of her being softening as if they wanted to become part of him.

Then his arms closed around her, and it felt good, so good, to be held by him, to feel his strength supporting her. She felt like a flower drinking rain after a long drought.

He drew her even closer, until it almost seemed they were welded together. Joni felt every last bit of resistance in her slipping away. She had dreamed of this for so long, and who was going to say it was wrong *now?* Certainly not she.

But before the joy in her could bubble up too much, Hardy released her and stepped back. "Come on," he said. "It's cold out here. Let's go home."

Home? She didn't have a home anymore. Even after last night, she wasn't ready to consider moving back in with Hannah. It was too close to Witt. But she didn't dare ask Hardy if she could stay with him. It was too much of an imposition. Besides…he'd probably just meant that kiss to be friendly. She didn't want him to think she was going to hang all over him because of it. She'd seen other women embarrass themselves that way and had always vowed she wouldn't do it.

Sitting in the truck, with the box of beautiful roses

on her lap, she looked out the side window and felt her chest ache with a sorrow and longing so intense it almost overwhelmed her. Everything that mattered to her in life was being stripped away. Her heritage, her uncle, even the man she had believed to be her father. Everything was a sham, it seemed, most especially the word *love*.

She was afraid to glance in Hardy's direction for fear all her anguish would come spilling out and he would feel obligated to take care of her again. That was all she was to him, an obligation. All of this had started because he'd found her stuck in a snowbank and upset. Not because he wanted her in his life, but because he felt a responsibility to her. Maybe because of Karen. Maybe because that was who he was. But it had never had anything to do with *her*.

She absolutely did not want to be an obligation. That was not what she wanted from Hardy, not what she had ever wanted...but all she had ever had. He'd let her hang around him and Karen like the kid sister who had to be humored. He hadn't really *wanted* her there.

And it continued today. Everything that had happened between them had happened because of his sense of responsibility. That hurt her.

He wasn't even talking to her now, and finally she dared to glance in his direction, wondering if he was annoyed with her or just impatient to get rid of her. She couldn't read his face, unfortunately. Except that his jaw seemed a little tight.

Well, it didn't matter, she told herself. She needed to get on with her plans to find a job elsewhere and move away from all these damn shadows of the past. Enough was enough. These last few weeks seemed to have chilled her soul.

Much to her surprise, Hardy drove right by Hannah's house and took her to his own. "You're staying here," he said almost sternly. "Until Witt straightens out, I don't want him coming anywhere near you."

Still an obligation, she thought. Her throat tightened painfully, but she managed to say, "I hope you're prepared to have me hanging around for the rest of my life, then."

He looked at her, his gaze strange, almost hot and hard. He *was* angry, probably at having to rescue her again. "You might be surprised," he said flatly.

At what, she couldn't imagine. Witt was as predictable as the rain every summer afternoon. Or the snow every winter.

Hardy helped her into the house, and Barbara, who had the day off, seemed to bubble over when she saw the roses. She helped Joni put them in a large vase, then asked, "Would you like me to take them up to your room?"

Joni shook her head. "Thanks, Barbara, but they're too pretty to be hidden away. Why don't we keep them down here, where everyone can enjoy them?"

"What a sweet notion."

Hardy had already disappeared to his shop, and Joni could faintly hear him banging around. "I guess he's mad at me," Joni said as Barbara poured them both a cup of tea.

"At you?" Barbara laughed. "My dear child, no! No man gives a dozen long-stemmed roses to a woman he's angry with. No, it's not you."

Joni didn't exactly believe her. The roses were just an apology for the accident.

Barbara poured milk into her tea and returned the jug to the refrigerator. Then she sat across from Joni and reached out to cover her hand. "Honey, he's mad at Witt. He's been taking guff from that man all these years, and he never much minded it. As near as I can tell, Hardy's always believed it was what he deserved. But he doesn't figure you deserve this crap."

"But Hardy doesn't deserve the crap, either."

"You and I know that. I don't think Hardy's heart would agree, though." Hannah sighed, let go of Joni's hand and stared down into her teacup. "I've never been able to find a way to make him believe he wasn't responsible for Karen's death. He wasn't drunk. He wasn't speeding. How can it be *his* fault that some drunk drove smack into him without warning? But that's the logic of the mind, Joni. The heart's not so reasonable."

"I know." Indeed she did. She'd had plenty of unreasonable emotional reactions herself.

"But he's getting angry now, and that's a good

thing. Anger is a sign of healing. But it might be uncomfortable for the rest of us for a while.''

"Well, I'll be gone as soon as I can find a job somewhere else. It shouldn't be too difficult. I really hate to impose on you like this.''

Barbara looked at her, suddenly still. "Really? You're still going to do that?''

"Definitely. I'm through with this whole situation. My uncle…'' Her voice trembled, and she paused for a moment to gather herself. "My uncle is poisoning other people's lives. Hurting other people. He's been hurting Hardy for years, and now he's hurt me…and he's certainly hurt my mother. I want to get so far away I don't ever have to think about him again.''

In that moment Hardy's mother reminded Joni so much of Hannah that it was almost uncanny. Barbara sat silently for a minute or so, sipping her tea. When she finally spoke, her voice was calm, almost gentle.

"Joni, I'm sure you've realized that running away is never an answer, because you always carry yourself along.''

"That's what they say.'' Joni felt her throat tightening again, and she suddenly ached so badly for her mother that she could have cried. Now, right now, she needed Hannah's arms around her. "But why stay here so that Witt can scowl at me every time we meet on the street? Why do that to myself?''

Hannah nodded. "I'm not sure I have a good answer for that. But before you do anything rash, you need to be sure that getting away from Witt is enough to make up for everything else you'll be leaving. Your mother, your friends, a town where you know everyone. I understand that young people get bored in places like this, but…there's plenty that's good about Whisper Creek, too.''

''Oh, I know that. I love this place. But…'' Joni shrugged. ''I give up.''

This time Barbara didn't seem to have anything to say at all.

Hannah was getting more irritated by the minute. She couldn't find Witt anywhere. What had that damn fool man done? she wondered. Gone off to Denver? He wasn't supposed to be driving until they were sure the medicine was working. Thinking he might have returned to work, even though he wasn't cleared to yet, she called up to the mine and learned that no one had seen him, and if they had, they would have sent him home.

She checked all his haunts, from the hardware store to the saloon where he was known to bend an elbow from time to time, but no one had seen him.

Fear began to sink icy claws into her, fueling her irritation. What if he'd tried to drive somewhere but had gone off the road? But no, his car was in his driveway. What had she been thinking, letting him drive home from the hospital last night? She knew he wasn't supposed to, but had figured a mile and a half wasn't anything to worry about. At least he hadn't taken it into his head to interpret that as license to drive anywhere.

But all this ruminating was doing nothing to tell her where he'd gone. He wasn't answering his phone or door, and his car was still in the driveway. Fear whipped her hard. What if he'd had another heart attack?

She stood looking at his door and his car. He could be dead in there. Finally, not knowing what else to do, since he'd never given her the key to his place, she went home and called the police.

Earl Sanders happened to take her call. "The dispatcher called in sick this morning," he remarked philosophically. "Not to mention that half my crew seems to have the flu or something. So you get the top dog, Hannah. What's up?"

"I can't find Witt. Anywhere. And his car's in the driveway, but he's not answering the door or phone. I'm worried he might have had another heart attack."

"Hell. Sam's out in that area. Just finished up a call. I'll have him come right now. Where are you?"

"At my house. But I can run over to Witt's right now."

"You do that. Sam'll be there in two or three minutes. So will the ambulance."

She was glad he had thought of the ambulance. She'd been so worried that it hadn't even occurred to her Witt might still be alive and in need of immediate medical attention. *Stupid,* she castigated herself.

She arrived back at Witt's just as Sam Canfield was pulling up, lights flashing. He climbed out, giving her a brief wave. "When did you last see him?"

"Last night at the hospital."

"Damn." He looked at the house. "Okay. You stay back here."

He didn't explain why, although she guessed he was trying to protect her. As if she hadn't seen the dead and dying on an almost daily basis during her years as a nurse. But she had no delusion that it wouldn't be worse if it were Witt. Closing her eyes, she offered up another prayer.

Sam tried the door, pounded on it with his fist, bellowing authoritatively, "Police. Open up."

Nothing. He peered through the windows on either side of the door but apparently couldn't see anything. Just then the ambulance pulled up, and two EMTs climbed out. Jack Jessup and Hector Cortes. They were the same young men who'd been on duty the night Witt had his heart attack.

"Another heart attack?" Jessup asked her.

"I don't know."

"Just stay back a minute," Sam called to them. Then, drawing his gun, he raised his foot and kicked the door open.

With her heart in her throat, Hannah watched him enter the house, his gun at ready. Oh, God, she hadn't even considered the possibility of a crime! What if…?

But before her mind could conjure up any addi-

tional horrifying images, Sam came back out the
door, holstering his gun.

"He's inside," he said, jerking his thumb over his
shoulder. "Drunk as a skunk, snoring booze fumes,
but still alive."

Hannah started forward at once, but Jack and Hector gently restrained her. "Let us check him first,
Mrs. Matlock."

Hannah started to shake her head, then caught herself. She understood. She would only get in the way.

Sam came down the walk to stand beside her. "I
think he's okay, Hannah. He seems to be sleeping it
off."

"I am going to give that man such a piece of my
mind...." Her voice broke, and somehow she turned
into Sam. He didn't seem to have any problem with
holding her or patting her back soothingly.

"He'll be okay, Hannah. Physically, at least."
Sam made a disgusted sound. "Beats me how he
could have spent all that time with you over the years
and never once seen how much you love him."

Hannah caught her breath, and freshly formed
tears stopped spilling, hanging on her lower lashes,
threatening to freeze there. "Sam..."

"Sorry, I was out of line, but it was plain as the
nose on the damn fool's face."

Hannah started to shake her head, then stopped.
What was the point? Denying it wouldn't change the
truth. Suddenly aware that curtains were probably
twitching all around, she stepped back. No telling

what the gossips might come up with. The unfortunate thing about small-town life, especially where it snowed so much for so long, was that gossip was the stuff of social life. Sam might be ridiculously young for her, but that wouldn't keep the tongues from wagging. She didn't care for herself, but she didn't want Sam to be victimized. "Thanks," she said.

Ten minutes later, Jessup and Cortes came out of the house. "He's conscious," Cortes said. "He'll be all right, but somebody should keep an eye on him for a few hours."

Hannah mentally rolled up her sleeves, and the light of battle came into her dark eyes. "Trust me," she said, "I'll take care of that jackass."

The two men looked as if they wanted to laugh, but only Jessup made a sound, something like a strangled cough. Together, they climbed into the ambulance and sped away.

"Call if you need anything," Sam told Hannah. "I don't know if he's a belligerent drunk, but if he gives you a hard time, call. I'll be over in a jiff."

"Thanks, Sam." Then, without a backward glance, Hannah marched into the house and closed the door behind her.

Witt was sitting on the couch, regarding her from puffy, narrowed eyes. The smell of bourbon was almost overpowering. "What did you call all those people for?" he demanded.

"Oh, I don't know," Hannah said with unusual sarcasm. "It might have something to do with the fact that you had a heart attack recently and you weren't answering your door or phone. For all I knew, you were lying in here dead!''

''I'm too mean to die.''

''You know, Witt Matlock, that may be the truest thing you've ever said!''

He blinked, as if taken aback by her attitude. Well, why not? Hannah asked herself bitterly. For a long time she'd refused to let him see any part of her except the calm, measured part. Not once in all these years had she really treated him to her temper. Oh, the occasional small flash in the pan, yes, but not the full force and fury of her anger, or her contempt, or any of the other things he suddenly appeared to deserve in spades.

''What's gotten into you?'' he demanded.

''You! That's what's gotten into me. Your self-centered, self-pitying, damn-everyone-else attitude. That's what's gotten into me!''

For a few moments Witt appeared almost shocked back to sobriety. ''Hannah, what the hell's gotten into you?''

''You, Witt. You and all your bitterness and anger. Justify it how you will, you've turned into a sour old man, one willing to hurt people he claims to love, over nothing more than a difference of opinion.''

''Wait one minute! What Joni did—''

''Oh, shut up! You're drunk, and I can run circles around you right now. I don't want to hear it.''

''Then get out of my house!''

"No way, Witt. No way." Hannah dropped into a chair and folded her arms, glaring at him. "You're stuck with me, at least until you're sober."

"I told you to get the fuck out!"

"And mind your tongue while you're at it."

His glare deepened, and she realized the anger *was* clearing his head. For a moment she felt a qualm, wondering if infuriating him this way was risking his health. Then he spoke again, and everything else faded into insignificance.

"When the hell did you become such a bitch?"

"It's been growing on me for twenty-seven years. Ever since that night we betrayed Lewis."

"Oh, hell, that was no betrayal. He was screwing around on you all along. He got just what he deserved."

"You have no idea what he got. Is that why you did it, Witt? To teach him a lesson? Or to get even with him?"

"No." His eyes widened. "What the hell are you talking about? It was just one of those things. I never meant to do it. It just happened."

"So I just *happened?* Thank you so very much. It's nice to know I was just one more piece of accidental wreckage in your wake."

"Accidental wreckage?" His faced darkened. "You're crazy."

"Am I? Maybe so. Nobody in their right mind would put up with the garbage you've been dishing out over the last twenty-seven years."

"Garbage!" His glare was almost enough to cut steel. "I don't dish out garbage."

"Yes, you do. Day in and day out. Hardy didn't kill Karen, and Joni didn't commit a capital crime. Both of them are guilty of nothing but youth and caring about somebody besides you. And what the hell is your problem, anyway? You know perfectly well that that drunk driver caused the accident, not Hardy. So what's eating you, Witt? That she cared more for Hardy than for you? It was nothing but normal teenage hijinks, and if you hadn't insisted on turning it into *Romeo and Juliet*, Karen wouldn't have been sneaking out at night to see him."

"You think I don't know that?" He thundered the words and rose from the couch. Much to Hannah's surprise, he didn't even stagger as he started pacing the small room.

"So what is it, Witt?" she demanded, refusing to give quarter, the way she had always given in to him in the past. "What is it that keeps you so mad at Hardy."

"He shouldn't have taken her out against my wishes."

"Bull. Do you *really* believe that he should have been better than Karen? More mature?"

"He was a year older."

"In terms of gender, that made him still about two years younger than Karen and you know it. It was normal teenage hijinks, Witt," she repeated, "and in your soul, unless you've managed to deceive yourself completely, you know that. So what's the real problem, Witt? What's kept you so angry that you've been hurting Hardy for twelve years, and now you've hurt Joni, too?''

He shook his head and paced faster.

"Quit evading the issue," she told him sternly. "Whatever's going on has wrecked you, and now it's wrecking this whole family. Are you feeling guilty?''

"Why would I be feeling guilty? I told her the right thing to do! I told her not to go out with that boy. He was trouble, I told her."

"But he wasn't, was he? Hardy got into a couple of scrapes over ordinary pranks, but by and large he was one of the better kids at that school."

Witt shrugged, still pacing and refusing to look at her. "I didn't want her hanging out with that family of drunks."

"Family of drunks." Hannah repeated the words disbelievingly. "Hardy's father was the drunk. Barbara never touched so much as a drop of liquor, and Hardy...I don't think I've ever seen him have anything but an occasional beer or glass of wine. And back then he didn't drink at all."

"He came from bad blood!"

"Oh, cow patties!"

For a few seconds Witt appeared arrested. "Cow patties? Christ, Hannah, just swear. Your tongue won't turn black and fall off."

"I don't like swearing and I never have. And I hate myself when I do it."

"Why don't you unlace that damn corset? If you get any more pure, there won't be room for angels in heaven."

"Don't be ridiculous. I'm not pure. As *you* should well know."

"Hannah, that was a lifetime ago. We agreed never to talk about it."

"Too bad. We're going to talk about it now. Because finally, after twenty-seven years, you've got me nearly as withered and desiccated in my heart as you are."

"What the hell are you talking about, woman?"

"Don't call me woman. It's not a word to be treated like a bad name. So what is it, Witt? Are you feeling guilty because you turned Karen into Juliet? Or are you feeling jealous because she picked Hardy over you?"

"That doesn't have anything to do with it!"

"No? You're lying, Witt. To me and to *yourself.* And there's nothing more disgusting than a man who lies to himself."

She rose, pulling her jacket closer around her, and zipped it up. "Apparently you're not still drunk enough to need a baby-sitter, so I'm going home."

"You can't just leave after saying all these horrible things to me."

"I can't? Why not? You left after saying a whole bunch of horrible things to Joni. Why shouldn't I be able to treat you the same way? Surprise, Witt. What's sauce for the goose is sauce for the gander."

Just as she reached the door, he called out her name. "Hannah…"

She turned and faced him then. "Oh. One more surprise, Witt. That night we had our little slip? You made me pregnant. You might not want to talk about that event anymore, but you're going to have to live with the fact that Joni is your *daughter*."

She had the pleasure of seeing his jaw drop and waited just long enough to be sure he wasn't going to have a problem with his heart. Then she stepped out into the cold afternoon, where sunlight as sharp as daggers bounced from the snow into her eyes.

She didn't know if what she had done was right. She just knew she could no longer tolerate what Witt was doing to himself and everyone around him.

Enough was enough.

19

Joni lifted her gaze from her plate and looked across the dinner table at Barbara and Hardy. Though she had cooked the meal herself—ham and scalloped potatoes—Joni thought it tasted like sawdust. She'd given up flailing in her mind against Witt, arguing with herself and thinking she was the worst person on the face of the earth to have wounded him so. The truth was, he was wrong. And she knew it.

"I'm going to see Witt."

Both their heads snapped up. It had been a quiet dinner, no one seeming to have much to say, and maybe the sound of her voice had startled them.

"Joni..." Barbara spoke her name uncertainly, trailing off as if unsure what to say.

Hardy's gaze was still stony, but it seemed to Joni that there was a little gentleness around his mouth now. He was coming back. "Are you sure you want to do that?"

"Yes."

"He might say terrible things."

"Well, I've got a terrible thing or two to say to him. And if I don't say them, I'm never going to stop worrying about this. I *need* to have it out with him. To really stand up to him for the first time in my life."

"I'll go with you," Hardy said.

Barbara spoke carefully. "That might make him think you're ganging up on him."

"Too damn bad," Hardy said. "I'm not going to let Joni face that man alone."

Something inside Joni warmed a little at his protectiveness, even though it reminded her that she was nothing but a responsibility to him. At least someone in the world cared enough about her to take care of her.

The instant she had the thought, she felt guilty, because after all, Hannah had come to the hospital last night to sit with her. It wasn't that no one else cared. It was that she still felt a little heartsore that her mom had kept her true relationship with Witt a secret for so long.

Of course, she thought with painful honesty, that information probably wouldn't have changed much of anything. Witt had always claimed to love her as a daughter, and it hadn't kept him from disowning her.

Hardy spoke. "When do you want to go?"

"As soon as we finish cleaning up."

It was seven-thirty by the time the last counter was

wiped. Night blanketed the world, and a cold, biting wind had kicked up. "And it's only January," she muttered as she stepped outside and walked to Hardy's car.

"'It's only January' can be a good thing," Hardy remarked. "If you take advantage of it. Wanna go cross-country skiing? Snowmobiling?"

"Skinny-dipping?" she retorted, drawing a laugh from him.

"Sorry," he said. "I'm too chicken. I'll stick to activities that let me keep dry clothes on. But what got you so down on winter?"

"This month. This month alone. It's lasted forever. The post-holiday blues don't even come close."

"It *has* been kind of exciting, hasn't it?"

They both climbed in, and he started the engine. It was still warm from an errand he'd run right before they sat down to eat, so the first blast from the heater wasn't icy, even if it wasn't exactly hot.

"Exciting?" she demanded. "This hasn't been exciting. It's been miserable and painful and hurtful, but it hasn't been exciting."

"Depends on how you look at it, honey. Painful situations usually put us in a position to grow. If we choose to."

"Grow? Ha. I'm going to crawl into my little clamshell and close it up. And caulk it with superglue." Had he really called her *honey?* Had he meant it? Or had it just been a slip? A slip, she told herself. A slip of the tongue.

Hardy laughed. "Your little clamshell, huh? I thought clams couldn't talk."

"Apparently you've never read the comics."

"It's a cute image. Except for the glue part. I hope you don't mean it."

"Right now I do." And the closer they got to Witt's house, the more nervous she grew. She'd never faced down her uncle—her *father*—over anything, so she had only a vague idea of how cutting he could get. He'd wounded her to her core when he'd disowned her, but she had a strong fear he could do worse than that.

And she already hurt so much, she didn't know how many more wounds she could withstand. But she had to do this. Before she moved away, she had to say her piece to Witt. All of it. She hoped he would listen, but if he didn't, it wouldn't really matter. All that mattered was that she get her own concerns off her chest, that she made her stand. At least then she could walk away with her head up, knowing she'd stood up to him.

When they pulled up in front of Witt's house, Joni was almost sorry to see the lights on and Witt's shadow moving across the living-room curtains. He was home, and he was awake. She had no excuse to postpone the reckoning. Her heart began to beat nervously, and her mouth went dry.

"What if Hannah's there?" she blurted.

"I don't see that it makes any difference," Hardy said. "But if it does to you, *I'll* go in there and give him a piece of *my* mind. I've been wanting to anyway."

Much as she feared Witt's reaction, Joni wasn't about to let Hardy be braver than she. Her chin setting with determination, she climbed out of the car...right into the snowbank left by the plow. Snow slipped into her boot and slid down, soaking her sock and making her foot icy.

Wrong boots, she thought. She should have worn her lace-ups. It was an irrelevant thought, but it was easier to be annoyed with herself than think about what was to come.

She climbed over the snowbank and slid down onto the sidewalk. Witt had salted it recently, so the pavement was free of ice. Salt crunched under her boots as she forced herself to walk to the door. Hardy crunched along right behind her.

Witt answered on the first ring of the doorbell. His eyebrows lifted when he saw them, but his face didn't take on the flush of anger that usually came when he saw Hardy.

He did not, however, look at Hardy for long. His icy blue gaze came back to Joni. "What is it?"

"I want to talk to you, Uncle Witt."

"I've had all the talking to I want today."

"Well, you're going to get some more."

After a moment he stepped back and waved her in. He didn't even object when Hardy followed.

Witt smelled as if he'd just showered. The living room was full of the aroma of air freshener, but it didn't quite conceal the odor of alcohol. Great, thought Joni, he'd been drinking. That would make this even more enjoyable.

"Sit down," Witt said.

Joni almost obeyed, out of long training, but she caught herself. "I'd rather stand."

Witt shrugged. "I'd rather sit." He sat in his easy chair. After a moment, Hardy sat, too, on the sofa. Again Witt didn't object.

Joni stood looking at him from the center of his living room, her hands clenched until her nails bit into her palms. She couldn't find the words to begin with, didn't know where to start to express all the roiling anger and hurt inside her.

"Well?" Witt said. "I guess you're going to tell me how much I've hurt you."

"You're damn straight!" The words burst out of her, and then the rest began to follow. "Ever since Lewis died and we moved up here, you've always told me you loved me like a daughter. But you know what, Witt? Since Karen died, you've hardly even noticed I was really here. Oh, you talk to me, and you remember my birthday, and you give me Christmas gifts, but you don't love me like a daughter. Not really. You haven't really loved anyone since Karen died!"

"Wait one minute!"

"No, I'm not going to wait. You listen to *me* for

a change. I've been walking around for a long, long time wondering why Karen's death seemed to have crippled us all so much. Wondering why she seemed to haunt us all. People die, Witt. I loved Karen, too. But healthy people grieve and then go on. None of us has ever been able to finish grieving."

He scowled at her. "I'm never going to stop mourning Karen."

"Of course not. We'll always miss her and wish she were here. But what's been going on with us is *pathological*. Sick. She's affected our lives more these past twelve years than if she'd been here. We're all caught in this…I don't know. Time warp. But I do know none of us has been able to move on. It's not healthy."

This time he didn't say a word, just looked at her from hot, angry eyes.

"So I got to wondering. What's different about us than the rest of the world? And how come we can't really heal? And it dawned on me, just this afternoon. None of us can heal because of *you*. Karen's death gutted me. She was my…like my *sister*. But more importantly, I loved her because she was my best friend. I wept as hard as anyone did, and to this day I still miss her. But I could have moved on. I could have built my own life instead of coming back to this morass of twisted feelings and sinking back into all this anger and grief. I thought Karen was haunting us, but then I realized, it's not Karen. *You're* the one haunting us."

"Joni…"

"Be quiet." She didn't want him to divert her now that it was all spilling out. And she was past caring whether she was right, wrong or just confused. She had to get it out.

"You withdrew from Hannah and me," she told him. "You stopped loving us the way you used to. That hurt me as much as Karen's death. I lost *two* people, but one of them was smiling at me nearly every day and *pretending* to still care about me when he didn't really. After a while it finally dawned on me that you had never really loved me. And that after Karen died you couldn't even keep up the pretense well enough. I saw through you, Witt. And if I had any doubt about it, you proved it when you disowned me."

Witt raised a hand but didn't say anything. Joni ignored the gesture.

"So I lost my best friend and my surrogate dad all at one time," she said bitterly. "And stupid me, I was crazy enough to come back here to live after finishing college. I kept coming back, Witt, because I kept trying to find your love again. Well, trust me, I'm through looking."

Tears were stinging her eyes now, threatening to run down her cheeks, but she didn't wipe them away. All the pain held so long in her heart was determined to spill out. "I'm going to leave, Witt. I'm going to leave Whisper Creek, and you're going to lose your only remaining 'daughter.' And the only person you'll have to blame is yourself.''

His mouth moved, as if he wanted to say something but couldn't find his voice. He just looked at her, his blue eyes dimmed.

''What's more,'' she continued in a lower, angrier voice, ''you should be ashamed of the way you've treated my mother all these years. She loved you. She's always loved you. I've seen it in the way her face brightened and her step lightened when you came by. But you've ignored it. And pardon me for asking, what the hell were you doing sleeping with her when you didn't love her? Did you even wonder if I was your child?'' She paused at his look of recognition. He did know. He had known. He had known all along. How could he have treated her mother, and herself, this way? Her anger flared hotter. Enough was enough.

''If my mother wants to tolerate your treatment, that's her choice, but I'm not going to tolerate it anymore. Not ever again. I'm sick of you acting as if you're the only person who matters.

''Which brings me around to Hardy. How dare you accuse him of killing Karen? It was no more his fault than it was yours. Or maybe it was *more* your fault than his. All Hardy ever did was give her a place to run *to* when she was running *away* from *you*.''

''Joni…'' This time it was Hardy who spoke. ''Joni, don't. He's already blaming himself enough.''

"Enough?" She rounded on Hardy. "He's been blaming everyone *except* himself. Hell, I think he's resented me for twelve years because I didn't die instead of Karen!"

"No!" The word exploded from Witt. "No. That's not true."

She turned on him again. "I doubt you have any idea at all what's true. You're so blinded by anger and bitterness, you've blighted everyone around you."

Witt stood. "Joni, let me talk."

"No. I've heard enough out of you." Turning, she pulled up her hood and stomped out into the night.

Hardy didn't follow. He stayed seated on the couch, waiting as Witt stared after Joni, watching as the man winced when the door slammed.

Slowly, moving like an old man, Witt turned and looked at Hardy. "What do you want to say? You might as well take your licks."

"Sit down, Witt. I don't want my licks."

Surprise reflected on his face, Witt returned to his easy chair. He looked shrunken now, a shadow of himself.

"You know," Hardy said, "I probably understand some of what you've been going through. I've been feeling guilty about Karen's death since the night it happened. I've lain awake more nights than I can count, running it over in my mind, trying to figure out what I could have done differently. I've gone out on empty roads in my car and practiced evasive maneuvers until I was exhausted. But I keep coming up with the same bottom line.''

Witt sighed and nodded. ''Tell me.''

''I keep coming up with the fact that any evasion I'd made, given the road we were on—and assuming I had time to do anything—would still have had the same result. There was nowhere to go. I was on the cliffside, Witt. We'd have tumbled a thousand feet or more. And the other car was between me and the other side of the road. But I didn't have time to do anything. No time at all. I saw that car start to drift, and I eased over to avoid him, and he turned right into us. *Right into us,* Witt. Did you know that drunks steer toward lights? Neither did I, until the cops told me.

''So the bottom line is, it wasn't my fault. I didn't kill her. But it still feels like I did. *Still.*'' The last word came out on the harsh edge of pain. ''I think I've forgiven myself, but I still feel guilty.''

Witt nodded briefly, but it was almost the rocking of a person in severe pain. ''I guess you do,'' he said slowly.

''So,'' Hardy continued, softening his voice, ''I've got one person left to forgive. You. And not so much for the way you've treated me all these years. I can actually kind of understand that. What I need to forgive you for is the way you've treated Joni. She didn't deserve any of the crap. All she ever deserved was the best you had to offer.

''But you know what? I can't forgive you. Not yet.

Not until I see you taking care of Joni. Not until I see you giving her the love that was hers by birth-right. Not until you make her your daughter in your heart.''

''But she is!''

''Then act like it, Witt. Act like it. Prove it.''

His piece spoken, Hardy left, too, glancing back briefly to see that Witt looked like a beaten man. He felt a qualm, but brushed it aside. Sometimes you just had to tell the truth. For the sake of your own soul. And sometimes, bitter though it was, painful though it was, you had to *hear* the truth. For the sake of your soul. It was Witt's turn to hear.

Outside in the truck, he found Joni shivering, shaking all over. ''I'll have you warmed up in a minute,'' he said as he turned the engine over.

''I'm not cold,'' she answered through chattering teeth. ''I'm not....''

He turned toward her, gathering her as close as he could with a console between the bucket seats, feeling a sharp pang as he felt the tremors that wracked her. ''What's wrong, honey?''

''I can't...I can't believe I said all those things to him. I can't believe it! I said horrible...hurtful... things.''

''Actually, I thought you were pretty restrained.'' He rubbed her back, but layers of nylon and polyester insulation in her jacket probably deprived the touch of most of its intended comfort.

"But...but...I accused him of things that might not be true."

"You felt they were true in your heart, didn't you?"

"Yes!"

"Then they were true, whether any of it was what Witt intended. They were true, and you needed to say them and he needed to hear them. Maybe now he'll get around to trying to repair some of the rift."

"No. No." Still shaking, she pulled away from him. "He'll never speak to me again."

"If that's the kind of man he is, then that would probably be for the best."

Even in her state of upset, his words must have sounded harsh to her, because she shot him a startled look.

"Listen," he said. "I'm getting tired of comforting people that man has hurt. First Karen and now you. He needs to start thinking about what he's doing to the people he claims to love. And if he can't, then he doesn't deserve your love."

"Love shouldn't have to be earned."

He shook his head and turned around, reaching for the gearshift. "Maybe not. But it *does* have to be deserved."

He let her think about that while he drove them back to his place. But he found himself thinking about Witt, too. And despite his every inclination, he found himself feeling pity for him.

* * *

Joni didn't want to talk about it after they got home, and when Barbara suggested a game of rummy, she leaped at the opportunity to distract herself. They played cards until finally Barbara announced she couldn't keep her eyes open another minute.

Like it or not, Joni realized, she was going to have to face her thoughts at last. Alone and in the dark. She didn't relish the night ahead.

"We ought to go up, too," Hardy remarked. "It's late." A yawn escaped him, and he stretched, reminding her of the gorgeous body he had beneath his clothes. A body she had once touched and held. All of a sudden, everything inside her seemed to go into a meltdown.

She wanted him, she realized. She'd thought she'd wanted him when she'd been in high school, but that had been puppy love, a virgin's desire. Now, since the night they had made love, she had discovered what it was to feel a woman's desire.

It was a desire that made her ache to her very bones. A yearning so deep it filled her every cell. Her entire body grew heavy with need, and she felt herself throbbing at her center, throbbing as if she wanted to open herself and take him deep inside her.

And everything, *everything* that had been tearing her apart seemed to fade into the background, driven away by a more urgent demand.

The air in the room became so thick that she felt as if she couldn't breathe. But Hardy seemed unaware of it. He pushed his chair back from the table, after gathering the cards and returning them to their case. "Come on," he said. "I'll walk you up."

He didn't feel it. But instead of crashing from her high state of tension, she seemed to be caught in it. She noticed how he smelled as they climbed the stairs. Like soap. Like man. Like Hardy.

He was close enough that his breath occasionally reached her, smelling of the cider they'd drunk while playing cards. Even the sound of his steps on the risers behind her reminded her of how big and strong he was.

At the top of the stairs, they paused outside her door. His room was at the back, above the extension he'd added when he put in his office.

"Are you going to be all right?" he asked.

No way, she thought. No way. She was going to lie awake all night trapped in an aching body, pinned by a need that was threatening to overwhelm her. A need she didn't dare act on, because he didn't seem to feel it.

Although, in her present state, she was stunned that he didn't feel it, too. The miasma must be so strong around her now. She must be making phero-mones enough to pack the air to a distance of ten or even fifteen feet.

But he was oblivious.

"Look," he said after a minute as she continued to stare up at him, "if you don't want to be alone tonight, we can bundle."

"Bundle?" she repeated stupidly, even though she knew exactly what it was.

"Yeah," he said. "You can sleep in my room. We can put pillows between us, or a rolled-up blanket. You don't have to worry. I won't touch you."

He couldn't have said anything that would have cast her down more. Her hunger for him burst like a balloon, leaving her feeling...empty. Emptier than she could remember ever having felt. It was as if something inside her died.

She almost told him she would sleep alone, but something inside her wouldn't let her say it. Maybe because she knew exactly how badly she would sleep if she started thinking about Witt and the whole mess. Maybe because some part of her hadn't completely given up hope.

Whatever it was that compelled her, she nodded and followed Hardy down the hall to his bedroom.

She watched him roll a blanket and put it down the middle of the bed. It was a king-size bed, so there was plenty of room left. Little chance that they might touch each other accidentally. Little chance of anything, except talk.

"There," he said. "You can go get in your pajamas, if you want. I promise, you're safe with me."

Safe with him was, she realized, the last thing she wanted to be. But she had no doubt she *would* be. Hardy was a man of his word. "I'll change," she said, her voice muffled by disappointment.

Then she remembered she hadn't even commented

on his room. It ran along the entire back of the original house, full of space, and in the daytime it was probably full of light coming through the row of windows along the back wall, windows now covered with closed wooden blinds. Unlike the rest of the house, where he had pursued the Victorian touch, here he had gone for clean, uncluttered lines. The carpet was a soft beige, the ceiling a study of lines and angles that played with shadow. The colors he had selected were a deep green and burgundy, warmth against the coolness. He even had a fireplace, and his own bathroom, which she glimpsed through a partially open door.

''It's a beautiful room,'' she said finally, then left before he could answer.

She changed into a white flannel nightgown that was dotted by rosebuds. Nothing exciting. Nothing tempting. Just warm and comfortable. It probably said something about her that she didn't own a single negligee. No temptress, she was just a back-porch kind of girl.

When she returned to his room, she found he had changed, too, into navy blue sweatpants and a gray T-shirt. He squatted before the fireplace, coaxing a couple of logs into flame.

''Make yourself comfortable,'' he said over his shoulder.

She doubted she would be able to do that around him. Awareness of him was like a perfume in the air, surrounding her, reaching all her senses. Inescapable.

Finally she forced herself to look away from him and sit in an easy chair.

"This is a really nice retreat," she said finally, trying to distract herself.

"Thanks. I like it." Satisfied with the fire, he brushed off his hands and sat cross-legged on the hearth rug, facing her. "You feeling any better?"

Slowly, Joni shook her head. "Not much. I said some horrid things. I don't like to say horrid things to people."

"No kind person does. But you needed to say them, Joni. You know you did."

"I guess."

"Didn't you feel any relief at all?"

She thought back over the evening, trying to remember her reactions. "No. I just felt sick to my stomach."

"I'm sorry. But all those things have been bubbling up in you for a while. You've said most of them to me over the last week. You just finally got around to saying them to the right person, that's all."

"I guess."

"Come on, let's lie down. We can talk just as easily, and maybe we'll even fall asleep."

Obediently, she went to one side of the bed. "This okay?"

"Fine. I'm not particular."

When he pulled back the covers, she noticed for the first time that the blanket he had rolled up to put between them wasn't a blanket. "That's a quilt."

"Yeah." He seemed surprised she had commented on it.

"The colors are pretty." Sitting down on the bed, she leaned over to take a closer look. "That's hand-stitched! Somebody put an awful lot of time and effort into it. Look how fine the stitches are. Is it an heirloom?"

"I guess you could say so." He sat on the other side of the bed and put his hand on it. "My mother made it for me, to take to college with me. She worked on it for years."

"Wow. I can't imagine how many hours she must have put into it."

"Well, she started it on my thirteenth birthday."

"Can I see it?"

He hesitated, and she looked up to catch something vulnerable in his gaze. She had the feeling she was trespassing into a place where he didn't really want to go.

"I'm sorry," she said quickly. "It's none of my business." After all, she just wanted to look at it to distract herself a little longer. That was a lousy reason to pry.

"No," he said. "No, it's okay. It's just a quilt."

Rising, he began to unroll it. She helped him, until they had it spread out on the bed. But as soon as they opened it up and she looked down at the blocks, she knew it wasn't just a quilt. It was memories. Lots and lots of memories.

In the lower right corner there was a boy dressed

in jeans and a red shirt, flying a kite high above some pines. It was a cute kite, with a smiling face and a colorful tail.

Next to it was a block showing a boy bent over a book with a piece of paper and a pencil next to him. Then there was another block with a carefully drawn bridge that appeared to have been done in a child's hand. Scanning the rest of the quilt quickly, she discovered that nearly every block held a boy or a man.

"This is about you, isn't it?"

Hardy looked uncomfortable. "Yeah. Sort of. She wanted it to be a quilt full of memories."

Fascinated, Joni knelt on the bed and studied the blocks one after another.

"Was that your first kite?" she asked.

"I, uh, made it."

She smiled at him. "You've always been talented. And the boy with the book?"

"I had to study hard. Especially math."

"Me too." She bent again to the quilt and followed the scenes of a little boy until she came to a plain black square. It was part of a pattern of three plain squares on the quilt. "What's this? Just pattern?"

He hesitated so long that finally she looked at him. Something in his face seemed tight, too controlled. "Hardy? I'm not trying to be nosy. If you want me to stop asking, I will."

Nearly a minute passed before he answered. "It's okay. That's my dad. A dark patch in my life."

"Oh." She caught her breath and instinctively reached across the quilt to take his hand. "I shouldn't have asked."

"It's all right. Everybody knows what he was like. Everybody." His fingers curled around hers.

"It was hard on you, wasn't it?"

"I guess. He was a nasty drunk." He shook his head, as if wanting to dismiss the memories, but his fingers tightened around hers.

"I'm sorry you had to go through that."

He shrugged. "Doesn't matter. I'm past it."

She wondered if he really was. He might think so, but she suspected some of those childhood wounds were the reason he'd taken so much guff from Witt over the years. The reason he still felt responsible for the accident.

"You have a lot to be proud of," she told him. "You've come a long way."

"Maybe." He shrugged again and changed the subject, pointing to the sketches on the quilt. The first was the bridge she had already noticed, the second was a tall office building, and the third was a dramatic-looking house. "I guess I was always headed toward architecture. Mom copied those off drawings of mine."

"Pretty impressive." She looked closer and realized that the drawings were full of intricate detail. More so than one would find in the haphazard drawings of most kids...unless, of course, they were drawing fighter planes or something similar. What was more, they were appealing. "You have real talent."

"I'm adequate. But no Frank Lloyd Wright."

"Not yet, maybe. I wish you could do the hotel for Witt. Hannah told me how beautiful it was."

"I kinda liked it."

She looked at him again. "Only kinda?"

"Well, it wasn't as much as I would have liked to do. But given the budget restraints..." He shook his head. "It wouldn't have won anyway. Concrete construction is cheaper than siding and gingerbread and porches."

"Another cold monolith, huh? I wonder if Witt's that stupid."

"It's not stupidity. It's fiscal responsibility." He shifted until he was facing her directly. "Everybody has a budget. Very few people want to throw in all the frills, bells and whistles. So I accommodate them and try to give them something special at the same time. They aren't always interested. That's the risk I run."

"It must be so frustrating."

He squeezed her fingers and smiled. "I'm getting used to it."

She looked down at the quilt again and felt drawn to the two other solid squares. One was pure white; the other was bright sunshine yellow. Something warned her not to ask. But curiosity wouldn't let her keep silent. "What's this white square?"

He glanced at it. "Something lost."

Karen. It represented Karen. Suddenly she didn't want to look at the quilt anymore. With shaking hands she began to roll it up. "Thanks for sharing it with me, Hardy. It's beautiful."

"What's wrong?"

"Not a thing."

"I don't believe you." He came around the bed and sat beside her, taking her face between his hands. Her hands still clutched the edge of the quilt. "Stop hiding from me, Joni. Stop lying to yourself. We're never going to get anywhere if you won't be honest with me."

She shook her head, feeling her throat tighten. God, she was getting tired of being on the edge of sorrow and despair.

"Talk to me, Joni. Just talk to me." His tone was gentle, gentle enough to provoke her into speech.

"That was Karen's square, wasn't it?"

"Actually…no. It wasn't."

"Oh, come on."

"I'm not kidding." His hands tightened just a little as they cradled her head, letting her know he didn't want her to look away. "That's not Karen. There was a time when I wanted her on that quilt, when we first started dating, but my mom wouldn't let me do it. You know what she said?"

"No…"

"She said a high school sweetheart was a passing thing, and I wouldn't want to carry a memory of her through my life. Friends, she said, are the ones you want to remember. That square is a friend, Joni. Someone I still treasure. It's not Karen.''

She believed him. Crazily enough, she believed him. Something in her heart seemed to swell, and she reached out for him, forgetting the quilt, forgetting everything else except her need to comfort him and be comforted by him.

''We're going to be okay, Joni,'' he murmured as they hugged each other. ''We're getting through this already. A brighter day will come for all of us.''

She nodded, wanting to believe him, but more, just wanting to be close to him. She never would have believed that being held like this could make everything else seem so unimportant. That a man's arms could make her feel so sheltered and safe.

But the step from sheltered and safe to the heat of passion proved to be a very short one. As if someone had thrown a switch, all the desire she had been feeling earlier came sweeping back. Every muscle in her body seemed to soften, and the throbbing deep within her returned as strongly as if it had never gone away. She wanted him. She craved him. And she didn't want to spend another night without being in his arms. Tomorrow didn't matter. She needed him too much to worry about consequences.

Dizzy with the feelings flooding her, she tilted her head back and kissed him on the mouth. He stiffened, just long enough to make her fear he would pull away, but then his mouth fastened to hers, drinking from her as if he were starving.

Which was exactly what she was doing, too. Her fingers began to dig into his back, trying to pull him closer still. Pulling him until they fell onto the bed, she on her back, he partly over her.

He tore his mouth from hers suddenly, catching her face between his hands. "Joni…Joni…look at me."

Hazily she opened her eyes, resenting this interruption, fearing he would call a halt.

"Joni, are you sure about this? Last time…"

"I'm sure. Hardy, I'm so sure…."

He needed no more encouragement. He began covering her with kisses as he struggled to pull away her nightgown, his shirt and sweatpants, hurrying to bring them as close as he could possibly get them.

Impatience rushed them along, both uninterested in dallying on this journey. Joni felt as if she needed something more elemental. Something as primitive as what was raging through her. Something…deep.

Moments later, he entered her. The sensation was so exquisite that a thrill raced through her, leaving her transported on joy and passion. Nothing, she thought dimly, nothing had ever felt so good or right.

He seemed to be arrested by it, too. For long seconds he hovered over her, his eyes closed, motionless, absorbing the sensation. Then his eyes opened sleepily, and he looked down at her. "I never thought I'd be here again."

"Me neither."

"Sorry?"

"No!"

His smile broadened. Then he sank down on her, and they took the time to pleasure each other in every way they could think of.

Later, a long time later, as they dozed wrapped in each other's arms, Hardy murmured, "Joni?"

"Hmm?"

"That white square was you."

"Me?" She was suddenly wide-awake, and her heart was hammering again.

"You," he repeated. "So is the yellow one. Yellow because you were sunshine in my life. White because you went away after...she died."

"Oh...oh." Tears were suddenly flowing again, but this time they were tears of joy. "Oh, Hardy..." She squeezed him as tightly as she could. "Oh, Hardy..."

They didn't sleep for a long, long time.

20

Witt didn't wake in the morning, he roused. He hadn't slept, except for a couple of brief bits of dozing in his armchair. His thoughts wouldn't leave him alone; they kept clawing at him until he felt as if he were in tatters.

He ate a bowl of oatmeal, not because he liked it but because Hannah would have liked him to. Standing at the sink, trying to rinse the sticky stuff out of his bowl, he stared out over the town as another clear, cold mountain morning dawned. Only when he realized the tap water was turning his fingers into icicles did he stir.

It was time to start being a *real* man.

He washed up and changed into fresh clothes, a heavy flannel shirt and a pair of new jeans. A couple of pairs of thermal socks went on his feet, which he then shoved into the work boots he always wore. Then his jacket and knit cap. He looked like Witt, but he wasn't at all sure he *felt* like Witt Matlock anymore.

He drove directly to Hannah's house, noting that he needed to get up on her roof and shovel some snow off it before the load got too heavy in the next storm. She would probably argue with him about it, insisting she would get some young man to do it for her, and he wouldn't listen. He wasn't that old, and despite his scare, he wasn't in that bad a shape, either. He squeezed his hands into fists inside his work gloves and felt the strength he'd always relied on. It was still there.

Her walk was clear, dusted with fresh salt. He hoped she hadn't shoveled it herself. Knowing Hannah, though, she probably had.

He hesitated on the porch, his hand raised to knock. He wondered if Joni would be there, too, or if she was still staying with the Wingates. Everybody was talking about that, and it shamed him.

Finally he knocked, and a few moments later, Hannah opened the door.

"Witt!" She was clearly in the midst of getting ready for work, a mascara wand in her hand. Though dressed in jeans and a sweatshirt, a requisite for dealing with animals all day, she was still wearing her house slippers.

"Can we talk?" he asked.

The hand holding her makeup lowered slowly. "Are you going to yell?"

"No. I promise. I just need to say some things."

He wasn't used to seeing Hannah looking dubious, but right now that was the unmistakable expression on her face. He felt another twinge.

"Come in," she said, stepping back. At once she retreated to her rocker and sat. He followed suit, sitting in the easy chair she always ceded to him.

He could hardly bring himself to look at her. Instead, he stared at his hands, fists dangling between his thighs. "You were right," he said finally, his voice strained. "I was being a jackass."

She didn't say anything, leaving him to wonder if her heart was already closed against him, or if she was listening.

He tried again. "I've...been afraid for a long time."

"Afraid?"

He nodded, keeping his gaze on his hands. "Afraid. I've been living with fear and guilt for twenty-seven years. I felt like I betrayed my brother and my wife. I felt like I betrayed my daughter, too, when we...made love. And ever since I've been... feeling like a slug. Like I deserved whatever shit the universe wanted to dump on me. I felt like losing Shari and Karen was...just punishment."

"Oh, Witt."

Her voice was soft, and finally he was able to look at her. "I was afraid after Sharon died because I thought...well, if God was punishing me, maybe my punishment wasn't done. If He could take Shari, maybe He'd take Karen, too. Teach me another lesson about not taking care of the people I loved. Then He did.''

Hannah looked infinitely sad. So sad he felt his own throat constrict again. He had to look away. "Maybe I did protect Karen too much. Maybe I *did* turn a simple high school romance into *Romeo and Juliet.* It just felt like…the harder I tried to keep her, the more she was drifting away. And then…''

He shook his head and squeezed his eyes shut. "You can't rail at God, Hannah. That's only asking for more trouble. Remember Job? I was beginning to feel like Job. So I…got mad at everyone else. I blamed Hardy. I think I maybe even blamed Joni. Because it was safer than blaming God.''

"Witt…''

"I'm sorry, Hannah. I never guessed Joni was my daughter. I always figured if she was, you would have told me.''

"I should have. I was wrong.''

He shrugged. "We've all been a little wrong. Anyway…I'm sorry. Maybe I've been hiding from my pain by being angry. Maybe I was afraid to really grieve. I don't know. All I know is, I've been scared for a long, long time.''

He stood. "And now I need to go talk to Joni and Hardy. But I wanted you to know…I've been wrong. And if it weren't too late, I'd marry you in a heartbeat. Because I've always loved you, Hannah. But…I was afraid God would take you, too.''

Hannah rose then, crossing the room quickly to

him, to put her arms around him and hold him tight. After a moment, he hugged her back, and to her amazement, she felt a warm tear fall on her shoulder.

"It's okay, Witt," she murmured. "It's okay. I've been feeling guilty and frightened, too. And...I've never stopped loving you. Never, for even one second."

He lifted his head to look down at her, and she could see his cheeks were wet. He started to open his mouth, but she covered his lips with her fingertips.

"There's time for us later. Go talk to the children. You need to mend Joni's heart."

Witt swallowed and nodded, then, reluctantly, turned and walked out of the house.

Joni was dressed for work, coming down the stairs for breakfast, when Barbara called to her from the living-room doorway. "Honey? Could you get Hardy down here? You have a visitor."

At this hour of the morning? Joni wondered. "Sure," she said and trudged back up the stairs, reaching Hardy's room just as he opened the door. He, too, was dressed for the day.

"Barbara sent me to get you. We have a visitor."

"We also have something more important to think about," he said, and swooped for a deep kiss that left her feeling light-headed and weak. "Us."

A blush stained her cheeks. She'd been hoping

against hope this morning that he wouldn't be casual about last night. Apparently he wasn't.

"But," he said with obvious reluctance, "I guess we need to find out who the hell comes calling at seven in the morning."

"I wonder why Barbara didn't say who it was."

"Weird."

Together they went downstairs. Visible from the hallway, standing in the living room with his jacket unzipped, was Witt.

"Oh, God," Joni said under her breath. She felt herself bracing for whatever awful things Witt was going to say now. He was probably going to give it to her over staying with Hardy.

"Yeah," Hardy murmured back.

They exchanged looks, as if for reassurance, then stepped into the living room together, as if announcing they were a pair. Much to Joni's surprise, Witt didn't glare at them. Instead, all he did was say, "Hello."

Hardy stepped forward a little, as if ready to place himself between Joni and Witt. "Something I can do for you, Witt?"

"Yes. You can listen to me for a few minutes. And you, too, Joni. There's something I need to say."

Joni sat in an armchair, determined to show him that she wasn't intimidated by him, even if he stood over her.

Hardy motioned Witt to take a seat. After a moment, Witt settled into the rocking chair. Hardy sat on the end of the sofa, close to Joni's chair.

"We'll listen," Hardy said, speaking for them both, apparently because he guessed that Joni wasn't going to say anything at all.

A couple of times Witt looked as if he was about to speak but then caught himself and drummed his fingers on the arm of the rocker.

This was, Joni thought, the first time she had ever seen him at a loss for words since Karen's funeral. Despite her determination not to feel anything for Witt anymore, she found herself feeling sad for him. Sad and sorry.

"Okay," Witt said finally. "I'm having trouble finding ways to say this, and I kind of figure the two of you have lots of reasons not to want to hear me out. It's probably too late, anyway, although…I hope it's not."

"It's rarely too late, Witt," Hardy said.

Joni wondered how he could speak so calmly to a man who'd been verbally and emotionally beating him up at every opportunity for twelve years. Hardy seemed to have an awfully kind and generous heart. But of course he did. Look at how he cared for her. That was straightforward Wingate generosity.

Witt sighed. "I'm having a hard time getting started. I guess, first of all…Joni, I'm sorry. I'm sorry I got so mad that I acted like a damn fool and disowned you. You didn't deserve that. You've never deserved that. There's nothing on earth you could do that would make me stop loving you.''

The ache in Joni's chest grew so great that she had trouble breathing. A noose seemed to be squeezing her throat. ''Uncle Witt...''

He shook his head. ''Let me finish. I need to say it all. Then you can decide what you want to do about me. –

''You said something last night about coming home and looking for my love and never finding it. It was there, honey. It was always there. But...I was hiding it. And I was hiding it because I was afraid.

''You see, I'd lost my wife and Karen, and I felt it was punishment for what I'd done with your mother. I know it sounds crazy, but I was afraid...and I was afraid I'd lose you and your mom, too. That maybe my punishment wasn't over. So...I kept some distance after Karen. Especially with you. I couldn't have borne losing you, too.''

Joni could only look at him from tear-blurred eyes.

''Which brings me to you,'' Witt continued, looking at Hardy. ''When I get scared, I get mad. Stupid thing to do, but that's what I do. And I had some other stuff I was worrying about. I felt guilty that Karen was dead, figuring I hadn't protected her well enough. I felt...responsible, because losing her must have been some kind of punishment from God. I don't know. It's all tangled up in my head. What I *do* know is that I was shifting blame. Moving it from myself to you. It was easier, I guess.''

"I understand," Hardy said.

"That's more than *I* do." Witt stood. "Well, that's all I have to say. I was wrong. I was very wrong. I'm sorry. Now you two go ahead and do whatever it is you were planning to do and don't mind me. But if you can...maybe you can find a way to forgive me. I don't want to lose you, Joni. You've always fit in my heart like a daughter." He started to walk away, but Joni stopped him.

She'd fit in his heart like a daughter? Did he fit in her heart like a father? Or was that merely a biological fact? She studied his face, remembered the times he'd been there, even if distantly. It wasn't simply that her mother had glowed whenever he was around. She'd felt it, too. Was that what it felt like to be with "Dad"? Or would he always remain...

"Uncle Witt?"

He looked back.

"I love you...Dad."

He took her hand. "I love you, too, honey."

"And what about the hotel?"

Witt suddenly cracked a crooked grin. "I already told my lawyer to give Hardy the job. I figure Hannah and I can be married there in the autumn. You two want to have a double ceremony?"

He left without waiting for an answer. Not that Joni could have spoken. Dumbfounded, she looked at Hardy.

Hardy looked equally stunned, as if he couldn't

quite absorb the news. Finally he cleared his throat and said, "Wow."

Joni nodded. But her mind was already leaping to something else, something even more important. And so, for that matter, was Hardy's. He cleared his throat again and began to steer in that direction.

"It's about time he married Hannah," Hardy said. "I thought all along that they should be together."

But Joni's attention was elsewhere. Her mouth was dry, and her heart was racing like a motor on a speedway. "He thought...he said..."

"That we were going to get married?" Hardy's eyes suddenly crinkled at the corners as he looked down at her.

"Why would he...?"

"Oh, maybe because it's written plain as day all over my face whenever I look at you," he suggested, trying to sound philosophical. "Then, of course, there's the possibility that other people are beginning to see in your eyes what I'm seeing. What I hope I'm not imagining."

Joni's breath caught. "What are you seeing?" she asked in a hushed voice.

His smile grew tender, hopeful. "That...maybe you're falling in love with me, too?"

Joni closed her eyes, scarcely able to believe her good fortune. "Oh, Hardy," she whispered, opening her eyes to look at him again. "Don't you know? I've always been in love with you. But...I thought because of Witt you'd never want me. That it was pointless even to hope."

"Well, I kind of thought the same thing," he admitted, drawing her into a snug embrace. "All these years…it was like you were behind a window and I didn't have the key to get to you. Joni, I love you. Will you marry me?"

She bit her lower lip as a smile began to stretch her cheeks. "Are you sure? You really believe what Witt said?"

"That was a pretty big olive branch he offered, building his hotel. I believe him."

"Me too. And I need to tell him so."

"Wait a minute," he said, squeezing her even tighter. "Us first. Then you can run after him. Are you going to answer my question?"

Her eyes began to sparkle, and her smile was so wide that it hurt. "What question?" she asked.

He shook his head. "I can't believe you're going to put me through this twice. Don't you know how hard it is to ask *once?* My future's on the line here. My ego…" But he trailed off and grew serious. "Joni, will you marry me?"

Her answer was as simple as his question.

"Yes," she said with all the joy in her heart. "Yes!"

From the doorway came two voices.

"Hallelujah!" said Barbara.

"It's about time," said Witt.

Joni and Hardy didn't even glance their way.

Hardy murmured, "It *is* about time." And then he kissed her.

BARBARA

NEW YORK TIMES BESTSELLING AUTHOR

DELINSKY

A burning fever, a raging snowstorm, a broken-down car…
Karen shuddered to think what could have happened if
Brice Carlin hadn't pulled her from the drifts and taken her
to his home. As a doctor, his healing instincts took over.
But being snowbound with the man who once tried to
have her put in jail was dangerous territory.

Years ago, a car accident changed all their lives.
But sometimes fates decides to offer the chance to heal,
to forgive and to understand that things happen for a reason—
and love is the best one of all.

T.L.C.

Available May 2001 wherever paperbacks are sold!

Visit us at www.mirabooks.com   MBD822

New York Times Bestselling Author

DEBBIE MACOMBER

Buffalo Valley, North Dakota, has become a good place to live—the way it used to be, thirty or forty years ago. People here are feeling confident about the future again.

Stalled lives are moving forward. People are taking risks—on new ventures and on lifelong dreams. And one of those people is local rancher Margaret Clemens, who's finally getting what *she* wants most: marriage to cowboy Matt Eilers. Her friends don't think Matt's such a bargain. But Margaret's aware of Matt's reputation and his flaws. She wants him anyway.

And she wants his baby....

Always DAKOTA

On sale May 2001 wherever paperbacks are sold!

MIRA®

Visit us at www.mirabooks.com

MDM800

New York Times **Bestselling Author**

FERN MICHAELS

BEYOND TOMORROW

Carly Andrews's predictable life as the manager of a real-estate agency was turned upside down the day Adam Noble commissioned her to find his dream house. The Noble family was the next thing to royalty, and Adam's obvious desire to make his relationship with Carly more than business had her feeling as if she was acting out a Cinderella story. But what could a man who had everything want with an ordinary, average, unremarkable woman like her?

"Her characters are real and endearing, her prose so natural that it seems you are witnessing the story rather than reading about it." —*Los Angeles Sunday Times*

*Available May 2001
wherever paperbacks are sold!*

New York Times Bestselling Author

JOAN JOHNSTON

Abigail Dayton has a job to do—trap and relocate a wolf that is
threatening local ranches, in an effort to save the species from
extinction. Abby knows the breed well: powerful, strong and lean.
As rare as it is beautiful. Aggressive when challenged. A predator.

But the description fits both the endangered species she's
sworn to protect...and a man she's determined to avoid.
Local rancher Luke Granger is a lone wolf, the kind of man who
doesn't tame or trust easily. The kind of man who tempts
a woman to risk everything....

Never Tease a Wolf

Available April 2001 wherever paperbacks are sold!

RACHEL LEE

66554	SNOW IN SEPTEMBER	___ $5.99 U.S.	___ $6.99 CAN.
66298	CAUGHT	___ $5.99 U.S.	___ $6.99 CAN.
66173	A FATEFUL CHOICE	___ $5.99 U.S.	___ $6.99 CAN.

(limited quantities available)

TOTAL AMOUNT	$_____
POSTAGE & HANDLING	$_____
($1.00 for one book; 50¢ for each additional)	
APPLICABLE TAXES*	$_____
TOTAL PAYABLE	$_____

(check or money order—please do not send cash)

To order, complete this form and send it, along with a check or money order for the total above, payable to MIRA Books®, to: **In the U.S.:** 3010 Walden Avenue, P.O. Box 9077, Buffalo, NY 14269-9077; **In Canada:** P.O. Box 636, Fort Erie, Ontario L2A 5X3.

Name:_____

Address:_____ City:_____

State/Prov.:_____ Zip/Postal Code:_____

Account Number (if applicable):_____

075 CSAS

*New York residents remit applicable sales taxes.
  Canadian residents remit applicable GST and provincial taxes.

MIRA®

Visit us at www.mirabooks.com   MRL0401BL